C000224831

The Shadows of Heaven

TRIALS OF FATE

KaliVictoria

Copyright © 2020 KaliVictoria Wilson

No part of this book may be reproduced in any form or by any electronic or mechanical means including information storage and retrieval systems, without permission in writing from the author. The only exception is by a reviewer, who may quote short excerpts in a review. This is a work of fiction. Names, characters, places and incidents either are products of the author's imagination or are used fictitiously. Any resemblance to actual events or locales or persons, living or dead, is entirely coincidental. All rights reserved.

ISBN: 9798566810966

For love, and those who spend their lives trying to find it.

The Shadows of Heaven

TRIALS OF FATE

1
Gale

The City of Aaron is my home. High above the clouds and overlooking the infinite skies that encircle the earth. Our rivers flow throughout the city as the canals of Venice do, waterfalling into the atmosphere and supplying the clouds with whatever amount of rain necessary for the seasons. I don't quite know the science behind it, especially when summer days like this mainly consist of clear skies, but it's not for me to understand. Theseus could draw a thousand pictures, maybe more, but he could never capture the magnificent structures of this city. It's a shame we taught the Romans our architecture and infrastructure, only for it to sit in ruins on the Human Plane. Theseus takes a bite of his apple, interrupting my gaze.

"You may as well be fated to the city, Gale," he says. He's not even done chewing before he speaks again, "I thought Guardians spent all their time fighting on the Human Plane, sending demons back to the Banished realm and whatnot." He karate chops the air, his deep, dirty-blonde hair flopping about as he lays onto the floor behind him with a relaxed sigh. "Now that I think about it, why are you in the city so often?"

I reach for our lunch basket, grabbing a branch of grapes before I respond. Theseus and I were sitting on top of the Temple of Disciples, letting the cool, marble rooftop keep our bodies comfortable as we waited for Ares to join us.

Despite his name, Ares cared about everything else in this world except for war. Between the three of us, he held his tongue just as much as he held his patience, and there was only one thing that could make him open his mouth until the end of time.

Knowledge.

Ares will always have an answer for anything that's asked of him. A lengthy, *lengthy,* answer. It's why he's chosen the path of a Disciple in the first place, to teach the angel children of our city the word of God for the rest of his days.

I'd be lying if I said the position interested me in the slightest. I've been trying to master the elements of the earth since I could walk. I can easily shapeshift water like the angels in Adira, I've never struggled with transforming the earth like those in Hannah, and I was born in the City of Aaron, where the wings on our back were our birthright, along with conjuring the wind. The only missing element from this equation was fire.

No matter how many times Theseus had tried to train me with the element, the flames that escaped my fingertips were pathetic. But like every other angel of this world, we had our element of preference. Fire was Theseus' element of choice, and I guess it made sense since his personality was just as untamed as his flames. Ares' choice of element was earth, which was unsurprising. He became the most confident whenever following or enforcing the rules came into play. And according to a joke Theseus once said—while drunk might I add—Ares was a grounded soul.

And despite the capabilities of every other element, I've always been called to the wind. The element flew off my fingertips like second nature, and there was no other feeling that compared to how I felt while flying.

I push out the wings in my back, feeling their sturdy, velvet-like weight float up with strength, then settle onto the flooring behind me. The sunlight dances in between my blunt, muted-brown feathers, creating a subtle shimmer on the ground before me.

"Show off," Theseus says, sitting up with a groan.

I shrug, not trying to suppress the smug look on my face.

Theseus is a Nurturer. Although he's trained in combat as much as I have, his job involves interacting with humans more directly than mine. He's glamoured of course, so humans will never see him while he works, but he protects their minds from the telepathic taunting of demons. From what I knew—mostly from Theseus' boasting instead of my own observations—Nurturers were the most empathetic angels we have. They can sense the collective energy within a room, yet differentiate the energy of each individual inside of it. During their shifts, they wear a golden ring band, which gives them an inkling whenever a demon has latched onto a human's mind. The heavier the inkling, the more dangerous the situation. One of the most dangerous—suicide attempts.

Fortunately for Theseus, today was his day off.

"Patching up the ozone layer has been our priority for several centuries. Without that work, all of us would be done for," I try to reason, mostly to myself. Truth be told, my desire to go down to the Human Plane and fight demons outweighed my desire to fix the ozone layer.

From the age of twelve, angel children are trained for their abilities. Our relationship with the elements, our speed, our strength, our mental and emotional capacities—all are put to the test until the age of seventeen, when we are finally selected into our areas of work.

I knew I would become a Guardian, it's how my mother and father met. It's in my blood. I just didn't realize I'd be doing the boring side of their job for two years straight. At the age of nineteen, I should be in the field like they were, utilizing my skills. I should be sending demons back to the Banished Realm—to Hell. Instead, I spend my time repairing the earth's polluted atmosphere from blotches of the sun.

I frustratedly rip a grape from its branch, only to watch it squish under the force between my fingers. Theseus snickers.

"Don't worry, Gale, you'll put that wingspan to use one way or another. You just won't do it before me again."

"You're a Nurturer with the mind of a child. I'll be just fine," I retort before tossing the entire grape branch at his chest. Theseus catches the branch with a hearty laugh.

His words amount to the humor of human children, similar to their myths involving humans and their cooties. Throughout our school days, girls would taunt boys about the size of their wingspans. They assumed that the size of a man's wingspan determined the size of his third leg.

It was why I lost my virginity first.

Theseus was the last of our trio to lose his virginity, and despite his silver wings becoming the lengthiest of our crew, he wanted his experience to be memorable. After developing his charismatic skill as a Nurturer, however, girls seemed to flock to his empathetic, blue-eyed facade. "Your words just have to win their heart," he'd often say with charm, but Ares and I knew his physique helped just as much.

Ares' story is quite the opposite. He didn't care about who he slept with until last year when he turned eighteen. Disciples take their role of storytelling and teaching seriously, which means they can't have children once they reach the age of thirty. This time limit was created as a way to honor Jesus, who died in his thirties, but it also means that if a Disciple wants to start a family, they'd have to search for their significant other from a young age. For Ares, the time to look for that one person was now.

I reach for another fruit in our basket. Right now, I didn't care about love. I've suppressed the idea of love into the depths of my mind. I'd rather focus on my duty as a Guardian now. I couldn't care about her...

"Ares is taking awfully long today, isn't he?" Theseus points out. He feigns a yawn and stretches, reaching his hand out for me to pass the lunch basket with an exaggerated, begging face.

So I do.

The sound of wings catches our attention and our gazes snap forward. Ares hovers in the air with a face of inquiry. The braids on his half-shaven head have been thrown into a bun, and the color of his kinky hair matches the texture of his black, velvet wings, complimenting his glistening, bronze skin as he crosses his arms. The Disciple gestures his head to us with a glint in his golden eyes.

"What's up boys? We have an assignment."

2
Havena

I'm an only child. Born and raised alone. And this bike ride on my way home from Leah's house reminds me of that.

The cool, summer breeze dances throughout the town, speeding in my opposite direction as I wind down another street. It's not quite a suburban area, but I wouldn't categorize it as a city. Newly constructed, two-family homes dominate one half of the town, separated by the various strips of shopping centers and restaurants in the middle. Meanwhile, I live on the boring side of town. The side that's been around for generations—and looks like it, too. Various shades of yellow, baby blue, and white two-story homes mirror each other on each side of the street. I've gotten used to the identical, white window panes, run-down shingles, and dirty front porches led by stone steps. As if to add a little spice, the contractors would occasionally incorporate different-colored front doors.

I'm almost near my house now. The hustle and bustle of the freeway at the end of my block is barricaded by a row of tall, birch trees. The other side of the freeway is just a thick, unnerving forest. I've always wondered just how deep it went. Considering it took the entire duration of middle school for the freeway to be built on the forest's edge, I'd say it was pretty deep.

The summers before the freeway came to be, my mother would set me down inside of a kiddie pool on the front lawn. She'd sit in our rickety, dark pink, lawn chair and study scripture while I would just float on my back, watching clouds take the form of different animals or shapes. I was only five then, yet my mother sat tall, determined, taking notes with her gel pen and often grabbing her highlighter to emphasize God's word.

Our next-door neighbors asked to join us one day, and that was the day I met Leah. Two yellow bows secured her black hair swaying in high pigtails. She was already prepared to join me in the kiddie pool, wearing a red, polka-dot one-piece that showcased a spanish cartoon character on her belly. Her grin grew with every step her parents took toward my mother, and I returned it. I think God knew we would become the sisters we didn't have.

It had become our daily routine to lay side by side and watch the clouds after lunch, and soon after, my mother had stopped keeping us company outside. A part of me thinks she only left because I wasn't alone. Somehow in this quiet town, I finally had a friend.

I used to keep my eyes closed in that kiddie pool, waiting to hear Leah's feet run across the front lawn before I saw her.

Waiting, until the one day she never showed.

I sat up in the water for half an hour, wading my fingers through the cold waves of the tiny, plastic pool.

Waiting.

Then I gave up. I flopped down into the water and watched

the clouds alone. I had gotten used to Leah looking at the clouds by my side. It wasn't until that moment when I had finally realized how boring it was to do it on my own.

I was about to stop my solo pity-party when I noticed one cloud. Just one. And it had stopped moving entirely. I shielded my eyes from the glare of the sun and squinted, thinking my five-year-old eyes were mistaken. But the figure hovered there, a shimmery silhouette of fog. I waved my hand slowly, moving my hand over the figure, then away. Then over, then away. I did that about three times. Then it flew down into the forest. A small, silver glint of fog that I hadn't noticed before trailed behind it, until they were lost in the horizon of trees.

The breaks of my bike began to creak as I slowed down near Leah's old driveway. She moved out of her identical, yellow house after grade school when her parents divorced. Her mother had moved a few blocks away, closer to the shopping mall, but still on the same side of town. Thankfully, Leah and I still went to the same schools. We wouldn't have survived it without each other. And now we were eighteen, fresh high-school graduates that planned on escaping this predictable town together.

Eventually.

Leah wanted to take a gap year before college, to help her mother out with bills, but I had gotten a full ride from our community college. Hopefully next year, Leah could join me.

I bring my bike to a stop and slip off the seat, my boots crunching onto the grass of the front lawn. My worn, leather satchel bumps against my wide hips as I nostalgically take in my home, then the quiet of my childhood street. The strong breeze from earlier goes still.

I ignore it, but I can feel myself gripping the handles of my bike a little tighter. Then a rumble sounds. I can hear the shifting earth from my left. I freeze. I whip my head around to see the row of trees blocking the freeway, shaking from their bases. I can feel their roots crawling deeper into the earth, cracking the street in two. The clouds overhead grow dark and the crevices of the street start to pool with liquid. It's dark, murky...

And red.

■ ■ ■ ■

"Havena, wake up!"

My eyes opened instantly to find my worried mother staring down at me. The dark, brunette curls that I inherited frames her oval, innocent face. We share the same delicate features, almond eyes resting above a soft nose. I even have her brown skin and tiny ears. I, however, did not have her eye color. I assumed my dad and I shared that trait, along with his subtle cheekbones and defined jaw.

Her small frame dips into the side of my bed as she pushes some of my hair out of my face, the worry leaving her countenance as I yawn myself awake. I tiredly try to bring the comforter over my head, but her hand stops me.

"You have to go to the store soon," she warns. She had reminded me to visit the grocery store every hour of yesterday, and I didn't need the reminder again. Her voice sounded tired, as if she had just woken up, but it still held that maternal tone I knew I should listen to.

I close my eyes, murmuring, "fine," before flopping onto the other side of the bed. She gives a soft chuckle—nearly a whispered laugh—and leaves the room.

I like to think that my mother wasn't always so drained. Everyone says she looks young, oftentimes mistaking her for my sister, but what they didn't know is that she barely sleeps, barely eats, and barely acknowledges that my father is gone. She told me he died before I was born, but the only photo I have of him is dated after I was born.

When he held me in his arms for the first time.

She doesn't know that I found that picture, or that I know my name is scribbled in script beneath his. Nor does she know that it's underneath my mattress, in a box with all of the childhood trinkets I've collected over the years. It's been eighteen years, and whatever she's been afraid to face has kept her from moving on. From finding new love. From creating a proper bond with me.

Besides the fact that she's my mother, that's the only connection to each other that we have. I've never been allowed to personalize my room, and she's never bothered to show me any pictures of my relatives—if I even have any. I blame it on the fact that my face reminds her of my dad, but I'll never truly know. And above all else, she values her faith, and the cross necklace that never leaves her neck serves as a constant reminder.

I lazily shift out of bed and head to the bathroom to freshen up. After blindly twisting the knob of the shower, I avoid the mirror and slip out of my clothes. I didn't mind staring into my reflection, I was just tired of seeing the same image. Colorless clothing always covered my skin, and the only features that made me stand out were my eyes. My father's eyes. But he wasn't here.

The heat of the shower jolts me awake when I step into it, but I take it. I close my eyes, trying to scrub away the weirdness of that dream under the heat. The image of the blood pooling out onto the street. It was like my memory of meeting Leah combined with my memory of that weird flying cloud.

Or clouds?

I dig into the recollection, trying to remember the small blur following the bigger blur I had seen. It was definitely just my imagination playing tricks on me as a kid. It had to be... just like the ground ripping apart at the end of my dream... and just like the blood...

"*Ahhh*," I wince as the water suddenly sears my skin. I jump into the corner of my shower, out of the way of the boiling water. I sigh in relief as the cool air of this drafted, tiled cube saves me, but then I look to the shower knob, through the steaming ripples of water attacking where I once stood.

It's set to cold.

3
Gale

Our feet echo across the polished, marble hallway. The temple walls are tall, exalting the glorious, diamond-shaped skylight in the center of the ceiling. Theseus' face of awe mirrors my own. He lets out a whistle of admiration as his blue eyes scan every inch of this place. It echoes throughout the bone-chilling, silent corridor, with only a few fully-cloaked Disciples tiptoeing around. Ares turns around, shooting the Nurturer an annoyed glare of disapproval.

"Quiet!" Ares whispers tightly. Theseus and I raise our hands, feigning surrender, and Ares keeps leading the way.

"What do you think of our assignment, A?" I whisper to Ares. He slows his pace with a shrug.

"I'm not entirely sure. I've never heard of three angels sharing an assignment before," he admits.

"SHH," Theseus whispers, mocking Ares' previous tone. Ares shakes his head before Theseus starts again. "I thought you requested our silence, A."

"No, Cupid, I requested *your* silence. You shouldn't *whistle* inside of the temple, but *whispering* is fine."

Theseus scoffs, ignoring his nickname.

"That's the most ridiculous rule I've ever heard of."

The Nurturer was a chubby child, and it didn't help that his mother would dress him up as baby-cupid whenever she hosted a Solstice event. He's replaced the chubbiness with lean muscle now, but his big, blue eyes haven't changed since his tenth birthday, so we'll never let him live it down. Ares sighs with an amused roll of the eyes. I turn to Theseus.

"For a Nurturer, you're not very nurturing," I tease.

"And you're very, *very*, challenging," Ares adds, slurring his words with a point of a finger. Just as Theseus is about to open his mouth again, Ares shushes him. I try not to laugh as Ares ignores Theseus' face turning beet red. The Disciple pushes open a large, stone door that stretches to the ceiling.

The icy temperature of this newly discovered room failed to compare to the rest of the temple. Silver swirls glided throughout the marble flooring in an intentional pattern, leading to the silver altar in the center of the room. The room laid completely barren and windowless besides that silver and stone slab. Stone torches, subtly trimmed with gold, hung from the walls in symmetrical rows.

And none of them were lit.

"Not it," Theseus hurriedly whispers, breaking my observation. I look from Ares to Theseus, who has already taken a step back.

"Do you fear the wrath of God—" I start to tease, but Ares takes a step back as well.

"I am also not it," he says. "But by all means Gale..."

He ushers out his hand to let me pass.

"Ares, you're a Disciple."

"And *you're* a Guardian," he retorts.

Theseus crosses his arms.

"Ditto-ed."

I sigh in defeat and turn around. With a huff of my breath, I walk into the room. The first row of torches light with fire as soon as I walk past them. The same action happens with the second row. I turn toward the scared boys again.

"Last time I checked, this is *our* assignment," I remind them.

A wind suddenly sweeps through the air, knocking out the light from the torches my steps have lit so far. I look around, scanning the room for any disruption as Theseus and Ares rush to my side.

We're back to back, our eyes darting around for the source. I draw up air between my fingers. Ares gets in his stance to conjure the marble in the room, the element of earth. Flames flicker from the fire dancing off of Theseus' palm. We're prepared.

"The three of you work well together, but you lack the fourth element for this fight." A voice shakes into the room. The three of us stay planted in our stances, our eyes trying to find the source of those words.

"Who dares trespass this holy temple? Show yourself!"

From Ares' demand, a gush of water erupts from the stone altar. It shoots straight into the air, then funnels down into a low bubble on the surface. We lower our defenses with hesitation as the liquid dribbles over the altar's edge, gazing upon the wonder of the water. It restricts itself, refusing to move an inch onto the marble floor.

"I need not show who I am to you, but I will show you the element you need for this assignment. The element that is dire for all of creation. The element you need to win the war," the voice echoes out.

My breath hitches in my throat as I realize who we're

talking to. I glance to Ares, who was too busy contemplating the words of this being. I glance to Theseus, whose mouth hung agape as he stared at the stone, too in shock to utter any of his words. I turn back to the altar.

"You're God," I breathe.

"I Am," is the response.

"Y-You've called us here?" I stammer.

"Indeed. I did."

Theseus runs a hand through his dirty-blonde waves. Ares puts up a hand to stop Theseus' words before they're said.

"Don't say His name in vain," Ares warns. A hearty laugh comes from the altar.

"You are not here to be reprimanded. That is for Judgment Day. Your days of judgment are not near in your future," He says. Before Ares can apologize, He speaks again.

"The purpose of your task is to find the new vine. She has been pruned and placed before a thicket, yet her enemies have left the land dry. Her blood will bridge every realm of this earth, though one realm wishes for her realm to die. Find this vine, train this vine, fight with this vine, for three will become four and four will become one with the earth. Then, and only then, will the prophecy be complete."

Just as I'm about to replay the words in my head, the water begins to subside.

"Wait!" I blurt out. I step forward, but the water doesn't stop retracting. "How will we know when we've found her?"

What was once a cascading waterfall has become nothing more than a puddle in the center of the altar.

It bubbles one more time.

"You will know, Guardian. You will know."

Then the altar is dried.

4
Havena

"Grapes!" I announce to Leah. She takes hold of the grocery cart and darts through the farmer's market toward the fruit.

We've only been here ten minutes and she was already getting the cautious side-eye from Mr. Pelowski. I look back to the old man and send him a grin. He let me work in this store throughout high school, even before I turned sixteen. Besides my mother—and Leah—I didn't have much family, yet he felt like the grandfather I never had.

Unfortunately for him, Leah felt the same way, and oftentimes she would give him a headache by visiting me during my shifts. Every single shift. She even helped me restock shelves without pay. When Mr. Pelowski noticed it had become a habit, he would slip her money from time to time. Eventually, he started paying her biweekly for her work.

Maybe it was because Mrs. Pelowski died, or because his grandkids never visited as adults, but Mr. Pelowski didn't plan on selling Mrs. Patty's Marketplace until Leah and I had children of our own.

Or so he's said once or twice.

Even though Leah had ruined his pyramid of oranges on more than one occasion, I knew he still had love in his heart for both of us girls.

I look at the checklist of groceries my mother gave me, then automatically cross pomegranates off the list. Deciding to grab cereal next, I look up to find Leah. She had stopped darting around with the shopping cart and was now talking to a boy we went to high school with. Ethan Morris.

She's had a crush on Ethan since as far as I can remember, and has tried getting his attention amidst the other girls that tried as well. Her black hair was thrown up into a high ponytail, which she pulls to the side of her face to laugh at whatever joke he's just told her. I shake my head with a smirk and turn on my heel, heading for the cereal.

Sometimes I wish I had her body. It was small like my mothers, the curves delicate. Instead, I got stuck with hips that I constantly bruised by bumping into things, which just so happens as I bump into someone's cart.

"I'm so sorry—" my voice trails off. The woman before me had yellow, cat-like eyes that blazed as she took me in from head to toe. Her lips were as black as night against her pale skin, and she quickly checks her nails, which resemble the long, raven claws of a leopard. Her disturbed scowl sends a chill down my spine before she even speaks.

"Ugh, a human child," she spits with disgust. I can only watch as she gestures to move her cart around me.

Human child? And were those fangs?

I voluntarily take a step back to clear her path and watch as she walks into a crowd of shoppers. No one notices her appearance.

Or her claws... her eyes...

"Havena!" Leah shouts. My head whips around to find

Leah rushing over with our half-empty cart. The huge grin plastered on her face tells me her talk with Ethan went well. She stops the cart breathlessly, "Havena you won't believe the conversation I just had. I can't believe he just asked—"

Her voice trails off when she notices I've looked back into the crowd. I quickly scan every face, every cart, every hand, but I can't find the woman. She's gone.

"Havena? You look like you've seen a ghost," Leah says. My gaze snaps back to hers and she winces in confusion, glancing between me and the crowd of shoppers, hoping to see what I see.

I shake my head.

"No, no I'm just uh—How is everything in this store already disorganized? We've only been gone for a month!" I exclaim with a joking breath.

Leah shakes her head with a laugh before turning the cart down the cereal aisle. I tried to return her smile as she changes the subject back to her and Ethan. And I tried to listen.

I tried.

But I could only think about how the lady with cat eyes had vanished from my sight.

■ ■ ■

"Do you ever feel like you're crazy?"

I'm reclined in the passenger's seat of Leah's comfortably-old minivan, looking through the sunroof at the clouds. Her dark-brown eyes turn to me curiously from the driver's seat, her burger in hand. After grocery shopping, we decided to go to Bucky's, the burger joint at the opposite end of the parking lot.

Grabbing a burger from Bucky's has become our tradition whenever we go to the shopping mall. We've cried in this parking lot, shared our crushes in this parking lot, hid from the popular kids in this parking lot. Most importantly, we've talked about our fathers in this parking lot.

Leah never wants to talk about her dad. He was abusive to her mom and started another family shortly after their divorce. In Leah's eyes, she doesn't have a father.

The picture of my father may be the only thing I own of my dad, but wherever he was—Heaven or Hell—I couldn't imagine him bringing that kind of pain into my life if he were alive. Leah knows about that picture, but there wasn't much to tell her when I found it. We haven't talked about our fathers in three years, and I wasn't going to start now.

"You're friends with me and you think you're crazy?" Leah asks. Then she pauses for a second. "Actually, yeah, Have, maybe you are crazy."

We burst out laughing and I recline my seat upright.

She's the only person that calls me, "Have." It's a simple nickname, but I don't even remember when she came up with it. Just replace the, "C," in, "Cave," with an, "H," and then voila.

Have.

"I just mean, have you ever seen things that no one else has? Like no one would ever believe you if you told them, but it doesn't change the fact that you've seen... things?" I elaborate. I think back to the moment underneath the scalding shower water this morning. Then, I picture the lady with cat-like eyes again. I have to be losing it.

Leah pauses her bite into the burger and considers the question. I'm so thankful to have her. She's genuinely open to my ideas, no matter how unorthodox they are.

"I think," she starts, cautiously, "that people are..." she pauses. Her eyes widen as they glance through the window

19

behind me and I turn my head. A car about three parking spaces from us has started swaying up and down.

"Weird..." we say in unison.

Our chuckles collide as Leah wraps up her burger, dropping it into the paper Bucky's bag before starting up the car. I grab my seatbelt as she puts the car in reverse. She starts to pull out of the parking lot as the streetlights turn on.

"As I was saying." Leah interjects the comfortable silence. "People are weird. But there's like a scale of weird, you know?"

I shake my head at her reasoning and she bites her cheek, turning down a road near my house. We're next to the forest now, and the night sky has quickly blanketed over the tri-state area. She just needs to make two more turns before I'm home. The streetlights are spread further apart now, making the road harder to see. She flicks on her car lights.

"Some things people say, or see, are weirder than others, but it doesn't mean they're crazy. Like... I could see an Australian spider and call it insane, but Australians would think it's totally normal," Leah reasons. She looks from me, to the road, to me again, proud of her answer.

"Oh, so like anonymously sending Ethan chocolates on graduation day?"

"It was a cute gesture!"

"He's allergic to nuts."

"*Mija*, how was I supposed to know?" she whines, and I roar with laughter. She goes to pinch my side, but a sudden bright light flashes in front of the car. I can't tell if I screamed, or if Leah screamed louder. I just remember the flash of yellow eyes.

Then darkness.

5
Havena

"Oh, mortal, mortal, *mortals,*" a slurring voice coos.

I strained my eyes to open, taking in the cut fabric on my sweater. The sound of scraping screeched against the hood of Leah's car, clashing with the purring sound of the car's engine. I didn't have to look to know who it was. The woman from the supermarket.

I turned to Leah. Her driver's side window was completely shattered and her head laid unconscious against the steering wheel. I gently nudged her.

"Leah," I whisper, and she gives me a small grunt in return. I sigh in relief at the sound. She was alive. Leah was alive. Now we needed to get out of here alive. I nudge her again.

"Leah, we have to go."

"GO?" The woman outside of the car shrieks. I shoot my head up at her shrill voice, watching the woman shift her weight on the hood of the car.

The windshield was cracked, but not completely broken, and the woman circled one long claw on the glass above my face. There were shiny scales on her fingers, embedded deep within her skin that seemed to trail up her arm until it reached her chin. She circles her claw above Leah's face now. Leah's eyes flutter at the sound and she cautiously sits up.

"Ha-Have," Leah sputters. Her eyes register the creature on the hood of her car before they widen with terror. "Have!"

Leah grabs my hand with a squeeze. She could see the woman now, and I couldn't protect her. I couldn't protect my family. Despite the terror in Leah's trembling hands, I kept my grasp firm. glancing around for some kind of weapon. Some kind of escape plan. The woman leans her head back with a cackle of pure amusement. As if the creature could see that I was contemplating how to escape, her bloodthirsty eyes narrowed, confirming just how useless any escape plan would be.

Leah's hand suddenly freezes. I look over to her, only to watch as the whites of her eyes slip into her head. Her hand slumps into the driver's seat.

"What did you do?" I yell. I lean over, placing a finger to Leah's throat. Then, I mentally thank God when I feel her heart beating. She had only fainted.

"Did I scare your friend?" the woman coos, feigning concern. I could only glare at the creature, with nothing but rage building inside of my chest. She circles her claw excruciatingly slow over my face again, the scraping sound of the windshield making my body flinch.

"Oh, *prophesied vine* of the earth." The creature pouts. "I'm going to enjoy killing you."

6
Gale

"Find this vine, train this vine, fight with this vine," Theseus repeats for the hundredth time.

After our unexpected encounter with God, the boys and I went our separate ways to gather equipment. Theseus traveled to his apartment in the heart of the city. He collected his gear for combat, which included his family sword, his titanium shield, and most importantly, his golden ring.

Theseus hasn't put the ring on since he arrived to my home, but as he sat in a leather chair by the balcony door—his equipment next to him on the floor—his eyes watched the gold ring trail about his knuckles as he recited our assignment.

It had been an hour since Ares had gone back to his dwelling at the temple. He was most likely going to shuffle through a bookshelf or two, possibly find anything that could serve as a reference to the prophecy. Theseus suddenly stops moving the ring on his hand and shoots his head up. His eyes latch to mine.

"She's near a forest," he says.

"A forest?" I question. He nods his head. I could see the

words of our assignment dancing within his eyes.

"Her blood will *bridge* every realm," he emphasizes. He scoffs in amusement at my confusion. "She has to be human."

"How can you be so sure?" I ask. He finally slips the ring onto his finger and shrugs with a sigh, leaning back into the chair.

"I just... *feel* it."

There was no point in questioning the instincts of a Nurturer. They were almost always right, especially when it came to the humans they've sworn to protect. And despite Theseus' usual outbursts, I could tell he was serious about this one.

I walk over to my olive-green wall beside the balcony. My home sat on the edge of the city, overlooking the clouds that cascaded beneath our realm on one side and the other marble houses that replicated my own home on the other. The city lights lingered in the distance as the sun began to set. This place is my family's legacy, and has been for generations, but its current vacancy reminded me of the family I no longer had.

Years ago, nearly eighteen years, an angel had fallen. Fallen angels are not uncommon, and are usually sent directly to the Banished Realm—to Hell—for the rest of their days. This angel, however, managed to slip out of Hell's crevices through a rift, as many demons do, and began an uprising. But unlike demons, this angel was powerful.

And he wanted revenge.

No one knows all of the details, but during his five years in Hell, this angel continued to plot against humans. He wanted them beneath his feet, bowing to his name.

He wanted to become the next Lucifer.

From what I heard, his ambitions were no surprise to the angels. Some of my teachers had even predicted the events that unfolded. The angel that fell was Lucifer's son, Atticus Bernheim. And when he opened another rift five years after falling, he killed my parents.

I glance over the map that I had painted onto my wall when I was younger. The paint was black, shimmery, and the names of countries and capitals glossed under the dim lighting in my room. Theseus flicks his hand, lighting a few more candles in the room so we could see better.

I hold a finger to the map.

"A bridge, a thicket—well forest—and what else?" I ask, looking back to Theseus. He shrugs.

"That's all I can feel."

I look toward the map again and Theseus gets on his feet, stepping beside me to study the map as well.

"He said *you'll* know. Do you think He meant all of us? Or just you?" Theseus asks, still studying the map.

I shake my head.

"Why assign a task for three if it only requires one person?" I ask in return. Theseus nods his head in agreement as he stalks back to his chair. I keep examining the map, but I couldn't sway Theseus' question from running across my brain.

Was I supposed to know The Vine's identity?

A knock sounds from the door, but before I turn, Ares walks through it. He has a pile of books in his arms, a withering, leather satchel hanging from his side, and he's covered in armor.

Thin armor.

Theseus snorts before I do.

"If I didn't know any better, I'd say you planned on fighting demons with paper."

"The pen is mightier than the sword, Cupid," Ares retorts as he moves to my bed. Before I can protest, he dumps the books onto my mattress and starts to shuffle through them.

Searching.

"Ares, where am I supposed to sleep tonight?" I ask.

"There are plenty of rooms within the house, Gale," he reminds me, not bothering to stop his search. I grind my teeth at the response, but give a dismissive nod of my head nonetheless.

My house has ten bedrooms, seven of them being guest bedrooms. The smallest room would have been a nursery for my little brother. I haven't spent much time in those rooms, except for the occasional inquiry from maids discussing seasonal bed sheets. I usually ignore the vacancy of the manor by keeping to my room, the armory, the dining room, and the study, but right now my bedroom has transformed into something else entirely.

As soon as I got home from the temple, I pulled my desk into the middle of the room and cleared it off. I had written down our assignment and began developing a plan, ignoring the mess of papers across my floor as I tried to map our next move. Theseus arrived shortly after, and unfortunately, he wasn't much help.

Since we had agreed that staying at my house for this assignment would be best, Theseus had already moved a few of his belongings into one of the guest bedrooms. And when he sat in that leather armchair by my balcony door, all he's done on occasion was throw darts at the map on the wall—failing to pierce the paint because of his lack of enthusiasm. We didn't know what we were looking for so we bided our time, waiting for Ares to arrive so we could make progress.

Ares' face washes over with excitement as his hand glides onto a book with a dark, satin cover.

He lifts it triumphantly and meets my gaze.

"Well, what is it?" I ask. From the corner of my vision, Theseus, who was briefly resting his eyes while he sat, perks up.

"This," Ares begins, "is the key to our assignment—"

"Hold that thought," Theseus interrupts.

He stares intently at his hand.

At the ring on his finger.

Then he looks to us with widened eyes.

"We have to go."

■ ■ ■ ■

The summer breeze whipped against my face as we dove from the City of Aaron. Theseus had taken the lead in our flight, gliding a few feet ahead of myself and Ares. Our eyes adjusted to the darkness hovering over this side of the United States.

It was currently nighttime over the east coast, and I began to take in the shape of the states, recognizing the place my parents had shown me as a child. We were hovering over the location of a rift that Atticus had attempted to open.

New Jersey.

Theseus halts his wings and Ares and I pause at his side.

We've come prepared.

Theseus' shield rests on his forearm, his sword ready at his hip. His long, silver wings flap in the air as he looks around, circling the ring around his finger, waiting for a sign. Beside me, Ares tries to follow Theseus' gaze. He's still in the same armor that he wore to my room, the thin metal completely covering him from the neck down. He quickly glimpses from Theseus to the various city streetlights below, as if he were Theseus' second pair of eyes.

I feel the wind twirl between my fingers and look down. It glides over my sword and wraps around my hand, gently pulling me north. I stare at it, knowing I wasn't the cause of this. I move my other hand, trying to conjure the wind against the cool, summer breeze.

It has to be clashing with my powers.

But then the breeze wraps around my wrist and jerks me north once more.

Harder this time.

I glimpse north and immediately curve my wings, making them stable enough to go against the wind.

And without a word, I dive.

7
Havena

"I'm going to enjoy killing you."

My breath catches in my throat as I stare into those cat-like eyes. A couple of hours ago, I didn't know who this woman was. Correction, I still don't know who this woman is. I draw in a shaky breath as the creature raises her towering claws. She's about to break the glass. She's about to kill us.

I grip Leah's hand tighter.

A sliver of foggy brown cuts across the windshield, throwing the creature onto the ground. The car jerks free from their weight and Leah squirms. I release her hand, unbuckling my seatbelt to get out of the car. I ignore the ache in my body as I push the door open. It groans at the pressure but I hoist myself up, leaning over the hood of the car to gaze at the object that had just hit the woman.

Except it wasn't an object at all.

I take in the brown wings first, I'd be blind otherwise. They glisten under the moonlight, glazed over with a subtle tone of gray, which gives it an almost purple glow. It somehow looks familiar. Suddenly, two other figures shoot down next to my savior. Their wings are different.

The one with deep, bronze skin has black wings, like a void within the universe had blanketed itself onto his feathers. His feathers are as blunt as the brown feathers of his friend, maybe even more so. The blonde-haired boy has sharp wings. His feathers were soft, and the tips of them touched the road so subtly due to the span of his wings. His feathers were shimmery and metallic, almost tinted with warmth.

The dark brunette with brown wings hasn't turned around yet, and neither have the other two. Their backs were facing us as they examined the damage that the brunette had done.

He's killed her.

My breath catches in my throat once again and I can't move.

He's killed her.

The driver's side door opens, swaying Leah's car as it does and causing me to almost lose my balance. The three beings start to turn around, but Leah breaks the chilling silence first.

"Holy. Shit."

The boy with black wings flinches at Leah's words, and the blonde-haired boy catches the mannerism with a smirk. Leah stands from the driver's seat, darting her eyes from me, to the boys with wings, to me again. I can't help but do the same.

"You see this right?—"

I point, but Leah's already freakishly nodding her head.

"I see it. Do you see it?"

She points. I freakishly nod, too.

"We both see them—"

"You both see us," the brunette finishes.

Leah and I latch our gazes onto the boys.

In any other circumstance, I would have been breathless at the sight of their faces. The flickering streetlight illuminates just enough for me to see them, but not enough for me to give either of these boys justice.

The brunette's face is structured with strong cheekbones and steady, grey eyes. His hand rests on the sword at his hip, a kind of sword that I've only seen in movies. His hair sits at medium-length, framing his square jaw which narrows at the chin, and his tan skin was toned, barely glistening with sweat despite how hard he had tackled the woman.

He was completely symmetrical, body and face.

The bronze-skinned boy is equally blessed. His jaw is less narrow and a little less defined. His eyes are golden-brown, his nose is flatter, and his cheeks don't appear as toned. The sides of his head were shaved, yet braids rested on top of his head in a bun. He was the only being whose body was covered in metal plates, yet I could tell he wasn't a fighter. Before I could take in the blonde boy, wielding a thick, silver plate on his forearm and a long, leather sheath on his hip, Leah speaks to him first.

"Who are you?" she asks, pointing at him.

The blonde glances to his peers with a cocky glint in his eye before locking his gaze onto hers. As he steps forward, I can tell he's proud that Leah thinks he's the leader of their group. His cheeks are hollow, his gaze is sharp, and his jaw is defined, but the color of his blue eyes are soft, like the calm of an ocean.

He bows.

"I am Theseus, miss. And you must be *our vine*."

His voice sounds light and charming. He slurs the last bit of his words through those full, pink lips as if being, *'The Vine,'* were a title. I shiver, especially since the—now dead—woman wanted to kill me over that title.

Leah's head twitches from confusion, unsure of a response. I almost picture her stammering when I catch the brunette boy glimpse toward the forest. I clear my throat.

"That woman..." my voice strains out. Everyone turns their eyes to me, but I keep my gaze on him—the boy with brown wings. He blinks. "That... being you killed, wanted to kill us."

The blonde boy—Theseus—turns to look at the woman's sprawled body. The brunette steps aside, breaking my gaze to look upon the corpse as well. Theseus kicks the foot of it.

"Well, that's not a problem now, is it?" he says as a joke. The bronze-skinned boy cracks a grin.

"Theseus, she's terrified," the brunette mentions quietly. His voice is solid. Kind, but firm. And so was his command.

I took in those dominating, grey eyes again as they shifted between the eyes of his friends, realizing I wasn't terrified at all.

I just wanted to know about the boy with brown wings.

Theseus reluctantly sighs, taking hold of the feet of the corpse. As if on cue, the bronze-skinned boy who had yet to introduce himself, grabs the creature's arms.

Together, they shoot up into the sky.

Leah's gasp collides with my own as we watch them soar higher into the night. I look back to the brunette, who's eyes were already taking me in.

"I'm Gale."

8
Gale

"Havena," she says cautiously.

Whether it was the subtleness of her cheekbones or the sharpness of her eyes—which didn't fail to draw me to the fullness of her lips—her features created a balance of innocence and grit. Her voice was soft, corresponding with the kindness I knew lingered underneath that hard exterior of a gaze. I immediately noticed the tension hovering within her shoulders, as if she couldn't trust the being standing in front of her.

Or trust the fact that I even existed.

Havena quickly glances between myself and her friend, the question of how dangerous I could be lingering within her eyes. I raise my hands in surrender and hold her gaze.

"I'm not going to hurt you," I reassure. I stay where I am, watching as Havena glances to her friend again. Then she slips her arms off of the roof of the car and stalks to the other side of the car door.

"Who are you?" Havena asks behind the battered hood of the vehicle. Her voice sounds more in control now, not strained like it was before. I take a step forward, dropping my hands.

"I'm Gale. My two friends are Theseus and Ares. We were sent here to—"

"She also means *what* are you?" the girl with the long, black ponytail cuts in. Her friend closes the driver's side door and leans against it, crossing her arms. I look to Havena, her hands no longer trembling. They both share the same look of expectation.

The same mannerism.

"You're sisters?" I ask. They answer simultaneously.

"Nope," her friend simply responds.

Havena calmly shakes her head and continues to wait for the answer to her question.

A gust of wind swirls onto the road and Theseus drops down with Ares. Havena's friend widens her eyes, but Havena remains calm. I couldn't tell if she was faking her unbothered composure, but I could tell that she was studying us.

All three of us.

Theseus begins stretching into a yawn, flexing his wings to their entirety. Havena's eyes travel from his shoulders to the edge of his wings.

"Theseus," she asserts. He turns to her with a raised eyebrow, still stretching.

"And Ares?" she questions. Ares nudges me in the arm but nods his head with a grunt, confirming his name. Havena furrows her brows at me.

"What the Hell are you?" she asks.

"Don't say that," Ares scolds.

"I almost died tonight," she scoffs at him. Her friend raises a finger from her crossed arms.

"*We* almost died tonight," she points out. Havena shakes

her head toward her friend.

"But she called me, '*The Vine*,' Leah," Havena corrects. Theseus stops stretching and nods toward Leah in surprise.

"You're not The Vine?" he asks.

"Jesus Christ—what the Hell is The Vine?" Havena asks frustratedly. She glares at Ares before he can reprimand the language. "And why the Hell did I almost die tonight?"

A sudden snap echoes within the forest. We immediately scan the trees, looking for any slimmer of movement, but it was too dark to tell. Havena moves around the hood of the car and stands next to Leah. The two girls look around nervously. Havena's frustration battled the fear creeping onto her face. And it didn't help when Theseus and Ares stepped into their fighting stances.

"Do you know of a place where we can converse further? A safer place where we can hide?" I question.

I knew the demon I killed earlier wouldn't be the first to hunt Havena down, but I didn't think the other threats would discover her location so quickly. Leah, wide-eyed with alarm, shakes her head, and almost instinctively, grabs Havena's hand. I couldn't blame her. A few hours ago, they had no idea that this side to their world existed. And they still didn't know that Havena's life was now under our protection.

"I can't go home, can I," Havena mutters.

But, it's not a question.

She bites her lip, nervously looking around as she thinks of a place to go. With a flap of his wings, Theseus slips a few feet into the air to get a better vantage point. I scan the wooded area behind the car, moving my hand to the handle of my sword.

"The marketplace," Havena blurts out.

"Mrs. Patty's Marketplace."

■■■■

It's a rundown little shop. The washed-out, green sign barely illuminates *Mrs. Patty's Marketplace* in faded, red, neon lighting. A sheet of metal has been pulled over the entrance of the building. Havena was reluctant to fly in my arms, but as we landed on the sidewalk in front of the store, I could feel her heartbeat ease. Her dark hair whipped across my nose one last time before she quickly stepped out of my hold and onto the sidewalk. Ares lands beside me.

I watch as she tiptoes around the cracks in the ground, peeking into the crevices of the concrete. Her thin sweater is ripped across the sleeves, and the navy fabric of her jeans shimmer from splinters of glass—little splinters that she had yet to notice from the demon attack. I can't help but furrow my brows. Theseus' guess was right—The Vine was human.

She gets to the base of the door and lets out a sigh of relief as she bends down. Rising with a key in between her fingers, Havena starts to unlock the store when I hear a flap of wings above us. I look up to see Theseus with Leah in his arms. Leah's wide-eyed with terror, gripping Theseus as if her life depended on it. And judging by the way Theseus was holding her, it did.

They land, and the bell above the shop door jingles, catching my attention. It sounds throughout the parking lot and I quickly conjure the wind, freezing the bell in the air to silence our arrival. Havena and Leah look at the bell completely stunned, then at Ares as he collapses his wings. The wings fold over each other, shrinking down until there's no trace of him even having wings to begin with. The only signs that remain are two slits in the leather piece of his armor, sliced across the shoulder blades of his back. He walks into the store without a word and Theseus gestures toward the door.

"After you, ladies," he says. With a roll of her eyes, Leah stalks into the store. Theseus grins as he follows behind her.

Havena stays put, watching as I slowly bring the bell down, letting it vibrate within the gust of wind surrounding it until it goes still. My gaze meets hers again, and I notice something new lingers within her eyes as she stares into my own. Awe.

She drops her hand from her chest, clearing her throat.

"We have until morning."

9
Havena

I tried to keep my voice calm. Collected. But as his brown wings shrunk into his back, I felt my breath catch inside of my throat once again tonight.

He was beautiful, and terrifying. A phenomenon I wanted to completely engulf myself in even though it could hurt me. Or worse—kill me.

When Gale had asked me for a safe place to go, I could only think of this store. I mentally kick myself in the head for bringing these creatures here without Mr. Pelowski's permission, but as I turn on my heel to cross the store's threshold, I know I have no other choice.

Leah was smart enough to lead the other two beings into the employee break room, letting the rest of the store remain dark as we hid. The only problem was that the break room was nowhere near big enough for all of us to sleep in for the night. And I needed to sleep. I may not have known if these creatures slept, or if they even needed it, but I knew my mind. It was exhausted.

Gale walks into the store after me, and I avoid his gaze as I stop short, directing him to the break room behind the cash register's counter.

"They're all in there," I murmur as I turn to shut the door. He doesn't speak until I click the lock.

"Are you sure this place is safe?" he asks.

"How do I know you are?" I challenge. He studies me for a moment. And I do the same to him.

A sneeze from the break room catches our attention, and we turn to find Ares walking into the market area.

"Why are humans so vulnerable? And so gross?"

"Your wings must be collecting dust, A," Gale teases. I fight the smirk that wants to slip onto my face.

"Ha-ha." Ares grimaces before strolling back into the break room. I head for the room, too, with Gale close behind me.

Leah was sitting on the sturdy, plastic, lunch table shoved into the corner of the room. She had her back against the wall and curled her knees into her chest. Ares took a seat in the chair at the opposite end of the table, and Theseus sat next to him on the floor.

"God, my car! Hell, I have my life, but if my mom finds that car..." Leah starts. She runs a hand through her hair, which she's now pulled out of her ponytail, and buries her head into her knees. Ares looks at her in bewilderment.

"You have your life, human, you should be grateful," he says. She shoots her head up, and I go to the counter to turn on the electric teapot.

"*Human*," she snorts with a laugh. Then she lets out another laugh, which turns into a fit of giggles.

We all look to her.

"What?" she asks in disbelief. "This guy with wings—with bird freaking feathers that shoot, *and unshoot*, from his back—calls me a human, but because I laugh, *I'm the crazy one?"*

Theseus raises his hand and Leah glares at him.

"Trick question," she snaps.

I grab five mugs from the cabinet and set them onto the counter before grabbing the teapot. My back is turned from their silent gazes as the aroma of hot, green tea floats into the air. I instantly feel my body relax.

I fill the first two mugs and hand them to Leah and Ares. Leah gives me a nod of gratitude and Ares curiously accepts it. I ignore him. Then I go back to the counter and fill two more mugs.

I ignore Gale's gaze, whose body was leaned against the door frame, and head over to Theseus, who awkwardly takes hold of the mug. There was no way he could spin this moment into a joke, but it was funny to see his blues eyes consider it before he muttered his thanks.

I turn away, ready to give Gale his mug when I notice the empty door frame. Gale has chosen a seat on top of the counter, his back leaning against the wall. I hear everyone's subtle slurps in the background as I walk over to Gale and extend his mug. His hand meets mine and the graze of his touch sends electricity across my skin.

I look into his eyes and those dark-grey orbs mirror my surprise. I quickly lower my hand, hoping no one saw whatever had just happened, and step away to pick up my mug. It was probably a friction shock.

I lean against the counter and face the group. Closing my eyes, I take a sip of the tea and just breathe. For a moment, everything feels okay. At ease. I open my eyes and look at Ares staring into his mug, then Theseus. His blue eyes were closed as he relaxed his blonde head against the wall. Without their wings, they looked like regular boys.

Human boys.

Then I look to Leah. Leah was captivated by Ares as he stared into his cup, then she stared into her own cup, then back to him. A grin plays onto my face until I feel the hairs on my neck suddenly stand.

Gale had put his mug down next to my arm. I almost miss the gesture, but I had glimpsed at his hand just in time to see it inch away from the proximity of my arm, settling back to his side. I clear my throat and look to the others.

"So, where do we go from here?" I ask. Theseus keeps his eyes closed, but the tip of his ears curl at the question. Ares looks up from his tea.

"Well, uh, we were told to train... you," he stammers. I narrow my eyes as his judgmental gaze glances over me.

He quickly looks away.

"Train me?"

"What he means," Gale cuts in, "is that we were sent here to find you. The Vine is prophesied to master the fourth element—"

"Element?" I interrupt.

"Water," Gale concludes. He waits a moment, watching my lips to see if I'll interrupt again. "Angels can conjure all of the earth's elements. Earth, fire, air, water."

"Wait a minute! You're telling me Havena's Batman and I'm Robin?" We turn our gazes as Leah chimes in with a shake of her head. "I've known this girl for the majority of my life. She's not an angel. They don't exist!"

Theseus finally opens his eyes and settles a curious gaze onto Leah. Ares speaks first with a voice of disdain.

"Correct me if I'm wrong, but were you not just freaking out about feathers that shoot, and I quote, 'unshoot,' from my back?"

Leah fails to think of a counterargument as she glares at Ares, her mouth hanging open without a rebuttal. Theseus closes his eyes again with an amused grunt and a snicker escapes Gale's throat. My eyes latch to his, unamused, and Gale stops laughing.

"The point is, there's a prophecy about a war that's coming. It's always been coming. But our assignment, and apparently a part of the prophecy, is to train you for it. You, Havena, are going to be the one to end that war—The Holy War—and bridge our realms together."

I catch Ares put down his mug at Gale's words, leaning back in his chair with a look dancing in his eyes.

A look I couldn't place.

"What realms?" I ask Ares directly. He's too quiet for my liking, as if he was forced to be here. And as if to confirm my assumption, he shrugs in response.

I look to Gale for the answer instead.

"Your blood will unify all four of our holy cities. Including Hell."

10
Havena

"I'm not an angel, or a demon, or—whatever the Hell."

Walking out of the break room was a stupid decision. I didn't know what to do—and I had nowhere else to go—so I started sulking between the aisles of carted fruit, hoping Gale would leave me alone. He followed me instead.

"I'm not The Vine, okay? I'm just a girl—who was a nobody—until I bumped into that cat-looking lady, and now I'm on Hell's most wanted list," I huff out.

Theseus kept silent in the break room, meditating against the wall as Gale explained my role for their assignment.

Why I was, *'The Vine.'*

Ares had finally jumped in to tell me that because the war was prophesied—The Holy War—it was going to happen one way or another, and that going with them guaranteed that I'd stay alive.

Alive... for their war... for now.

The word bounced around in my head as I rushed out of the room, knowing that Gale was close on my heels, but I didn't care. They weren't sure if bridging the realms together called for my death just yet, and that's what overwhelmed me the most.

I nearly bump into Gale's chest as I turn around, pausing my parade to protest the idea again. He takes a step back, patiently looking down at me with a sigh, and I notice the rim of brown around the grey of his eyes. The words I was going to say are forgotten, so I turn away from him and keep walking.

"Please, don't tell me your purpose in life is to stay in this town," he scoffs.

"Of course it's not. I know it's not!" I insist, but the tone of my voice sounds weak. I sounded as if I were trying to convince myself. "But having three random strangers say, *'Come with me if you want to live,'* isn't exactly the kind of purpose I had in mind."

Gale furrows his brows for a moment. "But, you really should come with us if you want to live—"

I wave my hand dismissively.

"No—that's not—It's a movie reference."

"We don't... watch movies."

"Well... humans do."

I sigh in frustration and lean against a fruit cart, only to watch him lean on the cart across from me.

Then we just stare at one another.

We've been trying to figure each other out since the moment our eyes met, but I couldn't deny the inkling in my body that knew he was reading me like a book.

"You're afraid," he says.

"Wouldn't you be?" I challenge. He only nods.

"Sure," he answers. "I guess if I were human and didn't have any knowledge whatsoever on protecting myself—"

"You'd go with three creatures who could?"

"I'd go with *three angels* to guarantee my safety," he

counters firmly. I bite my cheek as he watches me patiently, but he's not waiting for me to make a decision.

He's waiting for me to agree.

"I can't leave." I shake my head. "I can't leave this place behind. My home is here... my mom... But it's good to know that Hell is considered a *holy* city."

"But if you don't, Havena, you'll die," he says, ignoring my sarcasm. "More demons will come after you. Not just the one from tonight."

"You'll just save me again—"

"Actually, I haven't decided if I should just let you die yet," he says nonchalantly. My heart skips a beat at the seriousness on his face.

Then he cracks a grin.

"Not cool," I laugh softly.

He shrugs with a smirk on his lips, then leans off the fruit cart.

"Your purpose in this prophecy—this war—is so much greater than whatever you're leaving behind—"

"So you're saying I should go on a quest—where I could die—because it will be fun to leave my family?" I ask.

"No, no! That's not what I meant at all," he says. His cheeks start to flush red, and for a split second, I think I catch a slimmer of sadness glaze over his eyes. By the time I blink again, it's gone.

"I know what it's like to leave family behind. And I know loss. But loss doesn't mean you should stop trying to be the person you were called to be."

I drop my gaze from his, unwilling to see the sincerity in his face that sounded through his words. That may have worked for him, but it didn't work for my mother when my father died. And as much as I wanted to believe what he was saying, I didn't believe his advice could work for me either. A chuckle of disbelief escapes my throat.

"This is ridiculous. I'm not called to be the hero in your twisted, little world—"

"But you are, Havena. You're a part of our world because it's your world, too... somehow," he says, taking a step forward.

He quickly realizes I won't respond and lets out a laugh of impatience. "Why are you so in denial about this? This town isn't extravagant and your... clothes are worn... You're as bland as paper, and yet you would rather die here than be who you were called to be—"

"I am not willing to leave my mother behind! Not like this! She's already lost my father. And if you expect me to jump into a situation where she could lose me, too, then you should leave—because I am *all* she has left!"

I hadn't realized I raised my voice.

Or that I've said too much.

Revealed too much.

My vision turns hazy as I take in the whirlpool of air lapping around my face. My breaths cut in and out of my body in short waves and I claw at my neck, grasping at the air that was restricting my throat. Within a blink, the whirlpool evaporates and Gale is standing a few feet away from me.

His hand raised.

"What did you do to me?"

"You have powers."

We speak at the same time.

The lights above me—and only above me—sway, and my chest tightens as Gale glances at his hand in the air before lowering it.

"When did you gain The Sight?" he asks. I shake my head at his question.

"You just tried to choke me—"

"No, I didn't. When did you gain The Sight?" he impatiently asks again. He takes a step closer. I take one back.

"Have you ever moved a rock with your mind before? Just thought about it and then—swish?"

I shake my head. Gale takes another small step forward.

I take one back.

"Have you ever noticed water behave strangely around you? Maybe it would flicker in a random direction that made no sense at all..."

I think back to my time in the shower this morning. The water had turned scalding hot, but it didn't move unnaturally. It was nothing like his example, so I stay quiet.

But I also didn't shake my head.

With a raise of his eyebrow, Gale takes another step forward.

I take another step back.

"Have you ever seen something you couldn't explain? Maybe you've seen someone appear as someone or something else the next second?"

"Oh my god," I breathe out. I run a hand through my hair and back into one of the fruit stalls. The memory of the still-cloud dances across my brain as the realization hits me. I wasn't crazy when I was a child, but I'd be crazy not to believe Gale right now.

Gale takes another step closer toward me.

And I let him.

"Look at your pants," Gale commands. I furrow my brows, taken aback by the request, but he only nods his head.

I look down.

"What the Hell does that have to do with anything?" I ask.

Gale shrugs.

"You tell me."

I look back up to him with the same face of confusion I've worn before. A smirk plays onto his face as he nods again.

Glimpsing back down to my pants, I take in the little, glittery specks lodged into the fabric of my jeans. They weren't there when I put my jeans on this morning. I squint, my vision suddenly recognizing the sharpness of splinters that had nestled into the threading.

I meet Gale's gaze again.

"Glass?"

11
Gale

She's not human.

As soon as her foggy, amber eyes scanned my face in confusion, I turned on my heel.

I wove my way through the aisles of produce as she called out my name, the shuffling of her feet sounding behind me, but I refused to stop moving until I reached the others.

Theseus was still slumped on the floor, his head still leaning against the wall as he lazily opened his eyes upon my arrival. Leah was still seated on top of the table, yet she had scooted closer to Ares. He was busy murmuring something to her, their heads huddled over their mugs before they lifted their gazes to my presence. Finally, I heard Havena's footsteps reach the threshold.

"She has The Sight." I announce. Theseus leans his head off of the wall in surprise. Ares straightens up in his seat.

"She's not human?" Theseus asks, his surprised eyes beginning to trail over Havena's body. I step in front of her.

"I don't think so," I tell him. He gives me a look, then shrugs back into the wall, closing his eyes again. Havena steps around me and hops onto the counter, hugging herself as she watches us speak. Ares shakes his head.

"Well, she's not fully angel. We would've known," he reasons. I tilt my head expectantly and he sighs at my ignorance.

"She would have wings. And she would've had them as a child as well. There's no way she would know how to glamour her wings without training. Hiding them on this realm would be impossible," Ares explains.

"So, if we're on the same page here—"

"Then, that would mean I'm half-angel," Havena says. She looks from me to Ares. Even Theseus opens his eyes, seeming impressed by her input. She takes a deep breath.

"I'm half-angel... and half-human."

12
Havena

"I don't have wings," I confirm, sliding off the counter. "But I've seen... stuff." I look to Leah, silently watching with her head propped on her knees.

"I've seen weird stuff."

Her mouth forms an, "O," remembering our conversation in the car before the attack. She nods her head in understanding and looks to the floor. I look to Gale.

"Where do we go from here?" I ask him.

"Well, you have to be trained," he responds, crossing his arms.

"And we need an actual safe space. I hate fruit," Theseus pipes in with a grimace from the floor.

We all look to him, but his bored eyes remain closed.

"I'm sensing a lot of annoyed people inside of this room," he adds, a smirk playing onto his face.

Leah shimmies off the table and stands next to me. A bruise, forming on the side of her face, appears to be the only damage she's taken from the attack.

"I'm not letting her go anywhere alone," she says, and I nod in agreement. "We just met you—you angels—*and Jesus,* you're angels for crying out loud."

"And she almost died tonight. Who's to say they aren't hunting her so they can get to me?" I ask. Leah looks to me with surprise in her eyes.

"Crap, there's more?" she whispers. Ares lets out an impatient sigh again and Theseus chuckles. Unlike Leah, it was obvious to me—and to the rest of us—that this wouldn't be the last attempt on my life.

"So, instead of one potted plant, we have two," Theseus says with a sarcastic click of his tongue.

Gale rolls his eyes but doesn't disagree.

"Right now, we need to go back home," Gale says. I didn't know what home he was referring to, but I knew it wasn't mine.

Growing up I always considered my mother my home. Not the rickety roof over my head, or this familiar town full of familiar faces. Our relationship may have been dull through the years, but our silent bond as mother and daughter was secure.

Home.

My mother was probably worried sick about me right now, or wondering if I was even alive. But if one demon knew about the prophecy, then others did, too. And if I had to leave her behind so she could be safe, I would. I'd rather those creatures come after me and not her. Not home.

"*We* need to go home," I tell Gale, gesturing my head to include Leah. "We need to say goodbye."

■ ■ ■ ■

Leah and I took our time as we cleaned up the break room. It was the cleanest we'd ever seen it, and when Leah squeezed my shoulder before we turned off the light, deep down I knew it might be the last time we'd ever get to see it. I glanced at the clock before leaving the break room, just to remember the time I'd done my last task for Mr. Pelowski. The time my life would change forever.

It was midnight.

Ares, Theseus, and Gale shuffled behind us as we exited the grocery store and into the night. I locked the door, listening to the sound of wings flap behind me, and dropped the spare key into a crevice in the concrete. I turned around to see Theseus already taking flight with Leah in his arms. She was going to leave a note for her mom and her entire box of savings that she'd hidden in her closet. Leah was planning on using that money to get out of here, out of this town with me.

I feel a tang of guilt climb into my chest, but it stops short as Ares pushes his wings out of his back. He slips into the air to hover above me and Gale on the ground.

Gale hadn't taken out his wings yet.

"Are you ready?" Gale asks me, holding out his hand. I let in a breath, staring at his hand for a moment, then his eyes. They held nothing but determination.

Although I knew I was his responsibility—and felt like it—there was something about his presence that I knew I should learn to trust.

Eventually.

I nodded, putting my hand in his, and let him pull me into his chest. That shock of electricity I had felt before danced in my veins, but I suppressed it, distracted by the rustle of his wings escaping his back. I watched as his brown feathers folded around us like a cocoon for a moment, like an embrace before he rose from the ground, his wings unfolding around us as he slipped further into the night sky.

I closed my eyes.

My heart hammered in my chest at the thought of my feet off the ground. Gale's strong arm pulled me into him around the waist, but it still took everything in me not to scream.

The night wind came in sharp and cold, whipping about my face and throughout my hair. I grimaced at the feeling of it slicing my flesh. If I ever learned how to control this element, or tamed it enough to dance between my fingers, I wonder if it'd hurt the way it does now.

This flight felt longer than the first one until I started to feel the tilt in Gale's body. I snaked my arm around his back and buried my face into the toned muscles of his bicep, clinging for my life before he dived. And my hand grazed against the softest of his feathers for the briefest moment.

It was velvety, despite how sturdy and solid it had appeared when I'd first seen it. I brought my finger up to touch the feather again, longing for a distraction from my locked eyes, and started to pet it.

Gale shuddered from the touch.

"Please, don't do *that*," he murmured to me in a husky whisper. I lowered my finger instantly. Within a matter of seconds, we landed onto the lawn of my house. Gale opened his arm and I immediately stumbled out of it, planting my feet on the ground as I took in my childhood home.

The light on the front porch failed to illuminate the front door. I looked to the windows. None of the lights were turned on. Not even the nightlight in her bedroom on the second floor.

And without a second thought, I ran.

13
Gale

When she stepped out of my arms and froze, I knew something was wrong. Her delicate shoulders had gone tense as she glanced around the front lawn. Then at every window.

Then the front door.

"Havena," I called out, but it was too late. She darted up the porch steps to the front door. It burst open without a key. I flew onto the porch and hurried in after her. Ares entered behind me.

She paused in the living room, looking around at the scattered items on the floor. The house was a shell of a home, but whatever furniture that was inside of it had been ransacked.

The bland couches were torn to shreds, with evidence of claw markings that stretched across the cushions. No personal pictures were hanging around the house of any kind. The walls were barren and the TV was smashed to the ground, covering the carpet flooring with flecks of broken, black glass. The house had an open plan, but the kitchen was just as destroyed as the living room.

Every rickety, wooden cabinet laid open, with utensils and broken plates scattered all over the tile floor. Even the refrigerator was open, but it contained a sad amount of food that wouldn't have lasted any angel a day—let alone a human. Havena looked around, then her blank eyes looked at me.

No. Past me.

She clutched her chest and rushed up the stairs, stepping beside me and my wings like we were a part of the wreckage. I raised a hand toward Ares, signaling him to stay put and stand guard, just in case. Then I heard her scream.

It was blood-curdling. One so sorrowful, it's already pierced my ears for the rest of my days.

My blood ran cold.

I shot up the stairs, my wings scraping against the walls of the corridor. I tucked them into my back as I landed onto the second floor and listened for the sound of her sobs. The hiccupped tears led me to a small master-suite. The window in the center of the wall overlooked the street, and it was the window that made her freeze outside.

I took a light step into the room. Sitting in an old pool of her mother's blood, was Havena. She cradled the frail body in her arms and wailed. Her mother's wrists and feet were bound. The bruising had settled in now, roughly several hours old. There was a slice on her throat that stretched from ear to ear, as if the person who did this wanted to take their time.

To punish her with a slow blade.

The state of her body and the barren household told me enough about how she died. She was protecting Havena, and she died before Havena was attacked.

Havena tried to catch her breath—huffing in, huffing out—and ultimately failing. Her breaths came in short hiccups, sloshing through her tears.

"No," Havena huffs out. She cups her mother's face, then looks up at me in the door frame.

"No!" her voice raised.

Whether she realized it or not, she began to circle air around her head as she had done in the supermarket. I raise my hand, fighting the air she was conjuring to shut herself up.

To suffocate herself.

"NO!NO!NO!NO!" Havena screams.

The air she conjured has intensified, and I strain my hand to break the flow apart. She looks down at her dead mother and the cry in her throat shatters. The whirlpool around her begins to wither, but I refrain from lowering my hand until the entirety of it ceases. She chokes through her tears and cups her mother's face again. Then she lays her mother's head to rest on the floor.

"N-No," she whines quietly, rocking back and forth.

Havena glimpses at her hands, and pauses. She begins rubbing them against her jeans, as if she could rub off the blood that's stained her skin.

She ignores me until I slowly kneel beside her, allowing the blood of her mother to soak onto my pants. She stops rubbing her hands on her jeans and lifts her eyes to mine.

Those amber eyes were completely broken, like beautiful shards of glass dancing under the moonlight, yet they burned the core of my heart with her pain.

Havena shakes her tear-streaked face profusely.

"No..." she whines again, leaning into my chest. I bring out my wings again, circling them around her, hiding her from this scene. From this nightmare.

And I let her sob.

14.
Havena

I didn't think I would cry this hard. But I also didn't think I would lose her this early. I didn't say anything when Gale hid me under his wings, but then again, I didn't know what to say. I could sit here and list all of the things I didn't do in my head, or I could think about how I didn't say goodbye. How I was robbed of a goodbye for a second time.

Gale kept me encircled in his wings as he brought me downstairs. I kept my head against his shoulder, listening as his wings ruffled against the walls of the staircase, wondering if it bothered his delicate feathers.

I had cried until I was empty. Until my eyes burned dry from the tears that wouldn't come out. And now my mind felt empty.

My soul felt empty.

Numb.

I didn't have any immediate family in this world anymore, and this shell of a house had finally settled itself into my brain.

My mother had died in this empty home, a house that made me feel like life wasn't worth living. On most nights, it was only the two of us at our silent dinner table, and the Mother's Day cards I'd given her as a child always got thrown into the trash on more than one occasion. We had stopped celebrating holidays during my middle school years, and there had been no point in inviting her to the school band concerts to watch me play piano.

She wouldn't have come.

Yet, even so, the love I had for my mother outweighed the hate I had for her ways.

We got to the base of the stairs and Gale unfolded his wings. They shrunk into his back, but I still held onto his arm. If I let go of him, I knew I'd fall. Because that's what I felt like doing.

Falling.

Ares sat on a barstool at the kitchen counter. He had tried to clean up a bit by closing the cabinets and creating a pathway through the wreckage, but I couldn't find the words to thank him. For some reason, I felt like he did it more for himself rather than for me.

"My mother..." I barely registered the sound of my voice, as if I could hear myself talking, yet I didn't realize I was. I brought my eyes from the floor to Ares. "My mother's gone."

Just as Ares straightened up in his seat, a second away from opening his mouth, we heard a thump on the grass outside.

Ares jumped to his feet, racing out of the door and onto the front porch. Gale almost took a step forward to follow suit, but I squeezed his arm. He stepped back, letting me lean into him. I didn't care if there were more surprises that he couldn't protect me from.

I watch as Leah steps through the front door, now slanted off its hinges. She rushes over to me. I let go of Gale's arm and collided into her hug. She pats my back as my breath trembles.

"I know," she whispers, "I know."

She releases me and steps away, running a hand through her hair as she backs against the kitchen counter.

Theseus enters the room behind Ares now. His eyes gloss over my body, taking in the blood on my clothes—on my hands—before meeting my gaze. The ocean I'd seen in his eyes earlier is flat with sadness. A moonless tide.

I drop my gaze and slump into Gale's arm again, looking over the damage to the house.

My house.

I fight the weight of my eyelids. Nobody moves, nobody speaks, and I can barely feel myself breathe.

Ares breaks the silence.

"Our father, who art thou in heaven..."

15
Gale

Havena keeps her arm snaked around mine as Ares says the prayer. Her head rests on my shoulder, now damp from her tear-streaked face although she was no longer crying. She's placed her entire weight onto me as if she'd fall without my strength.

And in this moment, I refused to let her fall.

"Amen," Ares finishes. Leah murmurs a hesitant amen and Theseus draws a cross over his heart with a nod. They cautiously look toward Havena on my arm.

And our silence.

Havena keeps her gaze on the floor, numb to the attention.

A gaze I'm all too familiar with.

I've spent too many days numb to my own loss, questioning why God had marked the course of my life with death. With the tragedy of that fallen angel wiping away my entire family. But I've managed to suppress that question behind my duty as a Guardian.

Havena's squeeze on my arm reminds me that I'm not alone. That she was feeling the same pain that I've been through, even though she didn't know it yet. She lifts her head off my shoulder, her eyes staring at all of us and none of us at the same time, through the wreckage and distant memories that she's had in this house. And when she finally speaks, her voice is quiet, sounding throughout the room just as faded as those memories she was probably thinking of.

"Take me home."

■ ■ ■ ■

Theseus and Leah announced that they would stay behind, to which Ares and I took with a curt nod before walking out of the house. Havena's head may have been off my shoulder now, but her grasp on my arm remained as we stepped onto the front lawn. And without a word, Ares and I took flight.

I knew Theseus was going to bury the mother's body, but I had no idea why Leah wanted to stay behind. And I didn't ask.

As the night wind laps around me, my eye catches Havena shuddering. She's snaked her arm around me again, burying her face back into my bicep.

I hadn't realized the wind had bothered her before. As I tilt my body, changing its angle to redirect the wind, Havena brings her thin hand near the root of my wing, just as she had done on our last flight. I gulp, trying to ignore the slimmer of heat that's traveled down my spine, settling into my abdomen.

At the root of our wings, there's a small dagger-like limb in our shoulder blades. They're short, similarly embroidered to that of a tattoo, and it's where our wings start to develop.

Growing with length as we age, our wings can vary in shape and size, and our feathers are genetically determined. Although I've been told I share the face of my father, I prided myself on sharing the wings of my mother.

If our wings were ever ripped from their root—an

excruciating pain no one intentionally puts themselves through—it takes years for them to reach full length again. And with all of this, any delicate touch across that part of an angel's body is just... extremely sensitive.

I flap my wings once more and we breach past the clouds. The sun was starting to rise far off into the horizon, possibly over Europe, and the water funneling out of the City of Aaron shimmers under the light of the moon, like a liquid rainbow as it funnels into the clouds below. I pause my flight, taking it all in as Ares flaps past me with a childish laugh, flying in loops toward the city. Havena moves her head to look around.

Her eyes, now widening in awe, glaze over the floating city. The sun had yet to set over my home, but the hazy, deep blues and purples of the night sky reflected onto its tall, marble buildings, giving every structure a glorious glint.

I fly toward it, slowly gliding high above the sleeping city streets so Havena can take it all in.

She gazes at the canals running through the city. The fountains and museum-like structures spread throughout the heart of it. The cobblestone sidewalks and silver trimmed roofings. I fly lower, feeling Havena's grasp squeeze me a bit tighter. A large canal underneath a wide, white-stone bridge with copper trimming separates the city from the residential area.

My residential area.

The manors are tall and wide, with gated front entrances and winding streams separating the properties instead of fences.

I gently land onto the pathway of my house. White, glossy stone, now shining under the moonlight, stretches to the entrance of my home. Tall, colonial pillars glide to the second story of my manor, meeting stone angels within the frieze of

63

the roof. They look upon the entrance of the pathway with frozen greetings.

Havena releases my arm and stumbles two feet ahead, turning her head from one aspect of this place to the next, drinking it all in. She turns to me with wonder in her tired eyes, and I can't fight the smirk of pride that rises to my face.

"Welcome home."

16
Havena

Stunning. There's no other word for it. Maybe incredible, but that word wouldn't do this city justice at all. It was as if the Romans had settled here after their downfall; as if they preserved a chunk of their identity from the earth and found a way for it to float. Gale opened the frosted double-doors of his house and moved aside so I could step in.

Mostly everything was white—the marble flooring, the paneled, stone walls, the wide, curved staircases that paralleled each other inside of the foyer. A circular iron table, matching the swirled railing of the stairs, sat in the middle of the foyer, and a crystal chandelier hung from the high ceiling.

To my right, I peeked through the large, french double-doors that revealed a kitchen. Other angels—maids—were hustling around the kitchen island wearing pale-gold aprons. I looked to my left, toward the living room, to find a dominating, brick fireplace in the middle of the wall. The furniture, although white, looked inviting and fluffy.

Comfortable, for a family.

Straight ahead, between the two staircases, stood a light-wooden double-door that gave color and warmth to the foyer. That must be the dining room.

I turned around to Gale, who leaned against the front door with his arms folded. He was studying me with worry, as if he couldn't decipher my next step. And I'd be lying to myself if I said I was perfectly fine with that.

We'd just met, and something about him constantly raised the hairs on my neck. Just looking into his eyes made me want to forget my words. And when we sat in the dampness of my mother's blood, I didn't push him away. Couldn't push him away. I needed his strength.

I glimpsed at his pants, still stained with red from the night, then looked down at myself.

"I need to—uh—I need... I need to—" I stammer, but I didn't have the heart to finish my sentence. Gale propped himself off the door frame with a nod of his head.

"Follow me," he says, and he motions for me to follow him up the staircase.

He turned right when we reached the landing on the second floor, and I glimpsed back to the left side of the hall. The white wall-paneling upstairs was the same as downstairs, and the doors on the left side of the hall were identical to the ones on the right. The white wood of the doors had tiny engraved swirls of brushed pale-gold within their corners. Gale opened a door at the very end of the hall and stepped aside.

I stepped in after him to find a huge, fluffy, white bed centered against a marble wall. The canopied bed frame glistened under the dim rays of dawn, subtly showing the shine of pale rose-gold. The entire floor was marble, and archways rested at each end of the wall, showing a glimpse into the bathroom with stone sinks and tall mirrors. The curtains laying over the canopy of the bed were sheer, delicate, dancing within the subtle wind that came from the balcony across from it.

The balcony.

The open french doors revealed a cobblestone balcony that overlooked the city, the dark sky...

The atmosphere.

I walked onto it, closing my eyes from the stars as the breeze swept over me. I almost reached for the railing. Almost. But then I paused, remembering the stains. The blood.

My mother's blood.

I let out a shaky breath as I opened my eyes.

This wasn't my home. I didn't have one. I'll never have one. I backed into my room and turned around for Gale, but my eyes scanned an empty room now. The door was shut, and I was alone. Replacing Gale's absence laid folded towels and a thin, grey dress on the bed. A cotton nightgown.

I left them on the bed, refusing to dirty anything with my hands, and walked toward the bathroom for the one thing I needed first.

A bath.

17
Gale

I broke through the surface of water above me and leaned against the porcelain of my bathtub. I could only hope Havena would do the same before she slept. She needed to rest. I placed her room across the hall from mine so I could keep an eye on her. If she unconsciously conjured an element, like she had done twice now with air, I might be able to stop her from killing herself.

The image of her suffocating flashes into my mind, and I grip the edge of the tub at the possibility of it happening again.

Her hands grabbing her neck... Her fingers pressing for air...

I run a hand over my face, then through my hair, removing the water from my eyes with a sigh as I gaze at the ceiling, thinking about the prophecy.

"She has been pruned and placed before a thicket, yet her enemies have left the land dry."

The prophecy wasn't just talking about her location, it was talking about her family. Her enemies have left her with nothing now. Her land—her home—was left dry, and our vine had tried to take her own life because of it—more than once.

I let out a huff of frustration before scrubbing the rest of my body. Soon enough, a knock sounds on the bedroom door as I step out of the bath. I barely grab a towel in time before Theseus waltzes in with an obvious pep in his step.

"Where's Havena?" he asks. I walk behind my frosted wall divider, grabbing a change of clothes from the dresser.

"Across the hall," I murmur, pulling up my slacks. Theseus grunts as he sits in the leather armchair by the balcony door.

"How long do you think she'll mourn her mother before she trains?" he asks. There was no expectancy in his tone.

Only inquiry.

I yawn with a stretch. My light, cream, polyester sweater hung loosely over my body, letting the breeze from the balcony slip through the fabric. The dark brown slacks are a little thicker, but they hung just the same around my legs.

I step around the wall divider.

"She's just lost her mother, Theseus. Her home. She's not like us," I remind him. He sighs up at the ceiling.

"Well, she's... half of us. We mustn't leave her entire being at death's door so we can coddle her."

My weight dips into the edge of the bed as I sit on it. I push off the books that Ares had put on the bed earlier. They tumble to the floor, some staying closed while others fall with their bindings open, creasing the pages. Theseus, still in his attire from our trip to the Human Plane, snorts as I lean back. His sword and shield are leaning against the wall.

"Ares is going to have a fit."

"Yes, well, he's not the one on my mind," I groan, finally relaxing into my bed. We had bigger troubles than Ares getting mad over his books. Just as Havena's broken gaze flashes across my brain once again, Theseus raises a brow.

"How did you know how to find her?" he asks, snapping

me out of my daze. He gestures to his ring finger, where his gold band should be, but there's nothing there.

"My ring went dull when we were over New Jersey. Next thing I know, you dived," he points out. I shrug, remembering the moment the wind tugged on my hand. Twice.

"The breeze felt familiar... like it knew who I was before it pulled me north," I tell him.

"You say, 'it,'... So you don't think she conjured the breeze to you?" he asks.

"I'm not sure."

The lie slips out a little too quickly, and Theseus studies me a moment longer before dropping my gaze with a smirk.

I didn't want to tell him, or anyone, that she's conjured air already. When the whirlpool wrapped around Havena's face for the first time, I thought I had done it, but as her voice rose, I realized she was using the air to muffle herself. To muffle her scream. She had succeeded in the grocery store by trapping the sound waves within the whirlpool. It muffled her outburst just enough for me to hear. Only me.

But when she found her mother, I couldn't let her hide. Couldn't let her suffocate, even though she wanted to. I saw it in her eyes—she wanted to die.

I sigh at the thought.

That information seemed too personal for me to share.

"Where's Leah?" I ask, changing the subject.

"She's in a guest room. Left-wing," Theseus answers nonchalantly.

My gaze meets his at the same time.

"You're staying in the left-wing."

"So is Ares."

"We both know Ares is going to spend most of his time within the temple," I point out. He dismisses me with a wave of his hand but I press on.

"You have the hots for a human girl!" I laugh.

"I'm *intrigued* by the human girl," he corrects. "There's something in Leah that's... fascinating." He gazes at the ceiling with a short pause. "For a human."

I let out another laugh and the sound of feet lands onto my cobblestone balcony.

Ares walks into the room. His armor has been replaced by casual wear—a sleeveless, black T-shirt and dark pants. His gaze immediately drops to the floor by my bed.

"Seriously?" he asks with annoyance. He raises his hand, conjuring the air to stack the books onto my desk.

"Come on Ares, throw at least one book at him!" Theseus suggests enthusiastically.

"You'd be a fool to fight against a Guardian," I warn.

"Want to test that out when we train tomorrow?" Ares questions, a daring smirk on his lips. Theseus sits up in his chair before I respond, his brows furrowed innocently.

"We're *all* training tomorrow?"

"Sure."

"No."

With our humor gone, Ares lowers his hand with curiosity as the last book to be stacked onto my desk drops to the floor.

"Havena and Leah will not be training with us. At least not yet," I say, explaining my disapproval. Ares' eyes widen in realization and he looks to Theseus.

"You want the humans to train with us?" he asks in disbelief.

Theseus simply nods his head.

"Havena's half-angel. Besides, the faster they learn how to defend themselves, the better chance they have at staying alive."

"But Havena's training will have to be different than Leah's," I point out. Theseus shrugs.

"Then what do you suggest?"

I've been trying to think of how we could protect Leah ever since Havena implied they either come with us together or not at all. Besides training either of them, we also had to hide them within the city. Make them blend into our world and learn our customs. I just haven't figured out how to do all of that yet.

I look to Ares, waiting for him to add to the conversation again, but he's already placed a book in his hand, ignoring our discussion as he flips through the pages.

Despite the death of Havena's mother, our vine couldn't be a sitting duck. Hell was hunting her, and although demons couldn't breach the borders of this city, they'd figure out her location soon enough. Prophecies were patient, and one way or another, the Holy War would come to pass.

"They'll be taught individually," I propose.

Ares pauses his reading.

"As in one-on-one?" he asks. I nod my head.

"Precisely," I confirm. "Theseus is right. The girls need to stay alive. We'll train them individually for two weeks and then rotate teachers. That way we'll have time to monitor and improve their fighting skills."

"And you, Ares, could teach them our customs," Theseus adds. "The customs of our realm, of Hannah, of Adira..."

"You can't be serious." Ares looks to Theseus with a shake of his head. "Havena? Sure—the girl's half-angel. But the human? The human should stay out of our fight. Our weapons aren't made for humans anyway. She'd be collateral..."

Damage, I finish for him in my brain.

"Her name is Leah and she will train," Theseus asserts. "We can't just bring her here and leave her defenseless."

"Then we shouldn't have brought her at all," Ares counters. Instead of continuing the argument, they expectantly look to me to be the voice of reason. I should be used to this by now. They've always made me the tiebreaker for their petty quarrels, but those arguments pertained to food preferences or conspiracy theories.

Not life or death.

"Don't tell me you agree with him," Theseus says to me.

"Whether human or angel, it doesn't matter," I start. "We can mentor Havena with the elements we're strongest in, and we'll do so protecting *both* girls. They'll train."

And even though my words should settle it, Ares slams his book down onto the desk. "As a Disciple, I cannot give the humans knowledge of our secrets. Weapons, customs—the other cities—or training of the elements alike." He looks to Theseus. "I won't train either of them."

Theseus' eyes flare. "Would you be so pretentious—"

"Fine," I interject to keep the peace. I give Ares a nod. "But the three of us become four, Ares. I trust you won't forget that."

"Wouldn't dream of it."

Ares reciprocates my nod, then avoids Theseus' glare before walking out to the balcony. His midnight wings slip out of his back and he leaps into the morning air.

"I'd rather inflict a few wounds he'd wish were dreams."

"Calm it, Cupid," I caution. Theseus meets my gaze.

"If he plans on coming back, make sure he goes through you instead of me."

I can only sigh as Theseus walks back to the leather armchair.

Although their position was crucial for the legacy of our realms, a Disciple's knowledge surpassed the rest of ours by a landslide. Oftentimes, their purpose would get to their head, their knowledge mistaken for power that even their loved ones failed to humble. I had looked at Ares as he spoke, realizing this was one of those times. I don't think he expected our vine to be Havena, a mere half-human, but the prophecy included all four of us, whether he liked it or not.

"Adding fuel to the fire will only drive him away," I respond. "But he'll grow bored of the temple soon. He always does."

18
Havena

My eyes fluttered open from the sunlight boring into the room. I twisted my body, feeling the gloriously soft, silk sheets glide across my skin. I knocked out almost immediately after my bath. I don't even remember slipping under the sheets after putting on the grey nightgown. Feet pattered lightly against the floor and I shot my head up.

Leah was propped at the foot of my bed. Her black hair was out of its usual ponytail, resting against her back and out of her face to expose her sharp ears. She wore a strapless, pale-yellow, evening gown that seemed to flow into a train onto the floor. Her knees were brought to her chest as she looked away from me, toward the french double-doors that led to the balcony, taking in the view beyond the glass.

Two maids were in the room as well. The first maid was blonde and frail. With pursed lips and eyes of determination, she busily shuffled through the tall, white dresser that sat next to the bedroom door. The other maid, a plump redhead, hummed softly as she placed a tray of food onto an ottoman next to the balcony doors. I had only just realized a seating area had been moved into the room.

The redheaded maid plucked an orchard branch from her pale-gold apron and dropped it into a vase on the tray. She smiled down at it with satisfaction before meeting my gaze.

"Oh, I-I'm sorry I woke you, miss," she says startled. The maid on the floor looks up to me, immediately standing to her feet with a composed smile. Leah turned around as well, a grin brushed upon her face. I sat up.

"It's fine, I was already awake." I tried to return their smiles. "Thank you," I add, nodding my head toward the food.

"That's what I'm here for, miss. I-If you need me, I'll be in the kitchens." The redhead flashes a sheepish smile before she curtsies, her face turning as red as her hair as she leaves the room. Leah gestures her hand toward the maid at the dresser.

"This is Aelia," Leah announces. Aelia's purple eyes brighten from the introduction.

"It's an honor to serve you, Miss Havena. I've been assigned as the caretaker for both of you girls. The others were too nervous once they discovered who you are."

"And you know who I am? What I'm called to do?"

"Well, of course I do! It's not everyday I get to tend to the prophesied vine." Aelia lets out a laugh as she turns to grab the golden knob on the dresser drawer.

Although her face was young, and her smile vibrant, the smile lines and subtle sag in her healthy cheeks placed her around the age of forty at least. Her blonde hair, with only a few streaks of grey, had been pulled back into a bun, and her throat hummed as she contemplated the garments inside of the drawer. She finally pulls out a lavender, evening gown. It flowed delicately to the floor and I took in just how long the dress was.

"I decided to start with your wardrobes first. I've been told

I'm a bit extravagant, but I'm sure you'll love the options I've picked for you." Aelia beams with pride. Clothing must have been her favorite part of the job. She walks to the edge of the bed, laying the dress down before straightening her apron.

"If there's anything you need—anything at all—just tell someone in the kitchens and I'll be here as fast as I can." Aelia smiles sweetly at us.

"We will," Leah says with a smile.

With a content nod of her head, Aelia turns on her heel and leaves the room. I flop onto my back.

"What the Hell is happening?" I murmur, dropping the smile from my face. Leah slips off the foot of the bed and goes to sit on the side of it, facing me. Her smile is gone as well.

"I wouldn't know, I woke up an hour ago to her shoving dresses into my closet. She pulled out this before introducing herself," Leah snorts, gesturing to her dress. Then she flops onto her back next to me.

We stare at that pristine, stone ceiling like we're kids again, looking toward the sky to find shapes in the clouds. Except we weren't kids anymore, and we were staring at nothing in silence.

"I think," I start to say, breaking the silence, "I mean—is it weird that I think I'm meant to be in this world alone?" I ask, studying the blankness of the ceiling.

"Obviously," Leah mutters without missing a beat. I look to her in shock and she just chuckles. She takes hold of my hand and squeezes it.

"I didn't leave my life's savings and fly through the sky with an angel for you to be in this house alone. It was terrifying!" she adds and I laugh. I picture her gripping Theseus's body for dear life, cursing him as they soared higher through the clouds. She definitely didn't close her eyes as I did.

"You know, for a moment I thought Aelia was going to squish my cheeks," I admit. Leah nudges my side.

"You're basically a superhero now and I'm the sidekick. We just have to get used to the fame... and the perks."

"What perks?"

"You know, the perks famous people get. Free food, free services, free clothes... We actually have a maid now, Have."

I shake my head with a chuckle and look back to the ceiling.

"Are they even called maids here... in this... city?"

Leah shrugs, bringing her gaze to the ceiling as well.

"I don't know..."

We stay there for a moment more until Leah gets up from the bed. I watch her curiously as she picks up the train of her dress, sauntering toward the end of the bed again before leaning down. She straightens up with a small shoebox in hand. My shoebox.

I've had that shoebox for years, keeping little trinkets of my childhood locked away from my mother. My mother refused to keep personal documents or pictures around, and I could never decorate the house with pictures I had taken throughout the years. Key-chain class portraits, class notes from Leah, and whatever I wanted to keep were saved in that box—along with the only picture of my dad.

I sit up, watching as Leah places the box on the foot of my bed. She keeps a hand on it before she speaks.

"We've both lost our fathers, and you just lost your mother, but you will never—*ever*—lose me." Her voice is firm. Her black eyes pierce my own and I know just how much she means those words. Leah's never been the type to be so sentimental. She's always gone wherever the wind takes her, where there was laughter and fun, and I've only ever heard her serious tone when she denounced her father in the parking lot of Bucky's.

And she never talked about him again.

She clears her throat, grabbing the fabric of her train, and turns toward the door.

"I'll see you at dinner," she announces, her voice recovering to its normal cheerful state. I furrow my brows at the back of Leah's head as I scoot toward the shoebox.

"Dinner? How long did I sleep? Where are you going?" I ask. Leah opens the bedroom door to leave, yet turns around to answer one of my questions.

"Have, it's only past noon."

■ ■ ■ ■

I'd spent the next couple of hours in my room, no longer exhausted as I enjoyed the time to myself. I'd taken in the view from the balcony every so often, watching the sun go down little by little. I shuffled through the various novels on the bookshelf next to the small vanity, trying to occupy my time reading their summaries. On occasion, my ears would flinch at the footsteps that subtlety sounded throughout the hallway. My breath would catch in my throat with every silent thump, in fear of someone knocking. I knew once I opened those bedroom doors, I'd officially be jumping into whatever this journey of my life entailed. Into the stupid prophecy that felt too much like a dream. Except it wasn't a dream.

I dressed in the lavender gown Aelia had picked out for me. It was light, soft, and flowing in the breeze from the open balcony doors. The sleeves of the dress were small, sheer, and off the shoulder, like loops of delicate paper around my biceps. I sat on the velvet loveseat at the base of my bed, looking through the pictures that summarized my youth. Everything was here, except now I knew why Leah had stayed behind with

Theseus last night.

She had found my mother's driver's license and added it to my collection. My fingers carefully glided over the little plastic card, as if the weight of my fingers would smudge it.

Miriam Bernheim, mother of Havena Bernheim.

She was forty-five years old, 5'6", had brown eyes...

And she was dead.

I placed the license beside the picture of me and my father. Beside Atticus. I gazed at their features, wishing I could've seen them together in person. My mother always wore a wedding ring, and though I had never seen their wedding photos, I had found this baby picture of me in her room. It was small, hiding between the wood of her desk and the wall, except for the creased corner of the picture sticking out.

"Atticus + Havena," was written in script, and I immediately knew he was my father, despite the absence of our last name on the back. Either way, I knew he was the missing puzzle that made me a Bernheim.

Just as I moved my hand to lower the picture, a skid at the base of the box caught my attention. I moved the pictures around to reveal my mother's necklace. The last time I'd seen it, it was glazed with my mother's blood as I cupped her lifeless face. But now it was a clean, shiny cross. The silver reflected the light of the evening sun as I let it hang from my fingers, watching it curve in the breeze. I placed it in my palm, then shuffled to a mirror framed by frosted glass. I opened the clasp, letting the cool metal rest against my neck. The top of the dress was cut into a delicate sweetheart shape, and the chain traveled down my collar bone, resting the cross right in the middle of my chest. As if it were right over my heart.

I locked the clasp and dropped my hands, gazing into my reflection that resembled too much of my mother. Her brunette waves, the shape of her eyes. Her nose. I blinked back the sudden wetness of my eyes and shook my head.

I gathered the lavender fabric of my dress between my fingers and shuffled to the bedroom door.

My clenched heart didn't want to cry anymore.

It wanted revenge.

19
Leah

I pulled up the train of my gown as I walked down the marble staircase. When Aelia had surprised me earlier in my room, she informed me that dinners were ready by sunset and that the dining room was past the wooden doors in the foyer.

The second those hazy oranges and purples of the setting sun spilled through my bedroom window, I left my room. I've only been here a day, and everywhere I looked, I couldn't help but feel like the past twenty-four hours weren't real. Every bare-footed step I've taken in this place reminded me of the fact that I was on a floating rock in the sky of another freaking floating rock.

My room was similar to Have's, except it was located within the left-wing of the house and didn't have a balcony.

And I was grateful for the balcony's absence.

The idea of angels arriving to my room by flight instead of knocking on my door sent a shiver down my spine. Whether that shiver was an indication of excitement or fear, I couldn't tell just yet. But it served as a constant reminder that I was human, and they were not.

The bottoms of my bare feet pad against the last of the cold marble stairs. I step onto the foyer floor. Two maids, one male and one female, hurry out of the light-wooden doors that encase the dining room beyond. They send me a tight smile of acknowledgment before they shuffle into the kitchen. I slant my eyes, squinting through the glass of the french doors closing behind them, seeing other maids shuffle about in the kitchen.

"Don't tell me you're blind as well," Theseus' voice sounds out. I turn around toward the white living-room and find him sitting on a couch. He's dressed in white pants and a blue sweater. The pants are loose, yet they cling to his toned legs all the same. His sweater brings out his mischievously, piercing blue eyes that scan my face. If it weren't for last night, I'd have thought he was human. Except for the fact that he flew me into the freaking sky and didn't comfort me while I screamed.

After Havena's mother was killed, I stayed behind with him to find Havena's box of childhood belongings. I knew he was going to discard her mother's body, just like he had done with the creature that attacked us, but when I stepped onto the front porch, shoebox in hand, my heart wanted to shatter.

Havena's mother was gracefully hovering above a six feet hole in the ground. I hadn't seen the state of her mother beforehand, but as she floated in the air, her skin clean and full of life, I nearly cried. For once in all of my years of seeing her, Havena's mother was at peace. With a raised hand, I watched as Theseus slowly lowered her into the earth with the small hum of a hymn escaping his throat.

Even though I had assumed he was only a sack of sarcasm just hours earlier, I could see the sadness in his eyes that resembled my own. I almost apologized when he gave me her mother's necklace, thinking that there was more to him than the carefree attitude he spewed the entire night. That I had figured him out incorrectly...

Then he flew me into the sky, and all I felt was the rumble of his laughter at the sound of my screams until we landed in front of Gale's manor.

I straightened my posture and cleared my throat as he took me in. That smirk on his face raised the hairs on my arms; I just couldn't tell if that was a good thing yet either.

"I'm not blind, I'm curious," I retort, keeping the sound of my voice free of amusement.

Theseus uncrosses his legs and gets up from his seat. He gives me a shrug as he walks over to me.

"Isn't there a saying you humans have? Something like *'Curiosity killed the cat'*?" He leans next to my ear to whisper, and the heat of his breath makes me flinch. "Does it apply to bare-footed humans as well?"

I shoot him a glare and he steps beside me, cackling as he approaches the dining room doors. Then he opens it, showing me a glimpse into the dark-paneled room his blonde head was gesturing to.

"After you," he says.

I roll my eyes and walk past the threshold.

The flooring is wooden, not marble unlike the rest of the house. It shares the same color as the door, yet tiles the room in patterned squares. The paneled walls are darker, a rich, deep, wood that seems to be glossed over. Pictures hung from the walls, a combination of portraits and landscapes, visible by the candles that jutted out from the wooden panels, matching the candlelit chandelier that lights the entire room. Multiple picture frames showed Theseus, Ares, and Gale throughout the years, from the time they were children to the time they became young men. Thick bookcases, stretching from the floor to the ceiling, line the entire back wall. It's... homey.

Gale was already occupying one of the iron seats around the long, rectangular, oak table. I count about ten chairs around that table, elegantly dominating the middle of the room. The table has already been set with a glorious feast of breads, fruits, vegetables, and meats, and my stomach rumbles quietly.

"Welcome, Leah," Gale greets. His eyes are kind and he gives me a warm smile. He's no longer in his armor, his wings are gone, and he looks a bit more rested than last night. His brunette hair waves down to his chin, but he has it tucked behind his ears and out of his face, showcasing his chiseled jaw.

Theseus sighs behind me.

"Well, are you just going to stare at the man, or are you going to eat?" he asks in annoyance. I shoot Theseus a glare before huffing out a breath to my seat. I choose the iron seat in the middle of the table, away from Gale on the opposite side. It's slightly cold against my bottom, but it's surprisingly comfortable. I grab my hair from behind my back and my thin elbow hits something. I freeze my arm as I turn to look at what I hit, only to find Theseus's leg. The blonde obnoxiously clears his throat as he pulls out the chair beside me and sits down.

"You could literally sit anywhere else," I mutter under my breath. I twist my hair through itself one final time to secure the bun. I can feel the heat of Theseus' gaze, but I ignore him, reaching for the platter of meat in front of me. He reaches for the platter next to the meat and grabs a bread roll.

"I could, but it wouldn't be any fun," Theseus responds. He brings his arm back to his plate with a nonchalant shrug.

Gale snorts.

"I can't believe you're a Nurturer," Gale says. Theseus sends him a wink before diving into his food.

I look between the two of them.

"What's a Nurturer," I ask. Gale is in the middle of pouring himself a drink and nods his head at Theseus.

"Nurturers," Theseus explains in between his chewing, "are said to be the most empathetic of the angels. We go to the Human Plane and try our best to protect your kind."

"Protect us, how?" I ask. He swallows his food before leveling his gaze, his blue eyes no longer humorous.

"We try to stop demons from... mentally harming you." His tone alone tells me not to ask any more questions as he goes back to his food. Gale leans back in his chair, watching the two of us before sending me a quick shake of the head. A gaze that tells me not to press any further.

"Fine," I mumble. "So that makes you a Nurturer as well, huh?" I ask Gale. He shakes his head again.

"Not in the slightest," he chuckles. "My job involves two responsibilities. I'm either assigned to fix the ozone layer, or, I'm sent to fight demons on the Human Plane. We send them back to..."

His voice trails off, and his grey eyes slip past my head with sudden awe. I heard the click of the dining room doors open, but now that I've followed his gaze, I nearly gasp.

Standing in the doorway behind me, was Havena.

20
Gale

Her eyes widen as they scan over the room, taking it all in. She's moved her brunette hair to one side of her delicate face, which flowed down just below her breasts. A glint of silver hangs across her lean neck, enhancing the curves of her collarbones. The lavender in her dress makes her look soft, gentle, yet the embers in her eyes were amplified, dancing like a flame. No longer broken like they were last night.

Beautiful.

Havena turns to the maid by her side and gives a quiet phrase of gratitude. The maid gives a sheepish smile in return, and curtsies before closing the dining-room doors.

Havena moves toward the table, ignoring our gazes.

"Um, where I'm from, staring is rude," she says with a laugh. It sounds forced, but her voice doesn't shake as she walks around the table, her dress flowing behind her.

"I just—We didn't think you were—"

"Speak for yourself, Guardian," Theseus interjects. He raises his wine glass in my direction with a knowing look.

"Tonight, we feast to a new dawn... *All* of us."

My mouth opens pathetically from the disruption, but I straighten up in my seat as Havena pulls out the chair beside me.

Leah turns to Theseus.

"You've only had *one* glass," she mumbles with annoyance. Then she turns to Havena. "I swear it's like having a pet pigeon."

The statement is said as if Theseus weren't beside her.

Havena's hand reaches for a food platter and Leah shrugs, but a knowing smile creeps onto her face, mirroring Havena's. The Nurturer lowers his fork of food and turns his head to meet Leah's gaze.

"For someone who has incomparable strength to mine, you sure have a lot of nerve," he scoffs.

"And yet you won't lay a finger on her," Havena mutters.

It was a warning, yet her graceful hand picks up my wine glass, bringing it to her lips as if her words were nothing more than a childish dare.

They snap their eyes to hers, and Havena raises her brow at Theseus as she leans back in her chair, sipping my drink.

Watching him.

Leah's cheeks flush, and she suddenly takes interest in the different foods on the table.

"No wonder you're The Vine," Theseus responds.

He drops his gaze back to his plate with a smirk, and I suppress my laugh, coming up with the title of this scene.

The scolding of a sister.

I look at Havena, who takes another satisfied sip from my glass before setting it down. I barely knew her, but I could tell she was tough. Physically, and most definitely mentally. Then she catches me watching her.

"Did I spill something?" she asks obliviously, looking down to scan her dress. I chuckle and gesture toward the glass.

"You drank my wine," I mention quietly, not trying to fuel her embarrassment further. Her eyes latch onto mine immediately, but before her full lips part with an apology, I give her a dismissal wave of my hand.

"It's no big deal," I say, dropping my eyes to my plate.

She's sitting too close to me, and the magnetic pull she has over me makes my nerves tingle with warmth. I move my fork around, trying to ignore the voice in my brain that was wondering just how soft her lips were.

"I never got to thank you for saving my life," she says. Thankfully, she turns her head to Theseus before I bring my gaze to hers. "Both of you."

Theseus shrugs. "You should hold your thanks, Havena. I fear you'll hate me once we start training together."

Havena raises a brow before picking at her plate. "I doubt it... But, you never told me what you are... I know you're angels but... what do you do? Besides, you know, put random people in your witness protection program."

She brings the food to her mouth, not bothering to watch my eyebrows furrow in confusion.

Leah catches my face with a snicker.

"You know... Witness protection?" Leah tells me. Theseus questions the girls for me.

"A what?"

Leah's eyes go wide.

"When someone's in danger, there are people that use their resources to protect that person from bad guys..."

"Like me?" I ask.

"I guess..."

"So they're Guardians?" Theseus asks.

"No..."

Leah's eyes dart from Theseus to me, hoping for understanding to settle onto our faces. Unfortunately for us, it doesn't, but at least Havena laughs.

"Where we're from," Havena starts, "the people that are supposed to protect us are a part of the government."

"Oh," I say, my brain finally hit with realization. I turn to Leah. "You were talking about a human profession."

"Sure..." Leah says puzzled. "But the jobs here are similar, right? Like being a Guardian here is similar to being a cop down... there?"

"A cop?" Theseus questions under his breath.

We ignore him.

"I suppose there are some similarities," I tell Leah, "but there's definitely a distinction in terms of danger. Many of us go to the Human Plane because the professions there are... calmer."

"But if so many of you are there, how come we—I mean humans—don't think you exist? Yeah, there's religion, but angels are just—"

"A fairy tale?" I finish for her. Leah nods her head with hesitation, in fear of disrespecting me. I only smile.

"Our glamour keeps us hidden from human eyes. On the Human Plane, I'd be invisible to you, even if I were standing in front of you, wings extended and all. Our protocol—I guess you could say—has made it that way for centuries," I answer. I notice Havena slowly lower her fork, her ear perking up at my words.

"Our wings retract, we age the same way you do, and we bleed as mortals. Unless we choose to live on the Human Plane—"

"Or idiocracy," Theseus mumbles.

"We refrain from dropping our glamour otherwise," I continue. "It's safer not to be seen."

"And why is that?" Havena asks. "What if an angel wants to marry a human? Or have a child?"

My mouth opens with hesitation from Havena's eyes, boring into mine for an answer. But as I'm struggling to answer her very, *very*, intentional question, I'm saved by the bell...

Or by an idiot.

A slurp sounds into the silence of anticipation. We turn our gaze to Theseus, his eyes wide with a wine glass on his lips as he takes in our expressions. Then he pauses his drinking.

Leah nudges his arm.

"Ow!" he mutters dramatically as he lowers his wine. Leah gestures to me and Havena with scolding eyes.

"As you were saying, Gale," she redirects with a tight smile.

"Right." I clear my throat and turn back to Havena, only to meet her patient eyes still waiting for an answer.

My answer.

"Well... it's complicated but... it's safer—easier even—to keep our true selves hidden on the Human Plane. I couldn't imagine any of your kind facing the same dangers that we face here, and luckily, they never will.

"Demons will always be glamoured from human eyes, but if humans knew that demons were walking right next to them, they wouldn't know where to purge first. Humans would turn on each other just as they've done before, like during the witch trials of Salem, if not worse. So imagine if we let them see us, even though they couldn't see the danger we're trained to protect them from. The purpose of us—angels who choose to be Guardians, or Nurturers, or even Disciples—is to take care of the earth, which includes protecting the humans from destroying themselves. And those of us who choose to live on the Human Plane just want... a life with simpler tasks."

I watch as Havena's eyes study my face, her teeth releasing the lip she bit halfway through my explanation.

"Wait, then how was I able to see the thing that attacked us last night?" Leah asks. To that question, I shrug. Even Theseus leans back in his chair, examining Leah curiously.

"You don't have a single drop of angel blood inside of you? None at all?" Theseus asks. Leah simply shakes her head.

From that response, I jump in.

"What happened before we arrived, Leah? And what happened exactly?"

"Umm..." Leah starts, her eyes wincing as she recalls the event. "I was driving. Then there was a flash of some sort, like a car light or something, but there wasn't a car. I was on the road by myself. Next thing I know, I open my eyes and I'm in pain, but I felt, like, extremely tired all of a sudden. And some weird animal thing was on the hood of my car. Havena was holding my hand while I freaked out."

"Oh!" Theseus and I exclaim at the same time.

Leah's eyes widen.

"What'd I say?"

"You held her hand," Theseus answers. Then he looks to Havena. "Humans gain The Sight when we share physical contact with them."

"So, she can see demons now?"

"Not exactly," I tell Havena. "Humans gain The Sight for as long as we touch them. For instance, if I held Leah's hand right now, she could see everything in this room as we do. The vibrancy of the light, just how deep the colors in the room are—she could even taste the richness of our food. Once I let go of her hand, she'll see things as she normally would... as a human. Since you held her hand when you saw the demon, The Sight allowed her to see the creature for what it truly was."

"Wait, your food tastes better?" Leah asks excitedly.

We ignore her.

"How dramatic is the difference? If my touch is that powerful, then why isn't it a bigger deal? I've bumped into other humans all the time, not just Leah."

"Because, in order to see those differences, they'd have to focus. Remember when you had finally tapped into The Sight on the Human Plane? You focused on the splinters of glass within your jeans. When Leah held your hand, she focused on her fear," I explain. Havena's eyes widen with realization.

"*God*, this is amazing."

Leah's voice catches our attention, and we turn to find her fingers between Theseus' dirty-blonde waves, gripping his head as she bites into her food. Theseus grins down at her chowing down with pure astonishment in his eyes.

After a moment, Havena speaks again.

"You use glamour because you think humans would look at you in fear."

My brain turns to mush at her statement. Every time Havena says something to me, it immediately rewires itself to replay her words in my head. And as she looks to me with the expectation of a rebuttal in her eyes, I choose the latter. It's not a question, but I nod in agreement before I answer.

"Precisely... Chaos is simply an eruption of fear. It grows from within, from those who fear what they do not understand. And humans will never understand our world."

I catch a glint settle within Havena's eyes.

"So, should I choose the profession of an angel? Or hide who I am as a human?" she challenges. The smirk that she's been hiding from me slips onto my own lips.

"You can do both... You're The Vine."

"I *personally* believe being a Nurturer is the best."

Our gazes latch onto Theseus, his mouth obnoxiously chewing the bite of bread he's taken from the roll in his hand.

Leah nudges him again, but I have to admit that without his outburst, I wouldn't have realized how close my face had gotten to Havena's. Our faces must have inched closer as we spoke, but Havena clears her throat and leans away first. I follow suit.

"So, what does the prophecy say exactly? Do I just stop this war by existing?" Havena asks jokingly. She doesn't bother to mask the annoyance in her voice as she tilts her head in confusion. A lock of her hair sweeps against her bare shoulder as she picks up her fork again, and I fight against removing it.

"In a sense, yes," I start, dropping my gaze from hers. "Ever since we were children, we were told the initial prophecy in the form of a nursery rhyme—"

"Oh, yes," interjects Theseus sarcastically, "the prophecy that gave me nightmares as a child."

Havena sits up in her seat, her eyes intrigued.

"How does it go?"

"The realms will divide themselves in pursuit of power," Theseus recites, *"a holy war will spur at the thinnest hour."*

"Doesn't sound too scary..."

"Any thought of bloodshed is terrifying when you're a child, especially if it's between the realms," Theseus assures Leah. He lowers his fork and looks back to Havena. "We're not exactly sure how you fit into the prophecy yet, other than the fact that you're The Vine and your existence adds onto it. We were recently assigned to find you, and soon enough, we'll fight by your side."

I catch Havena bite her cheek.

"So... who assigned you to find me?"

Theseus smirks.

"Who do you think, petal? The Lord, himself."

Havena widens her eyes.

"The purpose of your task is to find the new vine," I start to recite. "She has been pruned and placed before a thicket, yet her enemies have left the land dry. Her blood will bridge every realm of this earth, though one realm wishes for her realm to die. Find this vine, train this vine, fight with this vine, for three will become four and four will become one with the earth. Then, and only then, will the prophecy be complete."

"And what a fun time training you will be," Theseus adds charmingly, raising his wine glass to the girl.

Leah nudges him once more tonight.

"Wait. Wait, wait, wait... the first line is—was—my location," Havena mutters to herself.

It had taken me hours to figure that part of our assignment out, and it wasn't even my idea. It was Theseus'. Training her on the basics of our customs and combat might be easier than I thought. Leah's brows are furrowed, but we continue to watch Havena decipher my words.

"Left the land dry..." Havena murmurs, looking down to her plate. She takes a bite of her food, although curiosity still dances on her face. Then she swallows, looking back to me. "They—that demon—wanted to stop my bloodline."

A flash of anger sweeps into her eyes and she leans back in her chair. "If I stayed home they would have killed me, too."

Leah shakes her head. "We don't know that—"

"We do," I interject softly. Even Theseus pauses his eating and puts down his fork to look at me.

"The pool of your mother's blood was cold... and some of the blood was thoroughly dried," I turn to Havena. Her eyes soften a little at my words, but she lets me continue. "She died hours before your attack. She had to have been protecting you."

Theseus nods his head in recollection. "That would explain the barren interior. No personal items... In fact, no pictures at all... You were a hidden child, Havena."

She looks to me for confirmation and I can only nod my head in agreement. Havena was in this fight for good, regardless of whether she wanted to be or not. And based on her silence, and the realization in her eyes, she's finally accepted that as a fact.

Leah grips the arms of her chair in shock. Her human wits catching up to ours.

"Oh my God," she breathes out. Theseus puts a hand on Leah's back with startled eyes, trying to slow down her breaths.

But Havena doesn't move.

The flash of anger in Havena's eyes has disappeared. Instead, it's been replaced, glazed over by a bone-chilling calm that focuses on the wood of the table. Then she brings a hand to her necklace, and her eyes to mine.

"When do we train?"

21
Havena

"Monday," Gale had said at dinner.

I awoke for a fifth time underneath silk sheets, letting out a yawn toward the sheer curtains that hung over my bed. I still wasn't used to waking up like this. A few nights ago, I was unknown, and today, and possibly every day from now on, I was going to wake up in a bed fit for a princess.

But I wasn't a princess.

Princesses were usually saved from their death wishes, meanwhile I was biding my time with fate, waiting for the day my heart finally stopped beating. After all, death seemed to run in the family.

We've had dinner together for the past few days, learning more about each other while pointing out our differences. Gale and Theseus were nineteen, only a year older than my current age. To Leah's surprise, the boys had never heard of cartoons, and to Gale's surprise, we've never heard of The Selected, a competition that pits angel children against one another for sport. The competition happened once every school year, uniting the realms together as if it were one big pep rally—a human analogy that Gale didn't understand. Leah tried her best to describe her favorite shows, the boys tried their best to explain their favorite weapons, and I'd sit there listening to it all.

But every time I asked about training—or questioned Ares' absence—Gale would deflect, thinking up different scenarios of the prophecy instead. I tried talking to Leah and Theseus at the table, but the two weren't capable of suppressing their banter for five minutes. So I'd sit there, in whatever evening gown Aelia chose for me to wear, and wonder about my father.

He must've grown up in this city... and now I was in it. Even though I anticipated training every day, I couldn't help the fact that I silently wished to take a stroll through the city streets, to feel a slimmer of what my father felt when he grew up here. The only problem was, there was no way for me to explore this city on my own.

All four of us were supposed to meet in the dining room at noon. We planned on training for hours and hours until the sun set for dinner. I've spent the last couple of days inside of my room. Leah would visit, and we'd try to reminiscence about how life was like before all of this. To my luck, unfortunately, she'd always turn the conversation and start talking about the prophecy, as if this journey was simply an exciting field trip. I guess she had finally realized my lack of enthusiasm because she didn't visit my room yesterday.

A part of me enjoyed the solitude. I kept busy by reading the books in my room, the only form of entertainment that let me drift away from reality. My face hurt from the fake smiles I wore to mirror Leah's excitement. To make her think I was enjoying any of this. It was the least I could do since I had to take her on this wild ride with me.

A yawn escapes my lips just as I begin to sit up, only for my bedroom door to whip open. Aelia saunters through with that signature pep in her step. I'm hit immediately with the smell of food flowing off the tray in her hands.

She sends me a warm smile.

"Good morning, Miss Havena," she greets. Aelia places the tray onto the foot of my bed. I'm still not used to her role in my life yet, but I tiredly bring a smile onto my face all the same.

"Good morning Aelia."

The fresh fruit and pastries on the tray call my name.

"Is there anything I can do for you today?" she asks expectantly. I was about to shake my head and dismiss her cheeriness, then stopped myself.

"Do you happen to know the time?" I ask tiredly. She looks into the pouch of her apron and pulls out a pocket watch.

"It's 11 O'clock, miss. A little late to start the day, but—"

I throw the covers off my body and shimmy off the bed. Startled by the interruption, Aelia takes a step back.

Even though I was half-angel, I think I failed to inherit the graceful movement of their kind. I grew up in New Jersey, where we yelled at bus drivers and honked our horns as soon as the light turned green. I start toward the bathroom, then pause again, turning around.

"Do you happen to know if I have jeans?" I ask. Aelia furrows her brows, dumbfounded, and I gesture to my legs beneath my nightgown. "Pants?"

"Oh, right. It's in the bottom drawer. Gale told me you'll be needing clothes for combat," she says.

Clothes for combat, I snort in my head. I guess I'll have to get used to wearing gowns every day. Walking into the dining room for the first time felt bizarre, like an awkward dinner date before prom. Especially by the way everyone looked at me.

Well, I think to myself, *by the way Gale and Leah had*

99

looked at me.

My mother was never the type to dress me up, nor the type to call me beautiful, so I became content. I usually dressed in a pair of jeans and long sleeves, but I was alive.

I was fine.

Now, I was in a floating city in the sky, hidden under the protection of creatures I'd just met, and the people—well angels—here thought pants were *'clothes for combat'*.

Aelia puts her hands behind her back and stands expectantly, waiting for another question or task that I wasn't used to giving.

"Thank you, Aelia... Truly, I don't need anything else," I tell her earnestly. I watch as she hesitantly curtsies and leaves the room. I can't help but wonder just how many people thank her as I turn on my heel toward the bathroom, only having an hour to get ready.

■ ■ ■ ■

"I'm here," I call out, swinging open the heavy, wooden doors to the dining room. Gale turns from a bookcase on the back wall, a small smile playing onto his lips as he takes me in.

Heat rises to my cheeks, so I look toward Theseus. He's seated in a chair facing the doors, his feet on the table. Leah is sitting at the far end of the table, away from him yet glaring at him.

Her nose, however, is crinkled, which I recognized as her attempt to suppress a laugh. She looks up at me.

"Good morning, Have," she turns to me.

"I believe you mean, 'good afternoon,'" Theseus corrects. Before Leah can bark back, he looks to me. "You're late, flower."

Suddenly, Theseus' feet slide off the table and hit the floor with a thud. We stare at him in bewilderment, but Gale's chuckle quickly sounds from the back of the room. One of Gale's hands was raised toward Theseus, to which the Guardian fully releases his laughter. I start to laugh, too, realizing he's just knocked Theseus' feet down with a conjure of wind. Then Leah howls.

"It's not that funny," Theseus says, clearing his throat as he gets up from his seat. He dusts off his cream button-up shirt and black blazer as if nothing happened, which causes Leah to laugh even harder.

"Oh, I think it's very funny, Cupid," Gale teases with a humorous smile as he drops his hand. Leah quiets her laughter.

"Cupid?" she asks, looking to Theseus. Before he can defend himself, she starts again. "Oh, wait, I kind of see it now."

My laughter collides with Gale's now and we look to each other. We study the joy in each other's eyes for a moment, as if we had our own little joke. Like we were the only ones in the room, despite Theseus' blathering to Leah. Our laughter subsides.

"Good morning... Havena."

"Good morning, Gale."

The scrape of Leah's chair catches my attention, and I find her looking directly into Theseus' face.

There's a twitch of uncertainty in his cheek as she glares up at him, but Theseus glares back.

"Unholy pigeon," she calls him.

"Unholy human," he simply retorts.

"Dim-witted, blonde bird."

"Short, *short*, creature," Theseus coos, emphasizing her height as he briefly flicks his eyes to her feet. She grinds her teeth and sits on the table, turning away from him with a huff.

Theseus laughs.

I walk to the other side of the table and sit next to her.

"So... training?" I look to Gale.

"Training," he responds, then raises his hand to pull out a book on the bookshelf behind him. The navy-suede binding of the book tilts toward Gale with a click. He releases it. The bookcase he's just touched pushes back into the wall. It presses back about a foot, then slides to the left, revealing another room. Gale turns back around with a smirk, watching as I don't do anything but widen my eyes, gaping at the hidden corridor.

"So cool!" Leah exclaims, jumping off the table. She shuffles without hesitation into the room and doesn't look back, her long, black hair gliding behind her. Theseus stalls for a moment, his eyes shocked by her energy, then quickly walks after her.

"It's your turn," Gale says hesitantly. I slip off the table and take a few steps toward the entrance until I reach his side.

"Are there any more surprises I should know about?" I try to joke. I nervously glance up to him, watching his lip curl reassuringly.

"You tell me."

22
Gale

"Breathe in." I watch her shoulders rise. "Breathe out."

Havena and I were sitting in the middle of the concrete armory floor, meditating. I glimpsed over to Theseus and Leah. They were in the corner of the room, huddled over the armory's illuminated strategy table. He was showing her a map of the city, teaching her the safest places to go just in case something were to happen if we weren't there.

Well... if he wasn't there.

I look back to Havena. She's sat across from me for two hours now with her eyes closed, focusing on the sound of my voice as I guided her breathing.

Her lashes were long and dark, delicately fanning out as they brushed against her cheek with every breath. The cut of her long-sleeve, combat sweater rested low, showing just enough of her defined collarbone to reveal the cross necklace she kept wearing to dinner. Her hands rested on her knees, and her long, thin fingers were cupping the black leather pants that covered her knee caps. Her hair was disheveled, clearly rushed into her ponytail since a piece of it had fallen by her face, swaying along with every inhale and exhale she made. Finally, she lets out a breath of frustration.

"This is pointless," Havena mutters, opening her eyes. She scans around the armory, at the different swords, daggers, and blades displayed upon the illuminated shelves of weaponry paneled within the walls.

"It's necessary. Once you learn how to feel the flow of the air, you'll be able to control it," I say patiently, but she ignores me, her eyes still searching around.

Since I had the most expertise with air, I planned on training her with the element first.

Every element was powerful, and although I've dabbled with all of them, air could be swift, silent. Deadly. Besides, I've already witnessed Havena conjure the air spontaneously; I just hoped she wouldn't hurt herself in the process.

Her wandering eyes freeze behind me, finally finding whatever they were searching for. I watch as she points to a sword.

"Shouldn't I be training to fight with... whatever that is? Instead, I'm just... sitting on the floor... hearing myself breathe." I look toward the blade she's referring to. It was thin, silver, and long. The platinum handle of the blade was sleek, engraved with swirls of rose-gold in the grip that stopped traveling just as it met the blade.

I can see why it caught her eye.

My father used to say that the selection of a blade was a vulnerable task. There's an inkling in your soul that knows what to look for. And once you've found it—the weapon that's captured a piece of who you are—that weapon is yours. Our weapons represent the qualities we subconsciously see in ourselves, yet are too vain to admit we own.

I get up, turning my back to her as I walk toward the blade.

The blade Havena has chosen rested on the shelf above mine. I've only picked up her blade once before, when my father had made my six-year-old-self polish the swords as a form of discipline, but as I lifted the blade again—really held it—I understood why she felt called to it. It was light in weight, and its double-edge was sharp and thin, which meant that it would be quick. With a swift twirl of my wrist, the sword sliced through the air. In silence.

I pick up my own sword—a thicker, heavier, double-edged blade with a bronzed handle—and turn around. Havena was still sitting on the floor, glancing at both of the blades in my hand as I walk over.

"Up," I bark. I didn't intend for my voice to sound so intense, but her eyes widened as she got on her feet. I held out her blade and she took it, her delicate hand gracefully wrapping around the handle but slightly faltering at the weight. She foolishly held it up like a kitchen knife and bent her legs, leaning her weight on her toes. The simplest maneuver would knock her on her ass.

"What kind of stance is that?" I ask, unable to keep the chuckle out of my voice. A blush forms in her cheeks as she scowls in embarrassment.

"I've seen it in movies," the octave in her voice jumps in justification. I laugh again and she lowers her stance in defeat, pointing the blade to the floor. I put my blade into the leather sheath at my hip and step to her side.

"Balance is centered from your hips," I tell her. I place a hand on each side of her waist and squeeze her into place. I push the closeness of her body to the back of my mind, but I can't ignore the shudder that runs through her. She jerks her head to the side in surprise, unable to turn to me fully because I've locked her hips into place.

"Look ahead," I assert.

Havena listens to my demand with a grind of her teeth. I lift her arm, and the blade follows, pointing it straight ahead. Her arm struggles a bit, but it was because she was barely using her strength. She was just simply... holding it.

"The blade is an extension of power," I tell her gently, sliding my hand underneath her arm to steady the trembling, "an extension that kills. Grip it like one."

She flexes her strength and the blade shakes a little less. Her grasp is better than before, but forming stability would take time.

Fortunately, we didn't know the prophecy's deadline.

I drop my hand from her arm and catch her glimpse at its absence. I bite back the curl of my lip as I take a step away.

"Bring your right foot forward and put a slight bend in your knees," I advise, circling in front of her. She follows the instruction but rises on her toes like before. I shake my head.

"Plant your feet," I suggest. And she does. The uncertainty within her eyes looks to mine for approval. I clench my jaw to suppress my smirk. I could put her in an orientation class full of Guardian younglings, but the only thing that would make her stand out is her age.

"I feel ridiculous," she says. I draw my sword, stepping into my fighting stance and she widens her eyes. "You're not going to hit me."

"Never underestimate the person in front of you," I warn.

Then I lunge forward.

My sword slices her own. A rippling clash of metal sounds into the air. The disbelief in her eyes seeps past our joined blades and bores into me, but to my confirmed hunch, there was no fear. The fighter in her was an instinct—a natural one—which meant swordplay was somehow in her blood.

We both step back into our stances and begin circling each other. One day, I'll have to ask her about her father.

"You should take your own advice," she spits at me with a triumph smile on her lips.

She thinks she's outwitted me, but I had lunged at her lightly, just to see if her instincts would kick in. I wasn't planning on pushing her any further.

But then she swings her sword.

I block it easily.

She sloppily swings at me a second time.

Then a third.

Determination masks itself onto her face, taking advantage of the fact that I wasn't attacking hard enough. She doesn't realize that I'm not showing my full strength. That I'm simply blocking every jab.

"For."

Havena huffs with a swing.

"An angel."

She swings again.

"You're not."

I block her once more.

"That hard to fight."

I finally swing this time.

The force collides with her blade and pushes her back. The sword slips from her fingers, clanging to the floor, and Havena falls like I knew she would.

On her ass.

"Hey, careful over there!" Leah calls out. We both turn to find Theseus and Leah watching us. Theseus looks at Havena impressed, seeing her potential despite her place on the floor. Leah, however, holds a glare of worry.

"It's fine," Havena calls back, brushing her hands off on her pants. "I'm fine."

She gestures to get herself off the floor but I offer my hand.

"I told you to plant your feet," I tell her. She analyzes my hand, then leans back to look at me, declining it.

I keep my hand extended.

"You let me hit you. Again and again and you... You let it happen... You played me," she scowls, nestling her legs into a pretzel. I lower my hand.

"You kept hitting me as if you had something to prove. If you were sloppy in an actual fight, you'd be dead right now."

Havena lets out a shaky laugh from my words and drops her gaze. So I extend my hand again.

The first thing I learned as a Guardian was to keep my emotions out of a fight. Feelings could cloud our judgment, and one distracting second could determine life or death. The sooner Havena learns that, the sooner I'll be able to trust her with the task of protecting herself.

Havena bites her lip, as if she realizes that too, and takes my hand. I pull her up from the ground, underestimating her weight and she glides into my chest. Her lips hover over mine for a moment, giving our breaths a chance to collide.

Electricity runs through my veins, a feeling I've experienced twice before when I've felt her touch. But then Havena steps back, releasing her hand and bringing it to her chest before avoiding my gaze. To her necklace. I clear my throat.

"Why do you want to train?" I ask, trying to get back on topic. She meets my gaze and studies my eyes before answering, as if she wants to say the right thing.

"Because we have to. The prophecy says—"

"Forget the prophecy. Why do you want to do this?" I repeat. That determination she had while we sparred was sparked from something inside of her, something that filled her with fury, but she was too numbed down to say it. To claim that the prophecy was its origin was a lie.

She rolls her eyes, looking around the armory for another excuse she could use.

"Because I'm supposed to—"

"Why are you training, Havena?" I demand. Her gaze latches onto me, and I watch as the amber in her eyes ignites into flames. Her knuckles pale as she clutches the necklace on her chest.

"I want revenge, Gale. Is that what you want me to say?"

Her steady eyes watch my face for a reaction, as if her answer was too unorthodox to be heard. "I want the person that killed my mother to burn."

Without another word, she takes a step toward her sword. But I conjure it. It glides off the concrete floor from the wind, and Havena watches as the cool, metal handle settles into my palm.

"You want revenge?" I question. She steps back to me, her calculating eyes serving as confirmation, her countenance more certain than before. I offer her sword.

"Then fight like you want it."

23
Havena

I'm sick of him.

I'm sick of him reading me like a book. I'm sick of his stupid, grey eyes that set the nerves in my body on fire. And I was especially sick of the way he kept knocking me on my ass.

We've been training with our swords for almost two weeks now and it's been nothing like I anticipated it to be. I was sore, I was anxious, and I was weak. My blocks have gotten better, I still needed assistance with my footwork, and the only noticeable difference was the stability I had with my sword. When I had first seen it—felt it—it was like I was lifting a piece of myself into the air. And even though it made me more confident—and less sloppy—I was tired of fighting with it. My body craved something different, but since Theseus was supposed to take over my training sessions, I guess I'd just have to settle for training with him as something different.

Today was Thursday, which meant I had just one more day to train with Gale before he rotated with Theseus on Monday. Although Gale said Ares would visit and help train myself and Leah, I haven't seen Ares since the first night I arrived here.

From what I was told, Ares was supposed to teach me the customs of the other realms, which meant that I'd be learning what Leah currently was, and possibly more, for another two weeks. Regardless of whether Ares decided to teach me or not, we all seemed to be approaching our new reality on whims and unpredictable planning.

Leah's been hovering over the strategy table with Theseus since the first day of training. On some days, I wished I could be learning the things she was learning instead. She had told me about how she was studying a map of the city, and instead of visiting me like she had tried to do before, she spent her time learning first aid procedures and mentally mapping the safest places to go. A part of me didn't mind the solitude sometimes. I would be too sore to socialize from the fighting I was doing with Gale anyway, but I couldn't fight the temptation in my heart that told me to go into the city.

I may not have known much about my mother, but I didn't know a drop of information about my father. Every time I opened my balcony, I felt a tug in the air, begging me to travel into the city. As I sat on the armory floor, letting Gale guide me through my breathing, I silently thanked the heavens he wanted us to rest on the weekends instead of training. Now, all I had to do was find a way out of this house.

"Breathe in... and breathe out," Gale's gentle voice instructed. Keeping my eyes closed, I decided to test my luck.

"If you're doing what I think you're doing, it's not going to work," I warn. Air has been the only element I've seen him conjure, and he was adamant enough to be the first person to train me with it. Plus, I wasn't stupid.

My outbursts with this element had probably scared him both times, but I'd be lying if I said I felt the same. Those whirlpools around my face reminded me I was alive, yet when they did happen, I didn't want to be. Oddly enough, this new threat on my life made me want to protect it now.

Avenge my mother. Research my father. As far as I was concerned, learning more about myself was the only objective amidst my prophesied purpose.

My eyes remained closed, but an image of Gale's confused face danced behind my eyelids.

"And what am I thinking, Havena?" he asks.

"It's like you said before. You think that I can breathe my way in and out of conjuring the wind, or the air—or whatever you call it. Like I'll get a feel for it or something." I open my eyes to see his own narrow at my face in subtle surprise.

"Then by all means, how do you suggest we harness your abilities?" His calculating gaze mirrors my eyes, but I simply suggest what my heart was yearning for.

"Take me into the city."

"Absolutely not."

The dismissal sends a thrumming through my fingertips, but I ignore it and begin rising to my feet. Gale follows suit.

"This has been the most pointless part of our training yet. I'd rather go back to swordplay than do... this. The least you could do is let me see the city," I huff.

"What you'd rather do and what you should do are two different things. You need to get a feel for your capabilities, Havena. If you want to randomly lash out like before, I won't stop you. But you've already conjured wind twice now. Just because you feel like killing yourself—"

"You don't know a thing about what I feel!"

I didn't have to look to feel the gusts of wind swirling about my fingers, looping around in the shape of an infinity sign. I kept my gaze on Gale, watching as a subtle smirk of satisfaction slid onto his face.

Then I sent him flying.

Within a single moment, Gale stumbled back, skidding across the concrete floor in a whirlpool of wind. I lowered my hand, letting the air subside, but I still felt a tingle in my fingertips that made me want to unleash my power again. Theseus' laugh distracted me from the urge, echoing throughout the room as his blue eyes settled onto Gale. Leah stayed silent, her eyes wide as she took in the element around my hands.

The Guardian winced, his face a combination of surprise and fatigue as he slowly sat up. I turned on my heel toward the armory doors.

"Push me again and I'll do worse."

■ ■ ■ ■

I kept my bedroom door locked throughout the evening, using the time to take a bath, skim through a few books, and practice conjuring the wind a bit more. If Gale hadn't made me angry, I probably wouldn't have known how to center my power like I was doing now.

From what I could feel, the wind would wrap around my fingers whenever I willed it. The problem was keeping it under control. The first two times I'd done it, I had let my emotions guide the flow of the wind. Thinking back to the grocery store, I realize now that I let my emotions skyrocket, and the key to getting the wind under my control was to simply command it. If I willed the wind up with a finger, it would follow, and if I decided to cease it, it would follow. I wonder if the other elements were guided by intent.

The hazy purple of the setting sun began trickling into the room as I laid on my back, now dressed in a satin, dark blue, evening gown that Aelia had left out for me. I'd have to get used to wearing dresses like this. And even though I wasn't entirely comfortable in them, I couldn't deny how the gowns made me feel. It haltered around my neck, exposing my back and hugging my curves in all of the right places. For the first time in a long time, I felt pretty. And that made me feel powerful.

I twirled my fingers, moving the fabric of the canopy curtains into the air once again. I had been doing this exact motion for the past hour before a knock sounded on my door.

"You're not welcome," I call out.

"How'd you know it was me?" Gale asks. I ignore his question. "Could we at least talk?"

The stubbornness in my bones keeps me from responding, but the disheartened sigh that sounded behind the door made me consider his request.

For a moment.

"You don't have to talk to me. You can just ignore me if you want to, but dinner is ready. You shouldn't starve yourself because you're angry," he says. I stop fiddling with the canopy curtain and sit up, listening to the padding of his feet fade away.

The sudden rumbling of my stomach didn't help the fact that my stubbornness felt foolish now.

I should've opened the stupid door.

My ears catch the sound of steps in the hallway again. I shuffle to the door, mentally preparing myself to look into Gale's eyes and appear unbothered. He pushed my buttons when he shouldn't have, and I wasn't ready to admit that he pushed the right ones.

A light tap barely hits my door before I open it, only to see Leah. She had changed into a flowy, lace, evening gown, and a tray of food for two rested within her hands. Her signature, magazine smile flashes up at me as she holds the tray of food up like an offering. I step aside, letting her shuffle into the room as I lock the door behind us.

"We had a feeling you weren't going to eat with us," she says with amusement lacing her voice. She places the tray on the ottoman and picks up her plate before taking a seat.

"We?" I question, but I knew exactly who she was referring to.

"Theseus and I," she simply says.

Never mind, I mentally kick myself.

She wasn't talking about Gale.

I shuffle over to the ottoman and look at the tray. My plate is filled with foods I enjoy, a crystal glass is filled to the brim with wine, and I can't help the smile that forms on my lips. I pick up my plate and sit down.

"Thanks for making my plate," I tell her, but Leah pauses mid-bite and still manages to shake her head.

"In all honesty, I was going to make your plate like mine. Gale practically took your plate from my hands with the wind.. power... thing before we came upstairs."

Leah digs into her plate full of meat.

Then she pauses after a few bites.

"You know, I really enjoyed watching you knock him on his ass though," she chuckles.

"Yeah, well, he deserved it," I scoff, thinking back to his stupid face of satisfaction.

Gale had known pushing my buttons would set my powers off, but it's the fact that he knew where to push that terrified me. I didn't even know he existed a few days ago, yet he saw—or was beginning to see—the deepest and darkest parts of me that I kept to myself. Parts that Leah didn't even know.

Maybe my powers simply acted as a defense mechanism

against letting someone in. And the part that scared me was the fact that he made me want to lower my defenses.

"I probably needed him to push me like that," I admit with a shrug. "But, I would've been a bit nicer if he agreed to take me into the city."

Leah snorts with a tilt of her head.

"You want to go into the city?" she asks. I nod my head, watching the gears turn in her brain.

"How is it that I'm probably standing in my father's birthplace and I haven't fully seen any of it?" I reason, setting my plate down to look into the night sky beyond the balcony. Leah puts her plate down as well and joins my gaze.

"You think your father was the angel? Not your mom?" She asks. I think about her question for a moment.

My mother spent her time studying the bible with every breath. The only time she wasn't cooped up in her room was when she decided to read scripture in the living room for a change. Or when she'd kiss me goodnight on the forehead. I shake my head.

"She devoted her time to God because she needed protection," I finally say. "If she were an angel, she would've felt more confident about protecting me herself."

I drop Leah's gaze and reach for my wine glass, letting another realization settle into my brain. My mother never talked about my father because she wanted to protect me from this world—his world. And I couldn't be mad at her. His enemies were mine now, and she hid me because of her love for him. Her love for me.

"Why don't we just go tonight?" Leah suddenly asks. I lower the glass from my lips with furrowed brows.

"Into the city?" I ask. Leah nods excitedly.

I go to shake my head in refusal, then pause. My bedroom

door was locked, and if we didn't leave the room, it would just seem like Leah and I have fallen asleep. I meet her gaze and find my smirk of excitement mirrored on her lips.

"Just like old times."

∎ ∎ ∎ ∎

Leah laughed at me for saying it was just like old times, but this moment truly felt like it.

Way into the night, after my mother would go to sleep, I used to sneak out of my window, creep across the roof of the porch, and climb down the column to meet Leah on the front lawn. The freeway during that time of night would be quiet, with only a few cars or so every couple of minutes, but empty nonetheless.

Leah and I would walk that highway in either direction. We'd peer into the different streets and stores that lined the highway's edge, drawing up scenarios about the owners of houses we saw. Some people, we concluded, had had affairs. Others would be goth or have a zoo of pets in their house. Some probably peaked in high school, and so forth. Our outings like this happened at most twice a month, because if my mother had found out she would have thrown a fit. But now she's gone.

And I only have Leah.

My balcony was a bit high on the second floor, so we took my evening gowns from the drawers and tied them together, heaving the rope we had made over the railing. Aelia would probably scream at the tied fabric, but this was our only option. I climbed down first, trying to be as silent as I could, but each time I looked up at Leah, we both struggled to hold our giggles of excitement in. Leah climbed down after me, and as soon as her flats tapped against the pavement, we didn't look back.

We took off our shoes to run across the front pathway in front of the house, hoping our bare-feet would be muffled on the glossed stone, but as soon as we stepped past the front gate, into the smooth stone street that seemed to bend into the horizon, we put our flats back on and took off. Leah led the way, and we soon reached the bridge I had spotted when Gale flew me to his house. The faint sound of music was on the other side, but we stopped to catch our breath before crossing it, trying to shake the exhilarated laughs that escaped our throats.

After calming down a bit, Leah nudges my shoulder.

"Are you ready?" she asks.

"I think so," I admit breathlessly. "Yeah... yeah, I think so."

A sliver of nerves started to creep into my stomach, but I shot it down as I looped my arm around Leah's.

Then we walked across the bridge.

The first half-hour in the city streets filled my heart with a feeling I don't think I've ever felt. Laughter flowed through every block, mixing with the musicians on the street that played harps at every corner. Glasses of wine were grasped in the hands of socializing angels, flavors of food wafted through the air, and when Leah had led the way to a circular courtyard, a grasp of tenderness clung to my heart. Angels were floating off the ground, dancing in the air over an elegant stone fountain. Water trickled over the structure, with flowers and vines sculpted into the broad stone, plummeting into the sparkling, clear water at the bottom that sprinkled into the air, illuminating the dancing angels above. Leah and I stared in awe at the sight, watching the intimacy between the dancing pairs and their glistening wings swaying with the music.

It was simply beautiful—until a strong grip took hold of

our linked arms and flew us into the sky. Within a flash we were thrown atop the roof of a building, rolling across the stone surface. Leah groaned as she tried to stand up, but I had gotten used to being thrown onto the ground from my sparring with Gale. I got on my feet, fighting the tension of my muscles that tried to rise within my body.

I almost ceased the wind swirling around my fingers as I took in our attacker, but then I remembered Gale's words.

Never underestimate the person in front of you.

Our attacker had vibrant, red hair that cascaded behind her thin, pale body. Her bronze wings fanned out wide, and she was wearing a flowing, cream, evening gown. The dress had a slit in the side, exposing her toned legs and a set of daggers strapped to her thigh. Her dark, monolid eyes rested above her subtle cheekbones, analyzing myself and Leah with bitterness. Although she wasn't a demon, I could tell she wasn't fond of our presence all the same.

"How did a pair of your kind slip into this city?" she asks, her voice unwavering. I stand in front of Leah, who nervously held her breath as she bunched her gown into her fingers and stared at the winged being.

"And who's to say I don't belong here?" I retort calmly, trying to push Leah out of the conversation.

If I could get this girl to focus on me somehow, and maybe use the wind to push her back a rooftop or two, Leah might be able to climb down and escape. I was half-angel, but Leah wasn't, and even though there was a chance this angel wouldn't harm me because of my blood, I had to make sure Leah's blood wouldn't be spilled at all. Within a moment, the angel finally plants her feet onto the rooftop floor and retracts her wings.

"Don't play coy, human, you don't belong here. My

questions come with mercy," she hisses.

"Mercy? You think throwing me on top of a rooftop is mercy?" I challenge. "What's my other option then?"

"The City of Adira," the girl answers without hesitation. "Ever heard of the Bermuda triangle, human? How do you feel about being reincarnated into the sea? You'd be nothing more than a fish."

I heard Leah's breath catch in her throat but I held this angel's gaze, keeping my face as hard as stone despite the threat. I had no idea what the other realms were like yet, but I suppressed the wheels that wanted to turn in my brain at the thought of the Bermuda triangle being a realm. This red-haired bird wasn't about to turn me or my best friend into fish.

"I have heard of it," I lie, "but have you ever heard of The Vine—"

My words were muffled by the sound of fluttering feathers. Two angels landed onto the rooftop. Their wings fanned out to their fullest length as to form a shield in front of myself and Leah. Our attacker's tough stance faltered as she took in our protectors with surprise.

"Gale, what in the world—"

"They aren't your concern, Ruth," Gale says, lowering his wings. Despite the intensity of his tone, I could sense the familiarity in his words.

"You've brought humans here? And you've shown them the city? *Our* city?" Her questions turn soft with disbelief.

I walk up to Gale's side, but he doesn't acknowledge me as he keeps his gaze locked onto the redhead. The psychological daggers they were sending each other couldn't slice the tension in the air. Theseus looks at me, a mischievous smirk on his face as if he were enjoying the trouble I've put myself in, then his gaze drifts to Leah. He raises a brow as he walks to her side, and I watch as she enters his arms and they fly toward the manor without a word.

Gale crosses his arms with a sigh before he turns to me.

"We're going to have to trust her."

"Trust her? For what? If you didn't show up she probably would have killed me," I protest. He raises his brows at me.

"And who's fault is that?"

"Yours! You should've given me a tour of this place!"

"You shouldn't have left on your own!"

"It's not like you said yes to my first invitation."

"Well, if I had known you were reckless enough to go anyway, I would have."

"Well—"

"Well, I need to know why the Hell you brought humans to our city," the angel—Ruth—interrupts. "But please, carry on with your argument. The night is still young."

I purse my lips at the sarcasm, but I'd be a fool to miss the flash of guilt that slips onto Gale's face.

He gives Ruth a tight nod.

"We'll discuss this at the manor."

24
Havena

The living room seemed much more inviting as the flames from the fireplace cackled into the room. The manor was quiet, and the only light source in the room was provided by the orange glow of the fire that reflected its color onto the white, parallel couches. Ruth sat in the middle of the couch opposite of myself and Gale. She crossed her legs, scowling at my seat on the arm of the couch before shooting that same scowl at Gale. He leaned back nonchalantly, watching her actions in amusement, to which she let out a scoff.

We had just arrived back from the rooftop, and I couldn't avoid the constant daggers Ruth's eyes shot at me every time I glanced at her in the air. Nor could I ignore the occasional shoves in the wind that hit Gale's body as he flew me back to the manor in his arms. I kept quiet, ignoring it as he did, but I could only assume those shoves were from her as well.

When we entered the manor, I turned on my heel to head toward the stairs, but Gale grabbed my elbow, gently pulling me toward the living room with them. He released me at the arm of the couch, to which I sat on, and I watched as Ruth plopped herself onto the opposite couch, leaving Gale to light the fireplace with a flick of his fingers.

I saw the way Ruth's eyes scanned over Gale as he sat down, as if she were comparing him to another image inside of her brain. A part of me wished I could see the memories of him traveling inside of her mind. Then her eyes latched to mine, and that's when her scowling began.

The two of them had a history that I obviously didn't know about, but as the light from the fireplace illuminated their features, like the glorious shine in her deep, red hair or the delicate, sharp curves of Gale's strong jaw, I felt like a sack of flour in my skin compared to these two.

"You know I don't like waiting, Gale," Ruth says. Although there was no sign of amusement in her voice, I could see it in her eyes as she waited for his response.

"Ruth Vardy, you've always been *so* impatient," Gale responds with a curl of his lip.

"And yet here you are, stalling," she replies. "I didn't know you were this kind of Guardian, Gale... You know, the ones who *toy* with the humans."

The way she says her last sentence forms a pit in my stomach, and the amusement that was on Gale's face vanishes. Her mouth twists into a sharp smile at his reaction.

"Her name is Havena, Ruth. She's The Vine," he says firmly. Ruth's smile falls from her face, but she quickly recovers by clearing her throat.

"The Vine has only been prophesied for a short time, and you mean to tell me that it's a human?"

"*She's* half-human," I correct. Ruh slithers her eyes to me at the reminder of my pronoun. "And she's also half angel."

"Who are your parents?"

"What does it matter?"

Ruth crosses her arms.

"Is your mother the angel or your father?"

"Easy, Ruth—"

"My father," I interrupt Gale. "My father was the angel, and my mother was human... Just human."

I turn my gaze to the fire, refusing to say more about my past for the night. Before Ruth can ask another question, Gale asks her one first.

"Did anyone else see her tonight?"

"I don't think so," Ruth starts. "They blended in pretty well, but the open back of her dress was a dead giveaway. The breeze moved her hair and I didn't see any wing imprints on her back—which you should be careful with by the way. I swooped her up the second I saw it... Or should I say, lack thereof."

I ignore the jab at my ego and turn my gaze back to her.

"Wing imprints?" I ask. Ruth nods her head with slight surprise in her eyes.

"It's similar to a tattoo where you're from—the Human Plane, if you didn't know—except it looks embroidered. Think of it as a patch on your shoulder blades. That's where you'll find the root of our wings."

I nod my head, trying to picture what she's just explained, and she turns to Gale.

"Gale Geffen! You didn't teach her our customs, did you? Have you taught her anything at all about the realms?" Ruth scolds. I raise my eyebrows at the sound of his last name. It was the first time I've heard it, and just confirmed how familiar they were with one another.

Gale shakes his head.

"Ares was supposed to do it, but we haven't seen him in a while. I've been training her in combat for now," he reasons.

THE SHADOWS OF HEAVEN

Ruth lets out a condescending laugh.

"Well, at least she's smart enough to lie about herself, that's for sure," she says. She even sends me an impressed nod. Gale's grey eyes shift to me, silently asking for an explanation, but I drop his gaze dismissively. I hadn't known the City of Adira was under the Bermuda triangle until Ruth told me.

Ruth suddenly stands from the couch. And so does Gale.

As they stand across from each other, I can't help but imagine how incredibly strong a union between the two would be. It's as if they mirrored each other's strength.

Ruth scans him over one more time with a small smile on her face, and her eyes soften when she meets Gale's gaze.

"I'll teach her the customs in Ares' place," she says, as if he's given her the offer, "It'll be fun to fight by your side again."

"Are you sure that's a good idea?" Gale asks. "What about your own assignments?"

"*This* seems like more of a priority." Ruth swiftly glances over me as she answers him. "Besides, I haven't seen you in a long time. It'll be fun."

Ruth jokingly places a light punch on Gale's arm before turning on her heel. Gale's eyes soften as he watches her head for the front door, but I pretend I don't notice and look toward the floor, fiddling with the hem of my dress.

"Goodnight, human!" Ruth calls out.

Then she's gone.

25
Gale

"What you did tonight was reckless."

Havena stops fiddling with her dress and brings her gaze to mine. There's no fire in her eyes as she stands from the arm of the couch, away from me.

"I know..." she says quietly.

The cackling fireplace flickers warmth across her dark skin, but it's not enough to brighten the dull tone of her voice. Her delicate hands reach down, sliding the pale-gold flats off her feet, and she starts toward the staircase. With a mind of their own, my feet follow the train of her dress on the floor.

"Then why'd you go?" I ask to her back. She's swooped the waves of her dark hair over her shoulder, framing the side profile of her face and leaving the entirety of her back exposed to the world. The open back of her dark blue dress cuts low into a dramatic V, revealing small dimples at the base of her spine. Just as Ruth had said, there were no signs of wing imprints on either shoulder blade.

The chance of Ruth finding Havena tonight was pure luck. I hadn't seen Ruth in three years, yet she still managed to look as radiant as ever. Ruth and I fell in love like many young angels do, growing up together and realizing that our flirting throughout the years had grown into something more. Then our relationship faltered when we selected our professions.

I've always wanted to follow in my parents' footsteps. The path of a Guardian was my only choice. Ruth always claimed she was unsure about what she wanted. But she had lied about that. She had chosen the path of a Disciple days before The Selection, she was just trying to find a way to break the news to me.

Just like Ares, she wanted to give herself the freedom to find the right person before she turned thirty, and despite how fond we had grown of each other—how much we loved each other—she said she was too young to know if she wanted to start a family with me.

Seeing Ruth tonight felt like looking at a healed wound and reminiscing on how you got it in the first place. And a slimmer of, "What if?" was making me want to open that wound again.

Havena turns around on the fourth step of the stairs and looks down to me at the base of it. I knew she wasn't going to answer my question. We both knew it was a stupid question. But even so, I found myself wanting to release Havena's voice from its somber state. I almost fumble my words under her gaze.

"I shouldn't have pushed you like that during our training."

I bite my cheek...

"No, you shouldn't have," Havena replies tightly, yet her eyes flicker over me for a moment.

"But I was an idiot to sneak into the city without you, so I guess we're both even," she says a little softer. A trying smile forms on her lips as she holds my gaze. I return it.

"There's a lot you don't know about this city, let alone the danger that's lurking around now," I tell her. She leans against the railing.

"That may be true, but I know this was my father's city once. I can feel it," she says. "If my family tree didn't have a death wish, I'd still be walking through the streets right now."

"Is that what your blood feels like to you? A death wish?" I ask. She simply drops her gaze to the ground, but she nods her head nonetheless.

"I've lost everyone so far, haven't I?" she mutters to the floor.

"You haven't lost me," I say after a moment. Her somber gaze glides to mine in confusion, but I continue. "Or Theseus, or Ares—wherever he is—or Leah. We may have been randomly brought together by fate, but we're in this together. And together, we'll see it through 'til the end."

"We've just met and you're asking me to what? Consider you family?" she questions, but it's not a question of protest. It's a question of hesitance.

"Anyone who fights by my side is family," I assure.

She studies my face, looking for any sign of falsehood. Then she nods her head when she can't find it, and I nod my head back at her, solidifying our silent pact of trust. She grabs her dress and turns to glide up the stairs.

My feet, once again, follow behind her.

"So, where did you go tonight? What did you see?" I ask to the back of her head. She doesn't answer until we reach the landing.

"I feel like I saw everything and nothing at the same time. I want to hear more of the music, see the city in the daytime... Leah took me to some fountain or something, and angels were dancing above it... I think." Her voice trails off like the recollections were playing before her very eyes. I step beside her as we walk down the hall.

"You went to the Fountain of Eden," I say, remembering where Theseus and I found the girls.

Theseus and I had planned on flying onto Havena's balcony to scare the girls—just for a bit of fun. But when we saw the tied dresses hanging over the balcony railing, we quickly put two and two together.

Fortunately, the girls didn't escape far into the city, and I figured we finally knew how reckless they both were. But as Havena tilted her head, waiting for me to explain the fountain's origin, I realize I mistook her genuine curiosity for recklessness.

"The fountain symbolizes the garden of Eden, and there's a myth that lovers who dance above it will have a blessed union. Like how Adam was blessed by his union with Eve."

"Hmm... But didn't they also get punished for having sex?" Havena asks. We reach our doors, but neither one of us reaches for a doorknob.

"Well... they got punished together," I reason pathetically. Havena pauses, and for a moment I think I've said something wrong, but then laughter escapes her lips. A snort sounds through her nose simultaneously, making her laugh even harder, and my own laughter joins hers.

This is the first time I've seen her with her guard completely down. Her usually tensed shoulders are slumped, her calculating eyes are filled with joy, and she's allowed the sound of her laugh to burst from her throat, echoing along the hallway walls for anyone to hear. She's not suffocating herself like before, and I'd like to keep it that way.

"Careful now, you're to learn our customs, not laugh at them," I point out, but the slight chuckle in my voice doesn't shoot down her amusement.

"I know, I know," she waves off, her laughter subsiding. "I've actually never learned how to dance, you know. But if I ever go into the city again, I think I'd want to try. I think my father would have... danced, I mean."

She turns to take hold of her door handle, and the words slip out of my mouth without a second thought.

"You can dance to your heart's content in two weeks' time."

Havena's eyes meet mine in a flash.

"What happens in two weeks?" she inquires.

I shrug, like the news will be no big deal, but the Summer Solstice is the biggest ball of the year. A tradition that's been around for centuries, and since the wind is strongest during this time of the year, angels flock to the ball in celebration of the element. Everyone shows up in their best and waltzes the entire night away.

"I'll tell you when we train," I say nonchalantly. I brace myself for a witty comment, maybe even an insult or two, but Havena rolls her eyes in amusement before turning the knob to her room.

"Goodnight, Gale," she sighs, then closes the door behind her, leaving me in the hallway face to face with her door.

Like an idiot.

26
Havena

My blade felt the sturdiest it's ever been in my hands.
Every jab, every nudge, and every slice felt like more of an
instinct instead of a pitiful request from my brain. I could
blame it on my father's blood that ran through my veins, but
deep down I knew the only thing that awakened this part of
me was Gale... even if he's blocked every attack so far.

Our swords collide again, and instead of pulling away, I
push into him. He does the same.

"You're getting more confident," he says, but I catch the
veins in his arms strain a bit.

"I think I'm just getting stronger," I retort.

His blade suddenly slips off mine, pushing me back, and
hits the base of my sword. The metal clatters to the floor,
leaving me empty-handed and Gale's sword inches away from
my chest.

"You've gotten stronger—I'll admit that—but getting
stronger is useless if you're not getting smarter," Gale says with
a smirk on his lips. He doesn't drop his blade, and I don't
expect him to. This is a test, and his eyes were daring me to find

a way out of it.

Wind sweeps off my fingertips, soaring to his chest, but it falls short, dropping down into the floor instead.

"Every angel can conjure the elements, but you must remember we can also conjure against them—even with a weapon in hand. Find a weak spot," Gale instructs, still pointing his blade. I nod at his advice, bouncing on my toes to look over his body, ready to attack. But attacking him anywhere wouldn't make sense. His feet are solidly planted, and every inch of him is practically covered in muscle. *Perfectly chiseled, and toned, and dripping in sweat—*

I bite my tongue and look to his eyes, hoping my cheeks aren't reddening as I bring my focus back to the task at hand.

But nothing could move him.

He lets out a chuckle at my no longer bouncing feet, as if they were a signal of defeat.

"You'll get it next time—"

His sword flings to the floor, skidding just a few feet away from us. He glimpses at his empty hand, now lowering to his side, and looks to me in surprise.

From the moment he laughed, his hand had faltered under his blade. So I attacked it. I started chuckling now, getting in a stance to fight with my hands now that I've found his weak spot.

Me.

"You told me I'd get to dance last night, so let's dance," I say. Gale scoffs with a raise of his eyebrow, but he gets into his fighting stance anyway. We start circling each other.

"I've been training my entire life. Do you really think you can take me with your bare hands?" he asks with amusement. I shrug playfully, keeping his gaze away from the pattern of my feet.

Then I lunge.

He grabs my arm within a second and twists it behind my back. It doesn't hurt, but I try to use my other arm to whack him with my elbow. He curves his arm under it, locking me into place. His chest rises against my back now, and his hand rests around the nape of my neck, making me look forward.

"So I'm only your weak spot when you're holding a blade?" I ask with a heavy breath. The heat of his chuckle hits my ear and I realize he's staring down at me. As if he's read my mind, his finger turns my face up toward his.

"Blades don't care about what they cut... I do," he says softly.

My brain goes blank as I study the intensity of his eyes, watching as they slip closer to mine.

"Sorry to interrupt."

My eyes slip off Gale's and settle onto the entrance of the armory. Ruth steps over the threshold, the heels of her boots clicking onto the concrete. She's already narrowing her eyes at the space between me and Gale.

"Ah, the *she-devil* has entered," Theseus announces with a clap from the corner. He was seated on top of the strategy table beside Leah. Their focus was no longer on the book in Leah's lap and Theseus leans back, smirking at Ruth.

Gale's hands fall from my body.

"Hello, Ruth. We weren't expecting you today."

"It's not like I haven't been here before. Besides, I wanted to see what you call training," Ruth answers dryly. Her eyes travel to me. "Glad to see it's going well."

"You wanted to kill us last night? Now, you have the audacity to train with us?"

Leah slides off the table and puts a hand to her hip. Ruth sizes her up and Leah barely bats an eyelash.

"I won't be training you," Ruth scoffs at her. "I'm sure Theseus enjoys making you his problem."

Leah takes a step forward. Luckily, Theseus catches her arm for me, stopping a fight before one starts.

"What did you have in mind for today?" I ask Ruth, trying to level out the conversation.

"So, what exactly are you teaching them, Gale?" Ruth asks, ignoring my input. Gale crosses his arms.

"You agreed to instruct them on Monday, Ruth. You'll teach them our customs then," he says firmly. Ruth tightens her lips at the dismissal.

"*God*, the punctuality of a Guardian... so tiresome," Ruth pouts. "How much time will I get with them?"

"Two hours or so after combat training. That way we'll have something to talk about during dinner," he says with a laugh.

He turns to collect the swords from the ground, clearly ending their conversation, but Ruth's gaze shifts from me, to Gale, then back to me. I can't help but grab my necklace as I stand in between them.

"That's not enough time," Ruth protests. "I want two full days. That way you can rest and I'll... take over."

She settles her eyes on him, and I can see the sincerity that was laced in her voice. Gale pauses at the sight of her face, his grey eyes taking in her words as if they were written over her body. If she already hates me now, then two full days with her would be a nightmare. Theseus groans from across the room.

"If only you were with us when we started our schedule. Unfortunately, I was planning on teaching this little gremlin here how to use a bow and arrow."

Theseus puts his arm around Leah and she nearly pushes him off the table.

"I'm not a gremlin, you bird."

"You're right. You're a very strong rat."

The sound of a slap echoes into the armory, and I catch Ruth roll her eyes at the sight of the two before settling onto me.

"Two days isn't necessary," I tell her.

"It's not your call to give, half-blood."

"You're right. It's mine," Gale cuts in firmly. He steps to my side with our blades in hand.

"Our history and customs are lengthy and annoying—you of all people should know that. Or do you have a newfound respect for books now that you're a Disciple?" he says. Ruth bites her lip, dissatisfied at the familiarity in Gale's voice, but he only shrugs. "Besides, I have to prepare her for the Summer Solstice."

"You're bringing her along?" Ruth's face suddenly falls completely, and the shock in her voice doesn't go unnoticed. This 'Solstice' was news to me, but her reaction showed just how important it was.

"What's a solstice?"

Our attention snaps to Leah's confused face.

"The Summer Solstice is a ball hosted by the City of Aaron. It's how we celebrate the wind," Gale answers. "Every realm hosts one in honor of the element they mostly use, but it goes further than that. On the Human Plane, you guys think astrology can predict your personality or... the future. In actuality, we use it to track when the elements will be strongest throughout the year. Only four solstices are held because they occur during the month when an element is most powerful. Air, our element, is most powerful towards the end of June. Fortunately for us, the Summer Solstice is around the corner." Gale looks down to me, adding quietly, "Besides, I promised you an actual dance."

"So you're preparing her for the committee waltz?" Ruth asks, gaining Gale's attention.

"Precisely."

Ruth clears her throat. "I'm sorry, I don't think I heard you right. You've signed her up for a dance she's never done before, yet she only has two weeks to learn?"

"I'm a fast learner," I cut in. I didn't know what the waltz was, but I had to give it a shot—more or less because I wanted to get under Ruth's skin. Based on her constant scowl, my very breath seemed to annoy her. "I want to do it, and I'd like to think my father probably did it as well... participated... I mean."

Ruth looks to Gale with a clenched jaw, but when he doesn't add any input she rolls her eyes, unable to argue further.

"Well, if you need me, you know where to find me." Ruth turns, leaving the armory without saying goodbye.

Leah's voice breaks the silence of Ruth's departure.

"Spot on, Cupid, she is a she-devil."

■ ■ ■ ■

Training ended shortly after Ruth left. For the few minutes after her departure, Gale seemed distracted by his thoughts, blocking my hits sloppier than usual. It's been a quiet day since, and I was just changing into my nightgown when my stomach rumbled.

I spent the majority of today playing cards with Leah in her room, but then I left shortly after Theseus stopped by to give her a book she had been asking for. I came back to my room after he showed up, and just as I was pondering over what dress to wear for dinner, Aelia entered my room with a tray of food.

I guess we only ate at the dining table during weekdays.

Even so, I left my bed tonight with a whining stomach, and my bare feet stepped into the cold hallway. Leah would want to see the kitchen just as much as I did, and I didn't want to raid the fridge alone. I took a few steps away from my door, but the faint sound of a piano drifted to my ears. The door next to my bedroom was slightly open, just enough for me to peek inside.

I gently pressed my head against the white wood, hoping to silently glimpse inside. The door, unfortunately, had other plans. As soon as the door creaked, the music stopped. I leaned my head off the wood, but before I could think of an escape plan, the door flew open, revealing the rest of the room.

Bookcases lined every wall—except for the wall in the back of the room, which was covered in floor to ceiling windows that showcased the night sky. Seated on a piano bench before the windows was Gale, with one hand still propped on the grand piano keys and the other hand lowering itself from my direction.

"S-sorry..." I wince with a sheepish smile. Gale only chuckles, pulling his hand toward his side. And me with it.

My feet hover an inch off the floor and the air he's conjured pulls me to the piano bench. He slides over with a smirk on his face and my feet touch the floor.

"That's... different," I manage with a soft breath, but I take the seat beside him. He smirks as he starts playing the piano again. His slim fingers float over the keys, mesmerizing me as he delicately hits every note. Then he misses one and lets out a sigh of frustration.

"Lift your wrist a little higher," I advise.

"What do you mean?" he asks, finally speaking. I ignore his gaze as I move my hand onto the keys, playing how the song should sound.

"Your hand stiffens over time as you play. It'll help if you—"

"Lift my wrist higher," he whispers. I look him in the eye to give him a nod as I lower my hand to my lap.

"I didn't realize you play," he says.

"I didn't know you had a piano," I counter. He chuckles.

"There's a lot we don't know about each other," Gale says softly. I watch as he plays for a few more seconds, wondering if I should say more or if I'll just interrupt his focus. Then he takes my hand—placing it over his—and keeps playing the same set of keys as before.

Before I can ask why he's moved my hand, he speaks again.

"Did your mother teach you how to play?" he asks.

I shake my head.

"No... I learned at school," I answer. Gale's eyes crinkle at the shy laugh that slips past my mouth from the memories.

"I started in school when I was about twelve. I didn't want to go home after school most days, so I'd stay with my music teacher. Eventually, she would just leave her classroom unlocked so I could practice." I settle my gaze onto the keys he's playing, finally unpacking a part of myself that I've compartmentalized. "I guess I started to play because... there was nothing to look forward to when I went home."

Gale's fingers start to slow as he takes in my words, but he doesn't say anything. The state of my house served as enough evidence for my story. And it's scared him off.

I start to slide my hand off his, but then he speaks.

"You can leave it."

He meets my eyes asking for his permission.

"Leave it," he reiterates softly.

Then he starts playing the song from its beginning.

"I was six when my parents died," he says. He keeps his gaze on his hand guiding mine. "My mother used to let me tap anywhere on this thing, even when she was playing this song... her favorite."

His small smile falls.

"An angel fell eighteen years ago, and my parents were assigned to stop him from the moment he became fallen. I was little then, but even I could tell he was plotting something big the year they died. That year they were just... they were restless. And I was too young to understand why my mother spent less time with me... and more time fighting."

He lets out a shaky laugh and turns his teary eyes to me. Our hands slide off the keys. "Everyone says she was brave. That honoring her duty was more important than being in my life... and more important than being pregnant."

He drops his gaze, searching the wood of the piano for the right words. After a moment, he says quietly, "Everyone looks to me whenever a decision has to be made and I just... I can only pray that I'm making the right decision. That I've taken everyone's self-interest into account... because if I don't... they'll go on this journey with us without realizing they're one mistake away from death. And now Ruth... she's jumped into this journey, too."

He lets out a breath, and takes hold of the piano cover.

But so do I.

Those grey eyes question me, wondering why I'm blocking him from bringing the wood down, but I keep the piano cover raised above the keys.

"We're not our parents," I tell him softly. I bring my hand down to the keys he just showed me, and start to play. He slowly lowers his hand and watches.

"Our fears are a product of what we've been through—maybe even what we've seen our parents go

139

through—but we weren't created to follow their footsteps."

I level my gaze to his. "I didn't know your mother, and I don't know what your duty as a Guardian entails, but I'm... starting to know you.

"Your name is Gale Geffen. You try your best to protect the people you care about, you've opened your home to a girl who no longer has one. And you lead with your heart... It's why we trust you... Why I trust you. Don't let your parent's mistakes tell you any different."

Gale blinks, taking in my words, and I almost do the same. I realize now that this was the loss he was talking about in the grocery store. It was also why he didn't let me lose control when I held my mother's body in my hands.

If he wasn't there to stop my powers, I would've been dead. And what's worse is I would've done it to myself. He didn't let me because he knows what it's like to doubt the purpose of his existence—the frustrating absence of identity—and he's fought that feeling longer than I have. And despite how much it hurt, he knew that the future—our future, whatever it may look like—was worth fighting for.

I softly bump his shoulder with a small smile as I play, thankful that he was there to keep me alive that night. He lets out a small laugh, as if he understands, and brings his other hand to the piano keys.

And we played his mother's song until we got tired.

27
Gale

Ruth stepped into the armory at just the right time. She looked fierce as usual, with her favorite daggers strapped around her right leg. I recognized the leather bodysuit that she wore. It clung to her body in just the right places, complimenting the deep red of her hair which was now braided to the side.

Ruth came here to fight, and as her slit, monolid eyes looked between Havena and I polishing our blades, I couldn't tell who she wanted to fight more.

"You're teaching her our customs, not how to kill," I joke. Ruth slyly walks forward, refusing to blink her dark eyes. A calculating smile slips onto her lips.

"I came prepared for both. I wasn't sure you two would finish fighting on time."

We used to train together when we were sixteen, and somehow every practice ended up the same way: with Ruth on my lips and our clothes on the floor.

And although she hid it well, Ruth was jealous.

"So what will I be doing today?"

I instruct her, gesturing to the corner of the room.

"Working over there."

Theseus and Leah left about an hour earlier, but they kept all of the books and notes they had used on the strategy table, just in case Ruth would need it. I was supposed to switch roles with Theseus today, but he was insistent on teaching Leah about different sword wounds and how to treat them. Ruth takes in the clutter and snorts.

"Am I teaching the incapable mind of a human or an incompetent angel—"

"You're teaching both," Havena interjects, handing her blade to me before walking over to the table. "So let's get to it, since you're such a great teacher and all."

I run my free hand through my hair, pretending not to see Ruth's lips pathetically part without a rebuttal. Havena lifts a brown, leather book and reads the title.

"Noah's Arc... I wonder what that's about..."

A chuckle escapes my throat and Havena sends me a smirk as she puts the book down.

"I may be doing this for Gale, but I won't teach you our customs if you treat our time like a joke," Ruth spits, but her face has flushed. I can't tell if she understood Havena's sarcasm or if she's embarrassed.

"Neither will I."

Ares steps into the armory and our laughter subsides. My eyes drift to his feet. He's wearing his usual slacks, but he's paired it with thick combat boots, an usual combination since Disciples rarely fight.

Ever.

"It's good to be back," Ares says with a satisfied sigh, taking in the room.

"Where have you been?"

"Why are you here?"

Havena's question catches me off guard. I knew that Ares would come back—eventually. But now that he has returned, I couldn't help but notice the tension in Havena's shoulders as she studies him. The uncertainty she was trying to hide behind her calm eyes.

"I've been at the temple," Ares answers my question. He turns to Havena to answer hers. "And I'm here to teach you... like I should've done weeks ago."

"Well, it's too late," Ruth cuts in, crossing her arms. "I'm teaching Havena now."

Ares looks to me for an explanation, but I don't give him one.

Not yet.

"Why'd you change your mind?" I ask. Ares shrugs, walking over to the strategy table. I catch Havena slide slightly away from him as he sets down the book in his hand.

"I realized I was being..."

"Arrogant," I finish for him. Ares nods.

"Disciples are known to let knowledge get to their head," he explains to Havena. "And sometimes we think we know best, only for it to cloud our judgment... Take Ruth for example."

"Hey!"

"Fair enough," Havena mutters under her breath.

"I will cut both of you!"

"Okay, okay!" I chuckle, easing Ruth's threat. "So, Ares, you're on board now?"

"Always have been," Ares answers. He turns his gaze to Havena, and a gulp subtly bobs across her throat. "There are many things you have to learn, Havena. Things that only Disciples can teach."

"Then Ruth will help you teach her," I blurt out.

143

All eyes snap to me.

I could sense Ruth's look of disapproval, but I kept my eyes on Ares. Impatience settles over his eyes, but I watch as he masks it with a smile.

"Perfect."

"Good." I mirror his smile, then walk to the shelves of daggers in the wall. "Then I guess you can officially start your teachings tomorrow. It's been a long day."

Havena looks at me curiously, but I look to Ruth. The Disciple slowly nods her head, understanding my signal, and starts walking toward me. "I'll help you polish the daggers then."

"So... we're done for the day?" Havena asks cautiously. She slips off of the strategy table.

"Yes. I'll see you later for dinner," I tell her. Havena lingers for a moment, watching between Ruth and I, then stalks to the armory door. Ares steps to follow her.

"Ares!" I call instinctively, giving Havena a head start to get away from him. It works, and he slows his steps. "Will you be eating with us tonight? I was hoping you would say the prayer before we eat."

He blinks at the suggestion. "Maybe another night? I have some errands to run at the temple, but I'll be back tomorrow."

"Perfect," I say with a nod. He sends Ruth a grin before stepping out of the armory.

"What's wrong?" Ruth asks. I turn my gaze to find her reading me like the back of her hand.

Telling Ruth that it's been a long day was our secret code. We've had classes together, trained together, and gone on our outings with Ares and Theseus a number of times, but when we just wanted to talk—or share an intimate moment between the two of us—we'd simply say it's been a long day and sneak off to be alone. And I was grateful she still remembered.

"I've never seen you and Ares so... weird. The boy barely speaks casually as it is."

"Something about him isn't right. He turned his back from our assignment—and he was sure about leaving. Now, he suddenly decides to come back? Arrogant Disciples are common knowledge," I remind her, but Ruth only furrows her brows. "Have you seen him around the temple lately?"

Ruth nods her head.

"Yes..."

Then she pauses.

"And... no. We occasionally pass each other by, but... I believe he's in the temple... sometimes. What are you trying to say?"

"He didn't want to bless the food tonight, Ruth. Disciples don't usually ignore that request," I hint at her. Her narrowed eyes widen with realization.

"You think he's... drifting?"

"Falling," I correct. "Three weeks ago, Ares wanted nothing to do with Havena—let alone Leah—and now he suddenly wants to join us again? Gain Havena's trust?"

"Are you sure about this? Or are you just being... protective?" she asks carefully.

Ruth's eyes were set like stone. She bites her lip as she waits for my response, something she only does when she's skeptical.

"I'm being protective of everyone, not just Havena," I tell her. Ruth rolls her eyes dismissively.

"Then do we tell her?"

I shake my head.

"We mustn't scare anyone..." I advise, mostly to myself.

Havena was visibly unsteady around Ares, and although I didn't know her list of reasons not to trust him, I could sense it. And I wasn't going to give her another one. Not when the accusation was this dangerous.

"As of right now, Ares seems fallen, Ruth. And I won't let him hurt her. I can't."

28
Havena

I couldn't breathe.

Aelia gave the strings of the corset another tug and I could barely register the fact that my body was tilting. Thankfully, my hands worked better than my feet, and I managed to catch myself before my body fell into the dresser in front of me.

"Sorry, sweetheart!" Aelia sighs reassuringly, immediately pulling me upright and letting her quick nimble fingers loosen the corset ties.

The Summer Solstice was tonight, and on top of my usual training, Gale had been teaching me the committee waltz for the past week. To my surprise, the dancing part was easier than I had thought. It was weird at first. I was used to closing the gap between Gale and I with my blade, but dancing—of course—took that blade away.

The first few minutes into practice were awkward, uncertainty running through both of our faces, questioning which areas we should or shouldn't touch, dangerously closing the gap inch by lingering inch.

Yet every time we did meet in the middle, that shock of

electricity we knew too well sent itself through my body—and every time I looked into Gale's eyes as it happened, I finally noticed he felt it, too. After five tries of awkward laughter, the shock happened again, but instead of stepping out of each other's grasp as we had done before, Gale pulled me back in. From that moment on we danced, and have been completing the entire routine for the past week.

Ruth and Ares weren't too pleased about cutting down their teaching time with me, but after talking with Gale, they figured that learning the waltz was a crucial part of learning their customs. Ruth made it clear to point out that I wouldn't be dancing with Gale at the solstice. The partners at the solstice were grouped by chance, and throughout the dance, partners were passed to other partners, which meant I would be dancing with three angel men that I didn't know. But, as far as I knew, the Summer Solstice was a time of celebration, and my only intention was to treat it like one.

Aelia had waited until the last minute to find a dress I could wear to the party—or so she had said. The entirety of yesterday was spent with her clung to my hip, taking my measurements and toying around with different hairstyles. I enjoyed it for a few hours, but the only time I got a slimmer of solitude was when she went to check on Leah.

That visit, unfortunately, was extremely short. Upon hearing that I was going to be the one doing the committee waltz, presumably from Leah herself, Aelia's visit with Leah practically never happened. And as kind as Aelia has been to me since I arrived, it sometimes felt foreign to have someone smother me with this kind of attention—especially when I'd find myself enjoying it.

"You must be excited to go to the solstice tonight," Aelia says softly to my back. Her fingers diligently focus on undoing the tight corset.

"Well," I strain through my suppressed ribs, "I think... I'm just excited... to get a break... from all of this."

The corset slips from my waist and I let out a breath. A giggle escapes Aelia, but she's already reached for another corset and wraps it around my waist in a flash, trying again. The corset is beautiful, entirely lacy with a floral pattern covering every inch of it. Aelia insisted on me wearing a ball gown for the waltz, so I'd *look like a butterfly among the brittle twigs and leaves.*

I've only been in this city for a little more than a month, thinking that the angels were more occupied with their duties rather than their appearances.

Aelia proved me wrong.

"Do we have to wear these?" I ask. "I think I know how Adam felt when God ripped out his rib."

Aelia roars with hearty laughter, then looks over my shoulder to study my reflection in the floor-length mirror. I send her my best sheepish grin.

"Oh, dear," she says, her smile dropping. Her fingers start unfastening the corset. "You know, if there's anything that you want to wear, like certain shoes, or a certain style of dress—or even a particular fabric—you can tell me... Just promise me I won't see it across the balcony like last time."

"I hadn't realized I had a choice," I laugh. Her fingers suddenly slow their pace a little bit, clearly stalling so I can keep talking. "I never did these kinds of things with my mother before. She just saw to it that I was alive... never... beautiful. This experience has been... fun."

The corset slips from around my waist and I can finally let out a breath, but it still seems caught in my throat since I mentioned my mom. Aelia places a strong, yet gentle hand, on my shoulder, peeking over it to look into my eyes in the mirror again. She hasn't even talked yet, but I can feel the stinging blur of my eyes under the intensity of her gaze.

"I see nothing except the prettiest soul inside of you. Selflessness that some angels I encounter every day do not possess. It has been an honor to be at your service, for the strength and kindness in your heart does nothing but elevate how radiant and beautiful you already are... I know your mother would be proud."

She gingerly wipes away the single tear that's fallen over my cheek as we stare into the mirror.

"Well then," Aelia huffs, pulling my hair to the side and turning me around. Her eyes, glazed with wetness, yet stubborn enough to keep the tears at bay, crinkle as she sends me a smile. "I know exactly the dress you'll need."

"But I thought—"

With a dismissive wave, Aelia takes my hand and leads me into the hallway.

"Where are we going?" I ask, but the journey's short. She's taken me to the first door in the right-wing of the house.

"We're going to get your dress," she simply answers, opening the bedroom door. We cross the threshold, entering a bedroom that puts my own to shame.

The bedroom is huge. It has the same white, marble flooring that runs throughout the house, but the floor to ceiling waffled windows spread along the back wall take my breath away. They reveal the large balcony that lies beyond, peering over the edge of this realm and into the clouds. On one wall, a large bed rests in an elegant, iron bed frame, and an archway rests next to the mirrored side table that leads to the bathroom. Although no one was staying in the room, it looked pristine, like it was regularly cleaned for a guest that would eventually return.

Opposite of the bed, large, wooden-paneled closet doors take up most of the wall, which Aelia walks over to. She slides the door over, revealing hangers upon hangers of dresses, and scans over them.

The amount of dresses in the closet exceeds my imagination. Ball gowns, evening gowns, Victorian-style dresses, clothing I've only ever seen through history books or TV. With the same composed smile I saw on the first day we met, Aelia pulls out whatever she was looking for.

"What do you think?"

■ ■ ■ ■

"We're going to be late."

"I second that. Are humans always this tardy?"

"Both of you, knock it off," I hear Gale intervene.

Aelia had taken her time preparing me inside of the vacant bedroom. My hair was done up into a bun, but she purposely left out a few of my waves to frame my face. My makeup was light, emphasizing my eyes with mascara and a bit of eyeliner to make them look slightly more dramatic. My eyes, to Aelia's reasoning, were too kind, and she wanted to make sure I looked fierce among the other angels. The attention from my dress, I figured, would already do that.

The lace top was cut into a low V-neck, with off-the-shoulder sleeves that cascaded down my arms, tear-dropping over my knuckles. The sleeves clung to my skin, yet the lace fabric still managed to give me enough flexibility about the arms. The V-neck on the front was replicated onto my back, leaving just enough fabric to cover my shoulder blades—and hide my lack of wings. The tulle skirt of the dress was fastened above my waist by a belt, doming out into a flowy cloud that layered the actual lace skirt of the dress, which flowed straight down to the floor. Etched onto the belt were flecks of silver, gold, and diamonds, giving just enough flare to the overall look.

For the first time in my life, I felt beautiful and unstoppable at the same time. Most importantly, my mother's necklace rested just above my heart, reminding me of how much I'd been through to feel this way, and how proud I was of it.

After stepping into the simple, pointed-toed heels that Aelia had chosen, she stepped to the bedroom door and gave me one final once over. Her proud smile trailed all over me, getting bigger and bigger until, at last, she met my face. I hadn't realized I was holding in my breath until she opened the door, a reassuring smile beaming on her face. She motioned for me to enter the hallway just as Ruth's voice echoed from the foyer.

"I could fly there and back and she'd still be late."

As I passed the threshold, turning to give Aelia a 'thank you', her grip on my arm halted my feet.

"Miss Havena, I must warn you." The maid quickly reaches into her apron, retrieving a small dagger with swirled etchings on the handle. I nearly jump out of her grasp, but the overwhelming worry in her eyes told me not to worry. And that the next few words she would say would be laced with utmost importance.

"Many of us know of the prophecy, but many angels tonight will not know who you are or what you look like. Beware of the ones who do. The Disciples, Havena. Beware of *The Fallen*," she whispers. For a brief moment, Aelia places her palm to my cheek. Then she attaches the small dagger to the belt of my dress.

"How do I know who's fallen?" I question, mirroring her

152

whisper. I couldn't help but think about my gut feeling towards Ares, wondering if she didn't trust him as well. She took my hand in hers, stepping out of the bedroom with me.

"You are The Vine, and the prophecy I know of implies that you will defeat the evil of the realms by bridging them together. Trust your heart," she finishes. She gives my hand a long squeeze, signaling the end of her warning and I swallow my breath. Without time to process, she begins walking me to the top of the stairs, to where I was going to have to smile down at the others below—including Ares.

Gale's voice sounds from the foyer.

"Seriously guys! She's coming, just wait."

Aelia brings me to the landing and I'm instantly met with their gazes. I study the faces of Theseus, Leah, Ruth, and Gale, wondering whether I should tell them about Aelia's warning, or if they even knew of the risk tonight. Then I looked to Ares, and the smirk that was plastered across his face as he glanced from Gale to me.

My original plan tonight was to join them in celebration, except now I had enemies to look out for, and I was pretty sure I was already looking at one.

So I smiled.

■ ■ ■ ■

"Beautiful."

The quiet remark made my eyes drop from Ares and settle onto Gale. It didn't take much for him to clean up since he was already breathtaking, but the attire he wore for tonight made my breath even more unsteady. All three men before me were dressed in formal suits, resembling the kind of clothing worn during medieval times. Their tailcoats were composed of different patterns and material, but from the moment I took in Gale's suit, I realized it coordinated with my dress.

His blazer was dark blue, and the trimming was etched with the same silver and gold pattern of my belt. A lace handkerchief hung over his heart and the cuffs on the sleeves were diamonds. I wondered if Aelia had planned this, and unfortunately for me, I wasn't the only one who thought so.

"I hadn't realized we were matching our outfits tonight," Ruth mutters, taking my gaze off Gale's.

Ruth wore an emerald, mermaid gown, with a subtle slit down the side. It's probably there to give her access to the knives I know she has strapped to her legs. As usual, she looks stunning, even now as she scowls at me from the foyer floor. I can feel the heat of Gale's gaze boring into me but I avoid it, taking a step at a time as I travel down the stairs.

"Trust me, this was very last minute," I say with a nervous laugh, glancing to them one step at a time.

"Well last minute or not, I agree with Gale. You look beautiful, Havena," Leah pipes in with a reassuring smile.

She's standing next to Theseus, wearing a simple, red, satin ball gown. Her skirt is less dramatic than mine, and she has her hands in the pockets of it. Lucky.

"She's not the only one," Theseus murmurs. I barely heard it, but I can see the heat in Leah's cheeks rise as she looks to him without saying another word.

The only person who hasn't spoken yet is Ares, and I turn to him when I reach the foyer floor. He's wearing a white suit, and the etching trimmed onto his coat resembled the color of coal. He looks good, yet even less inviting than he already is.

"I'm happy you're joining us tonight," I tell Ares with a smile. I can hear Aelia's warning sound throughout my brain, but I keep my cool. As if playing the same game, Ares winks.

"I hope you enjoy tonight as well," he says. The satisfied

calculation in his golden eyes confirms one thing: it's a threat. I can't help the gulp that goes down underneath my smile.

"Sorry, I'm late," I apologize, stepping to Gale's side and out of Ares' gaze. The glint in Gale's eyes immediately causes my mouth to mirror his smile onto my own, but I couldn't keep my brows from furrowing in confusion, my mind wondering about whatever surprise he had planned. Then, with a wave of his hand, he opens the front doors.

In the middle of the driveway were three identical carriages. Golden wheels supported the iron vehicles, trimmed with multiple shavings of copper, bronze, and silver. I turned to Gale, in awe, but still confused.

"Where are the horses?" I ask.

Gale mirrors my confused face.

"We don't use animals here for that sort of thing," he says gently. Leah and Theseus exit the foyer, her arm wrapped around his as they head toward a carriage. I share a look with Gale, seeing the wheels turn in his grey eyes just like they were currently turning in mine. Theseus and Leah's constant banter made them an odd pairing, but it also made sense for whatever was budding.

Gale extends his arm, silently asking me to take it. And I almost do...

Until Ares turns our heads.

"I guess we should split up in pairs then," Ares suggests, not asking for our input as he looks to Gale. "Why don't you and Ruth take this time to catch up?"

The suggestion is sly and unsettling. I take Gale's arm and give it a squeeze, hoping he would know my answer.

And he does.

"It'll be a long ride. I'll probably just bore you to death," Gale declines, looking to Ruth. To my surprise, Ruth gives him a nod of agreement.

"Besides Ares, I'd love to hear you critique my teaching skills," she says, shooting Ares a tight smile. Ruth grabs his arm and they head off toward their carriage before he can protest.

Gale and I walk to our carriage.

"If I ever had a gut feeling about something, would you trust me because I'm The Vine?" I ask. Gale turns his head down to me, but I avoid his gaze. "Or would you simply trust... me?"

Gale pauses for a moment, pondering over my question, but I slip my hand from his arm and take the next few steps to the carriage alone. He hurriedly goes to open the carriage door and steps to the side, leveling his intense gaze onto mine.

"I trust you regardless of your title. The Vine isn't who you are, Havena, it's what is expected of you. And I'll always trust you because you'll always exceed my expectations," he answers.

I blink, unsure of my words. He offers his hand to help me up the carriage steps, and I accept it. I bite my lip as I step up and settle onto the plush seats inside. Gale sits down on the opposite seat, closing the door behind him.

"I trust you, too," I admit, feeling my face heat up from my words. I look out the window.

It was unfair of me to ask him that question. It'll be even more unfair when I tell him the hunch I have against Ares. They've been friends for years, and I couldn't expect him to take my word over his closest friend. Not when we've just met.

I'd be breaking his trust for even thinking of the idea.

The breeze suddenly picks up and the carriages start to roll, trailing down the driveway and onto the street on their own.

"Are you doing this?" I ask, turning back to Gale.

"It's the solstice," he says with a cool smile, looking at me as if my eyes never left his in the first place. "As you know, the

Summer Solstice is a celebration of wind. Since today is the strongest day of the breeze..."

"The carriages run on air," I finish. He leans back into his seat with a nod, and I peek out of the window, watching other carriages pull into the street and follow our path. After a few minutes, I turn to Gale again. His eyes are rested on my belt, studying the dagger attached to it.

"Aelia had added the dagger, just in case I would need it," I explain, looking to him to see if he'll brush off her worry.

But he doesn't.

"That's exactly why the dress was made," he says. A small smirk plays onto his lips reminiscently.

"Who was it made for?" I ask. Gale's eyes soften when he brings his gaze to mine, still holding warmth in his eyes from his fixation on the belt and dagger.

"My mother."

29
Havena

My journey to the solstice was spent listening to Gale talk about his mother. His eyes crinkled with happiness every time he said her name—Rose. And he spoke about her so delicately, with nothing but pride in his voice. I learned that his father, Nathaniel, was also a Guardian, just like Gale's mom, and I quickly concluded that Gale chose to be a Guardian because his parents were.

He was their legacy.

The carriage came to an abrupt halt, almost sliding me off the seat. Gale, unphased by the movement, starts to laugh at me.

"You could've warned me, you know? I thought these didn't run on horses," I huff.

Gale unlocks the carriage door before answering.

"You'll get used to it... one day," he says with a chuckle, then he steps down from the carriage and onto the pavement. He extends his hand, just as he's done before, but I step past it, too captivated by the sight before me to accept it. I turn in circles, the skirt of my dress orbiting around me as I try to take in my glorious reality.

We were standing in the middle of a courtyard, surrounded by thick, museum-like buildings on each side. The buildings replicated each other, yet the crests at the top of their entrances seemed to distinguish each buildings' purpose.

A crest of swords to the East, a crest of symbols I didn't understand to the West. A crest of a cross to the South, and a crest of doves to the North, engraved onto the building where overdressed angels currently flowed together like a river.

Marble steps slid up to the stone columns of every entrance, leading to archways filled with conversation, laughter, whispers...

It seemed as if everyone had dressed in their best, my eyes getting caught in the glint of diamonds and gems every time I turned, but just as Aelia had wanted, I stood out. All of the dresses were colorful, nowhere near the color of cream—let alone white—and I found myself trapped under a few envious glances.

I looked overhead to find angels flying into the scene instead of using carriages as we had done. The sun was starting to set, and some angels—dressed in all black—were busy hanging fairy lights from one roof of the building to the next. I stop spinning to watch them.

Gale explains before I question him, stepping to my side.

"Those lights are for later tonight."

"And what happens then?" I ask. He curls his lip.

"You tell me."

An excited grip on my arm turns my attention to Leah, who's managed to keep Theseus locked around her other arm. The Nurturer shares the same startled look I have, probably because he couldn't handle Leah's spontaneity, but he also looks like he doesn't mind it.

"God, this is so cool," Leah gushes, sighing at the view before her. Then she looks to me. "I wonder what they eat during this kind of thing. Do you think they eat cake like we do?"

"I... hope so?" I shrug, taking her arm and starting our walk to the entrance with the crest of doves above it.

Theseus lets out a grunt.

"Must you drag me everywhere with you?" he asks dramatically, but he doesn't sound annoyed.

Leah keeps her gaze straight ahead.

"Yes," she responds matter-of-factly. "I want to see this place for what it actually is. What if the buildings look like a stupid cloud or something if I don't hold onto you?"

"Oh, the exaggeration," Theseus chuckles. Still, he pauses his stride within the crowd and gestures to the building south of us.

"That building with the cross is the Temple of Disciples. Pretty self-explanatory, but the Holy Council is inside of there as well. Six angels govern this city, two from each profession and all of them at the top of their ranks. They're the only council that's ever governed a holy city—*ever*. The other cities have rulers. Archangels, as a matter of fact."

Theseus points to another building. I squint, trying to comprehend the symbols of the crest.

"*Datum perficiemus munus*," Theseus recites. "Latin, meaning, 'We shall accomplish the mission assigned.' From the age of twelve, that building is where we go to school. We learn every area of academics we can. Mathematics, literature, the sciences... Competition, both on paper and in combat, so we can be prepared for our future tasks as Disciples, Nurturers, and Guardians, which brings me to the next building...

"The public armory," Theseus announces, pointing east to

the crest of swords. "An extension of the school, yet open to anyone who wants to train all the same."

He turns again now, directing us back toward the building with doves.

Our feet join the flow of the crowd again.

"At sixteen, we're selected into our professions. Of course, we decide which job we want to do, but you can't be a Guardian if you flinch during swordplay. Nurturers and Guardians spend their last school year with swords attached to their hip, so you'll usually find us in that building from the age of seventeen and beyond. Guardians receive their tasks there, and Nurturers and Disciples receive their tasks from the temple. They spend most of their time around books, the Disciples, so their temple is where they can usually be found..."

"You must be exhausted then," I say thoughtfully. "I couldn't imagine fighting my classmates to find my purpose."

"Well, I can only imagine what it's like on the Human Plane," Theseus says. Leah snorts.

"Boring, tedious, a scam—"

"Academically focused," I answer for Leah correctly.

Theseus cracks a smile.

We're halfway up the marble steps now, almost near the entrance, when Theseus raises a curious brow.

"So, your plane sends its youth into the world unprepared?"

"And your city trains its youth to clean up the mess in mine," I counter. He laughs.

"Yeah, yeah," Leah says with a disinterested shrug. Her eyes were dancing around the event before her, but now, a playful glint settles into her gaze as she looks to Theseus. "Actually, now that I think about it, having a blonde bird for a bodyguard is kind of cool."

"Sounds more like a date," I laugh quietly. My hand slips

from Leah's arm and I look toward the crowd behind us trying to find my bodyguard.

Trying to find Gale's eyes.

No luck.

"Ew, Have, he's like my annoying, little weapon. I'd rather jump off the city's edge," I hear Leah reason.

"As a Nurturer, Leah, I'd have to catch you. As your friend, I think I'd jump first."

"And as your voice of reason, keep your feet on the ground," I sigh, turning back to the pair. I find Leah's furrowed eyes examining me, examining my hand—which I haven't even realized has found its way to my collarbone.

To my mother's necklace.

Suddenly, she takes my arm, connecting our trio once more, and weaves across the threshold of the building.

The room is huge, with pillars and pillars of stone set up around the perimeter. The yellow, marble floor has been polished to perfection, and I can see my racing reflection in it when I briefly look down. At the far back of the room are tables of food. Waiters trickle into the massive crowd, offering various glasses of liquid as red as blood. Before I can finish taking it all in, Leah pulls us into a vacated corner.

"Why do I feel like you're nervous about something?" she asks me. She's got me cornered between her and Theseus, and they both look to me for an explanation.

"Is it that obvious?" I ask.

"Yes," they say in unison.

I give them a look for their mirrored behavior, then sigh, looking back to the crowd to scan for Ares. He hasn't entered the building yet, which means he's still probably outside with Gale and Ruth. I bring my voice to a whisper.

"Aelia gave me a warning after I got dressed," I explain.

Both sets of eyes calculate my face.

"What kind of warning?" Theseus asks.

"She told me to, 'Beware of The Fallen' tonight. How am I supposed to know who my enemies are? Or if there's more?" I ask him. Worry hovers onto Leah's countenance.

"What do you mean, 'if,' there's more?" Theseus asks.

I wave it off, realizing my slip up.

"Nothing. It's nothing."

"You've discovered one of our enemies and you won't tell us?" he presses further. Leah puts a hand on his arm, but his concern doesn't falter.

"What does being, 'fallen,' even mean?" she asks. I look to Theseus, unsure how to explain, but then I see gold eyes out of the corner of my own. I see *him* walking toward us.

"Ares."

I didn't mean for it to slip out, but I couldn't stand the way Ares was walking over. His eyes settled onto me like a moth to a flame, filled with an underlying determination that I didn't think anyone else could feel. Except for me.

Leah furrowed her brows, but Theseus stared at me intently. I could see the gears working in his brain so I nodded to confirm his calculations.

"Ares is fallen—and he's coming," I whisper quickly, practically pleading for Theseus to understand. Those blue eyes study me a second longer before turning around with a charming smile plastered onto his face.

"Ares! I was wondering where the rest of you were," Theseus greets him. It takes Ares a few more steps to reach our corner before he responds. My breath catches in my throat, hoping Theseus wouldn't reveal anything.

"And I was wondering why you three were in a corner. The festivities are about to begin," Ares says.

"Why yes, they are." Theseus responds with his usual tone of enthusiasm as he looks back to the crowd. He offers his arm to Leah, then he turns to me. The wink he sends me is subtle, but it doesn't go unnoticed as he extends his arm to me. And I take it. "Shall we?"

We start toward the dance floor. Ares walks by my side, but I keep my head high, looking ahead towards Gale and Ruth in the crowd. I can hear other angels muttering about my dress more than I can see their eyes as they take me in. I'd have to let Aelia know about her success.

Gale and Ruth were engaged by another pair of angels, but I catch Gale's gaze as we walk over. Ruth laughs in her conversation, oblivious to our arrival. Theseus turns his arm toward Gale, allowing me to slip next to Gale and away from Ares. He gives me a quick nod before heading to the food table with Leah, and I let out a subtle sigh of relief.

"I'm sorry you had to third wheel," Gale whispers down to me. I mirror the smirk on his face, but it falters when I catch Ares watching us. Ruth is still engaged in her conversation.

"Actually, I came over here to make you the fourth wheel," I tell him. "I could use a drink."

As I lead him toward the back of the room, I spot Theseus and Leah at the very end of the food tables. Leah waves us over with a plate of food in her hand.

"Have you told him about Ares?" she asks, inhaling the grapes and cheese from her plate. Curse her big mouth.

"It's barely been five minutes—"

"What am I supposed to know?" Gale cuts in curiously. Theseus looks to me, and I bite my lip as I look up to Gale.

"You said you trust me, right?" I ask. He nods.

"I always will."

"Then you'll trust me when I say... I think Ares has fallen."

It wasn't a question. It was more of an expectation. Because when Gale had said I exceeded his expectations, I couldn't bring myself to tell him that he did the same for me. But my stomach dropped as soon as he opened his mouth again.

"I know."

■ ■ ■ ■

"You knew?"

I drag my dress to an empty corridor that sat just behind the columns surrounding the party. Classical music starts to play, which meant the committee waltz would start soon, but I didn't care. Gale's footsteps follow close behind me.

"I was beating myself up for the past hour trying to tell you information that I had just received—but you—you knew for God knows how long!" I yell, turning around to him. The music has drowned out my voice anyway, but Gale surrenders to me with his hands all the same, warning me of my volume.

"I've suspected it for a while now, but I didn't tell you to protect you!" he reasons, and I couldn't blame him. I didn't trust Ares. And Gale being as observant as he was must've picked up on that. The worst part is that he probably guessed how paranoid I would be. And he was right. So I couldn't be this furious. I shouldn't be. But I could feel my eyes searing into him with a fire that his cautious hands were trying to tame.

"Well, I don't need protection, Gale. And I don't like being left in the dark. Stop trying to be a leader and just... be a friend."

My heaving chest slows its pace of fury, and he lowers his hands away from me.

"When Ruth found you three weeks ago, you looked like a girl who needed protecting," he retorts.

"Oh, spare me—"

"Absolutely not, I've done nothing but spare you, and I've done it because I am your friend. Grow up, Havena—"

"You're only a year older!"

Trumpets sound out, announcing the committee waltz.

I straighten my posture, dust off my skirt, and push the dagger under the fabric of my dress, concealing it. Gale's eyes plead with me to say more, but I go to walk past him instead.

Then he grabs my arm.

"We'll talk later," I say through my teeth, avoiding his gaze. His hand reaches up to my hair in one swift motion, pulling out the pin that's been keeping my bun in place. I meet his eyes, feeling the weight of my hair hit my back. He brings my hair to the side of my face. My breath softens as his hand rests near my cheek, his finger brushing alongside it.

I step out of his grip and join the other women partaking in the waltz. As I step into line and bow, I try to wipe the scowl off my face for the stranger that would dance with me soon. Now that I'm waiting, I can't tell which part of the argument infuriated me more. Was it because he didn't tell me about Ares?

Or because he let me go?

The room is silent, watching and waiting for the waltz to start. I let in a deep breath, reassuring myself that everything will be okay, that I would get through this dance and have a fun time. A violin starts the symphony of the waltz, and I plaster a smile on my face as I rise with the women in line with me, ready to meet my dance partner.

Then I see Gale.

We meet in the middle of the floor, like the other dance pairs do, and slowly begin to circle each other. Our hands are so close, yet refuse to connect, and he won't drop his gaze from mine.

"I thought I was supposed to meet someone new," I say.

A glint of annoyance settles into Gale's eyes.

"We weren't done talking."

We bring our arms down and he takes my waist.

My heartbeat goes a little unsteady, and I can feel that familiar shock run through my body as he guides my movement through four more steps. Then we circle each other again.

If he felt it as well, then he was suppressing that electric tug just as much as I am.

"Am I talking to a friend? Or are you just here to give me a stupid command?" I question.

"You're talking to me, Havena," he says softly. He brings a hand to my waist and I slip my hand into his, letting him guide the dance again.

"Well, you should've talked to me about Ares. I may be half-human but I'm not weak... I'm... not fragile," I reply flatly, breaking his gaze to look at the other dancers.

I see Ruth among the dancers, and spot Leah and Theseus in the crowd, observing. Gale brings his mouth to my ear.

"I know you can handle yourself, but I don't put myself on the line for you because you're weak," he whispers. The heat of his breath makes my ear curl. "It's because I care."

He turns me out of his body, giving me no time to respond, and I glide to the middle of the floor, falling in line with the other women again. I try to stay focused, battling the heat on my cheeks—in my gut—as I twirl with the music.

Then I'm in his arms again.

"You're supposed to switch me out for another partner," I remind him.

This time I keep his gaze as we dance, trying to keep my eyes hard as stone as he looks down at me. My heart hammers at the way his eyes melt into mine, as if I were the only one in the room.

"And why would I do that when I could dance with you?"

My brain goes blank under his gaze.

So I step on his foot.

He fights shouting a curse behind his lips and I let out a laugh, swaying with him to the music.

"God, you drive me mad," he grumbles, already recovered.

"You'll get used to it."

"I already have."

His arm wraps around my waist and hoists me up, spinning me around like the rest of the pairs on the dance floor. My hand has a mind of its own, and I cup the side of his face as we go, admiring just how soft his chiseled features are. His feet start to slow with the music, and I don't notice how dangerously our mouths hover over each other until my feet touch the ground again. I slide my hand off his face, and he releases his hand off my waist. Just as we practiced, I take a few steps back, toward my new partner, but unlike the other women, I walk backwards, keeping my eyes on him. On Gale.

"We'll talk later," he mouths to me. I give him a nod, fighting the urge to go back and finish the dance in his arms, but as I turn to look at my new partner, I pass the angel taking my place.

Ruth sends me a wink, before setting her sights back to Gale. My heart hammers in my chest, but it skips a beat entirely as I focus my gaze onto my new partner.

Ares.

He sends me a friendly smile as he holds out his hand. I try to return his thin smile, placing my hand into his calloused ones. He politely keeps his other hand at a respectable level on my waist, but I can't keep my longing eyes from watching Gale and Ruth dance—even with the nuisance of the ring on Ares' finger scratching my skin.

"You're awfully tense," Ares says.

His voice forms a pit in my stomach.

"I don't know what you're planning, but I'll find out," I say coolly, meeting his gaze. If Ares wanted a fight tonight, he was going to get one. But then he furrows his brows in confusion.

"Havena, I've given you no reason not to trust me."

"Then why does every smile from you feel like a threat?" I question. He lifts me to his side and spins me, but his breath on my ear sends a tickle down my spine.

"I've been monitoring The Fallen."

In one swift motion, Ares puts me down, keeping his mouth to my ear. And I let him.

"The Fallen have infiltrated the temple. I've been away to monitor them because they plan on killing you. Look at the hands of the waiters in this room."

I glance around and scan the crowd. The waiters have gathered near the food tables. To the common eye, they would look normal, restocking trays and refilling goblets of wine as they usually do, but then I looked to their hands. The majority of them had markings of a vine that stretched from their ring finger and traveled up, under the sleeves of their uniforms.

"The ones with the tattoo?" I ask, finally staring into his eyes. Ares nods silently in confirmation, no trace of a threat or deceit in his eyes. I relax my shoulders.

"And why should I trust you?"

"Because Gale was trying to plot against me with his ex. He kept you—and even Theseus—out of the loop, as he usually does, didn't he?" he asks. As if to answer his own question, he turns his head in the direction of Gale and Ruth. I follow his gaze and my throat clenches. "Besides, the prophecy doesn't give you a choice, does it? The four of us become one, remember?"

The music comes to an end. Ares spins me out of him one last time, away from the direction of Ruth on Gale's lips. Without Ares' strong grip on my hand, I would've stumbled coming back into his arms.

I swallow my breath, trying to steady it so he couldn't hear the shattering of my heart through my voice.

"Fine," is all I manage. We step apart, bowing as the crowd claps in approval at our performance. I plaster a smile on my face, fighting the air around my fingers as I look back up to Ares.

Then I see Aelia.

My eyes scanned into the crowd of onlookers instinctively. I wouldn't have spotted her familiar, blonde bun in the back of a crowd like this, but the maid uniform she was wearing only amplified the fear on her face as she stared right back at me.

Two waiters were behind her, one of them with their hand on her shoulder. And their hand was tattooed with a vine.

"We have to go."

I grab Ares' hand, barely hearing the protest escape his lips, and start shoving through the crowd.

"Havena, what's going on?"

"They have Aelia!"

I turn my head back once to inform him and he doesn't ask again. We reach where Aelia once stood, but she's no longer here. I turn around, trying to scan the crowd again, but this time Ares leads me away. We enter the hallway, and I catch a glimpse of the two waiters carrying Aelia to the courtyard.

"I'll go get the others—"

"No!"

He hesitates at my outburst so I take a breath, calming

myself down. I couldn't look at anyone else right now, least of all Gale, but I didn't want Ares to know that.

"We stall now and she could die because of me. No one else dies because of me. If you really want to gain my trust, you'll come along. No questions asked."

My hand brings itself to my necklace, and as Ares captures the movement, he nods in understanding. My mother would be the last person that died for me, and Ares will be the only angel I trust. The only one. I slip the dagger off my belt and start walking toward the courtyard.

"We go alone."

30
Gale

"Are you out of your mind?"

I slip my arms from around Ruth and she takes a step back. She brings a hand to her lips.

"I thought this was a part of the plan."

"We are not a part of the plan. *We* never were. We trick Ares, but we don't hurt Havena," I reiterate. I mentally kick myself and quickly scan around the dance floor.

Havena was gone, and so was Ares.

"Over there," Ruth points. I look in her direction.

Waiters were filing behind the columns of the hallway, heading for the courtyard.

"C'mon," I mutter, rushing off the dance floor. As I shove through the crowd, I can't help but feel that annoying electricity in my veins clenching onto my heart.

The plan tonight was for Ruth and I to look rekindled so Ares would be baited into dancing with Havena. If he was persistent enough to get close to her—maybe even tell her sudden intel about The Fallen—it would confirm my doubts.

I had a feeling for a while now that Ares only came back for

Havena, except it wasn't a friendly feeling at all. Every time he came around her at dinner, or even in the armory, he studied her just as much as she studied him. They both walked on psychological eggshells around each other, like two dogs meeting for the first time, unsure of the other's presence.

It took everything in me not to slam him onto the ground and interrogate him at every uncomfortable moment. His eyes lingered a little too long for my liking. I didn't know his true intentions, but I knew I would keep him at bay. Until tonight.

What I hadn't planned on was getting into an argument with Havena. She looked radiant from the moment she walked into the foyer— even when her delicate eyes bored into mine with anger. The maids outdid themselves by putting Havena in my mother's dress, and I couldn't help but feel the pride that my mother would've felt if she knew who wore her dress tonight.

I couldn't put Havena on the dance floor without letting the other angels see the fire in her, the same ferocity that she wore in her graceful heart. So I let her hair down, and it took everything in me not to let her dance with someone else—anyone else who wouldn't appreciate all of who she was.

So I didn't.

I steered off course from the plan because of her, and nearly kissed her during the second part of our dance. Ruth, however, was not supposed to kiss me at all.

I shoved my way into the corridor, the panic in my body rising to my chest. I didn't have a plan to solve this, to fix what Havena saw, but I walked into the hallway to find Theseus and Leah rushing in with me.

"Have you seen her?" I ask. They both shake their heads.

"We saw you two rush in here so we followed," Leah explains.

Ruth, right on my heels, steps forward.

"Well, have you seen Ares?" she asks breathlessly. For some reason, her question sends adrenaline through my body. I look amongst the crowd, scanning for Ares' face again.

He's not here either.

Something bumps my shoulder and I turn, coming face to face with a waiter.

"Sorry," the girl says quickly without looking back. She continues shuffling toward the courtyard.

"Why are the waiters leaving?" I ask aloud, still watching the waiter walk away.

Theseus follows my gaze, followed by Ruth and Leah.

"There's still some by the table," I hear Leah mutter, but I'm already walking toward the courtyard.

Something wasn't right.

The meteor shower that we're supposed to see tonight wouldn't happen for another hour or two, and no one usually enters the courtyard until then. It was tradition for everyone to experience that together. A tradition that even waiters wouldn't break. I followed after the waiter who had quickly blended into the shadows of the night.

Theseus', Ruth's and Leah's footsteps faltered trying to keep up, but I didn't bother to slow down as I stepped onto the courtyard steps. The sun had been gone for a while now, and the lights that hung above the courtyard were slashed, hanging limply from their posts. Angels have gathered around, fearfully murmuring as they ignored my presence for the sight in front of them. My wings rippled out instinctively, and I flew up, watching the center of the commotion.

In the middle of the courtyard stood one of my maids, the crest of my family slashed on her uniform. She was held in a chokehold by one of the waiters of the solstice. A line of other waiters stood behind them, witnessing my maid gasp for air with satisfied smirks on their faces. The waiter glanced up at me, and I could see the knife in his hand pressed upon my maid's throat.

"You don't have to do this!" Havena shouts. She's standing with Ares by her side, a safe distance away from them. Air was conjured between her fingers, but she was hesitant to use it. I swoop down next to her, and another pair of wings flap down with me. Ruth and Theseus land by our side.

"This isn't you, Ezekiel!" Ares shouts.

Ezekiel lets out a laugh. He presses the knife a little deeper into my maid's throat.

"Stop!" Havena cries as the maid whimpers.

"For far too long, Angels have wasted away, serving those pitiful creatures on the Human Plane!" Ezekiel announces to the crowd. A murmur runs through the onlookers and he continues. "For centuries, we've let them plague this world. We've let them denounce our God!"

"Just as you have," Havena shouts back. "You've chosen to denounce God for your ego. Sacrificing your discipleship for power you think you have."

"I have not!" Ezekiel spits. His voice stings like acid, and as I look into those blazing, yellow eyes, I can tell he's too far gone—too fallen. I only see our enemy now.

Our prophesied enemy.

"Disciples have studied the word of God for centuries, and we've seen his flaws," Ezekiel says, using his hand with the blade to gesture to the waiters behind him. "We don't need another flood to correct those flaws! We need to refine Revelations. The Fallen will bring it into fruition—"

Suddenly, he's knocked back into the line of waiters behind him. Havena pulls back her outstretched hand and the maid glides through the air, into her arms. She embraces Havena with her whole body, and Havena returns it. I ready my stance, getting ready to protect them and fight the angels on Ezekiel's side.

The Fallen.

They help Ezekiel onto his feet. Then one by one, they all spread their wings and take flight. Ezekiel falters for a moment.

"Join me, Ruth," he says breathlessly, still winded from Havena's push. He stretches out his hand as an offering. "Ares?"

In one swift motion, Ruth slips a knife from her leg and hurls it toward Ezekiel. He conjures a slab of concrete in front of him, and the knife pierces the stone instead of his head.

He flaps his wings.

"Shame," Ezekiel murmurs with feigned disappointment as he hovers above the ground.

"You shame every Disciple—everywhere—and so has every Disciple that has joined you. We will not be one of them!"

Ruth's voice rings steady, and the crowd behind us starts to yell shouts of disapproval with her.

Ares' face distorts in disgust.

"I'll be back. And you'll regret it," Ezekiel spits. With a final, sour look at all four of us, he flies into the sky. Into darkness.

■ ■ ■ ■

Our flight back home was swift. Havena flew back with Ares, leaving me to carry the maid back home. We traveled in close range and landed onto the driveway of the manor simultaneously. Then we all stood in a circle on the pavement, taking a moment to catch our breaths, studying each other for a plan—and a quick one—because we knew we were no longer safe here. I chose to break the silence.

"Theseus, collect our weapons in the armory. Ruth, Ares, gather books we could use of any kind—"

"There's something I must show the two of you," the maid interrupts, looking to me and Havena.

Theseus and Ruth have already started toward the house, but I catch the way Ares sweeps Havena's hair behind her ear before leaving her side. He no longer made her tense, but the gesture made me bite my tongue.

"What should we know, Aelia?" Havena asks the maid, avoiding my gaze. Aelia gives her a nod.

"Follow me."

Aelia turns on her heel toward the house, expecting us to follow, and as we do, I turn toward Leah.

"Pack any personal belongings you have," I tell her.

She furrows her brows.

"We're leaving?"

"We have to Leah. We all do," Havena answers, glancing at me before facing the manor again.

"You danced with Ares tonight."

"I did." Although it wasn't a question, we both knew I wanted more of a response. My plan tonight had gone completely wrong. Ares wasn't the enemy, yet now that I knew she trusted him, I could also see her pushing me away.

"I'm sorry," I tell Havena quietly as we cross over the threshold. Leah runs up the stairs and Havena and I pause. I can see her searching my face for sincerity, but it's the fact that she has to that tells me I've broken her trust.

"Tell that to Ruth—"

"Now is not the time!" Aelia warns as she walks around the table in the foyer and into the dining room. We follow her, dropping our gaze from each other as Aelia walks toward the bookcase hiding the armory. She tilts the blue book on the shelf and the armory door slides back.

"No maid has ever entered the armory," I tell her. In fact, no maid has ever known its exact location—except for her.

Aelia turns to us with a satisfied smirk on her lips.

"I'm no maid, Mr. Geffen."

Wings of light escape her back, and the maid uniform melts to cinders off her body. Her skin starts to glow, beaming like the sun, and I instinctively put Havena behind me.

"You're an archangel," I gasp. Aelia nods her head, and the next moment, she returns to her normal angel state, dimming the glow of her skin. Replacing her maid uniform is a flowing, white gown with a thick gold belt. A heavy sword is attached to her hip.

She gestures toward the armory, and steps inside.

I go to take Havena's hand, but she dodges it and walks around me to follow the archangel. I trail behind.

"I thought an archangel's dwelling was in the Temple of Disciples. And we haven't had one for centuries since Aaron died. Where have you been? And why have you been *here*?" I ask, my feet shuffling across the armory floor.

A clang on the floor catches our attention and we look over to find Theseus, a crossbow at his feet. He gasps as he looks at Aelia, but when he takes in her scowl of annoyance, he hurriedly picks up the bow and turns to the shelves of weapons again.

"He is wise to not ask unnecessary questions. Whereas you, Guardian, are not," Aelia says. Havena lets out a snort. We follow the archangel to the strategy table. She begins to glide her hands over the table as if she were looking for something.

"Aelia, weren't you scared when Ezekiel took you?" Havena asks. The archangel ponders for a moment, then continues searching the table.

"I knew you would save me. All will fall into place just like the prophecy entails," Aelia responds. "You're stronger than you think by the way."

A click sounds from the table, and another smile of satisfaction crawls onto Aelia's lips. A compartment juts out from the side of the table, and she slides out the drawer.

Inside are three thick journals. They're identical, with papers tucked between the withering pages and worn at the seams. Aelia takes out the first two, and hands them to me.

"Your parents," she says gently, and I take the books from her hands. She gingerly gives my forearm a squeeze before taking out the last journal. She gives it to Havena.

"Your father."

Havena holds the journal in her hands as if it'll break. Her eyes tenderly trace the initials "A.B." that are etched across the cover.

"Atticus Bernheim."

My blood runs cold.

I almost fail to hear her mumbled words entirely.

"What did you say?"

Havena turns to me, her brows innocently furrowed from my sudden question.

"Atticus Bernheim?" she asks in return. I nearly drop my parents' journals to the floor. Havena's hand reaches out to me but I step back, staring at the journal in her possession.

"He killed my parents."

31
Havena

"What?"

Gale backed away from me as if I were poison, and stared at my father's journal as if it could kill just as much as I could. Or as if he could kill it first.

"Your father became fallen eighteen years ago. I was six when they died, I would remember the name of the man who did it!"

"You're wrong!" I protest, slamming my father's journal on the table. I kept my hand on the table's edge, gripping it to suppress the wind that wanted to fly from my fingers.

"How would you know? He didn't raise you, did he?"

The regret washes over the anger in Gale's eyes within a flash. Through the blur creeping into my vision, I could still see him take a small step toward me.

I take one back.

"Havena—"

"There's no time," Aelia interrupts with a scolding tone. She makes sure to lock her eyes on ours—on Gale's a little longer—before continuing. "Her father did not kill your parents, and you'll discover the truth in what has been given to you."

She gestures to the journals we've left on the table, and with a flick of her finger, they fly into our chests. I hug the journal and sigh a sigh of relief.

The same man in the photo, who stared down at me with all the love in his heart—his baby girl—couldn't have done it. He couldn't have killed Gale's parents. And for a moment, I almost thought he did—because of Gale. Because I truly didn't know the kind of angel my father was.

If Gale wanted to shatter my heart tonight, he'd done so.

Twice.

Leah steps into the armory with Ruth and Ares behind her.

"I've gathered our things! Have, I brought your box!"

"And I've gathered the scriptures we'll need," Ruth adds.

They both pause, studying the anger in my eyes.

"What the Hell happened?"

"Are you okay?"

I nod my head, avoiding eye contact with Gale as Ares immediately steps to my side.

"I'm fine."

Gale parts his lips, but Aelia raises her hand.

"Time is not as endless as love, dear."

She turns to the wall, then begins twirling her arms in a circular motion. A vortex of bright light begins to sprout.

"You'll be meeting Hannah on the other side. Tell her that The Fallen have arrived," she directs, stepping aside.

Leah walks to Gale's side, along with Ruth and Theseus.

Each of them are carrying heavy satchels of our belongings at their hips. Theseus, however, also has four sheaths of swords on his back. He stares into the portal in wonder, just like the rest of us, if not more.

"I thought portals were legend. Hell, I thought you were legend!" he stammers to Aelia.

"It looks like a sparkler. Like the ones we use for the Fourth of July," Leah adds in awe, looking to me. Theseus looks to both of us now, confused.

"A what—"

"Oh, shut up," Ruth grits through her teeth. She grabs his arm, then Leah's, and with a nod at Aelia, she steps into the portal with them, leaving me behind with Ares and Gale.

I can see Gale hesitate as he extends his arm, but I take Ares' first. I look to Aelia for reassurance.

"Will we see each other again?" I ask. Aelia smiles that kind smile that she's shown me since the day I arrived, then gestures to Gale's arm, silently telling me to take it.

So I do.

Her smile falls as she watches my hand rest on his arm.

"Your bond is fated," she mutters, wide-eyed with alarm as she looks to the Guardian.

"Fated?—"

A crash echoes from the foyer, cutting off my question. We turn our attention to the armory door before Aelia heeds one more warning.

"Go. Now!"

Without another second to waste, Gale rushes into the portal. I turn my head behind me just in time to see Aelia's skin glow again, her wings shielding us from the silhouettes she was about to fight. The light of the portal swallows us whole.

And we were gone.

32
Havena

My heels skidded onto a soft, almost dirt-like floor. Wherever we had traveled into, it was lukewarm and dark, and the only thing that broke the silence was the sound of our breathing.

Gale's arm pulled me tighter into his side, and my eyes adjusted enough to see him scanning into the darkness as I was.

Suddenly, a lantern of fire appeared in front of me, held in the hands of a brown-skinned, middle-aged woman. The light illuminated just enough of the room for me to see her. She wore dark pants and an adorned long-sleeve, and the dark orange cloak that hung around her neck must've been concealing the lantern a moment ago.

"Gale... Havena..." she whispers, stepping closer to examine our faces. The fire in the lantern dimmed as she took a step back.

"My name is Hannah—"

"Where's Ares?" I immediately ask, dropping my arm from Gale's. The weight of my dress turned with me as I searched around the room.

"Ares arrived shortly before you," Hannah replies with a furrowed brow.

"But he was linked to my arm before we left Aaron," I reason. Hannah seems to scowl at the information I've given her. Footsteps suddenly shuffle from a corridor I couldn't quite see, but it catches Hannah's attention and she steps away from us.

"We have to be quiet and we have to be fast. I'll explain everything once we're inside the common room."

"Common room?" Gale asks. She walks across—what I took in to be—a mosaic floor without answering his question, carrying the light of the lantern with her. Hannah's feet don't make a sound, and I squint down to her feet to see that she wasn't wearing any shoes. I immediately bend down to slip off mine.

"What are you doing?" Gale whispers. I gesture to my feet.

"We have to be quiet."

"Is that really necessary? You're wasting time," he whispers. I straighten up, raising the heels in my hand.

"I have to learn your customs, remember?" I retort, mirroring his volume. I turn my back to him without waiting for an answer.

He gives me one anyway.

"You spend a second with Ares and now I'm the bad guy."

I ignore him, my bare feet shuffling toward the back of the room to meet Hannah. Gale's shoes pad closely behind me.

Hannah holds open a hidden door within the wall with her free hand. The stone panel is large and seamless, yet it opens up to a small, clay hallway.

"You're observant." Hannah nods at my hand. "That's good."

Then she slips into the hallway first. I step in after her,

feeling the rut of sand and cold dirt against my toes. The door closes behind Gale and Hannah makes the fire in the lantern shine brighter. My eyes trailed over the sandy walls.

"Hieroglyphics," I mutter. Hannah chuckles at the observation. "But that's—"

"Impossible?" she asks with a smile inside of her voice.

She holds the lantern up to her face so I can see her dark eyes twinkling with pride.

"You're in the City of Hannah, *Vine*. Welcome to Egypt."

■ ■ ■ ■

The sounds of our feet scratching across the floor filled the silence of the secret corridor. I kept up as best as I could, holding the skirt of my dress as we moved through the hall. Hannah moved fast, and the flickering light from her lantern made the hieroglyphics resemble a picture book that my eyes couldn't decipher fast enough. After a few minutes, Hannah slowed her pace and trailed a hand along the wall until she found what she was looking for. Her fingers hovered over the carving of an eagle with flat eyes and gold wings. With a pause, she turned around to Gale and I.

"Your friends are inside," she says.

Then she pressed onto the wall.

Light poured into my eyes and I blinked, stepping over the threshold. The yellow, marble floor was shined to perfection, and the charcoal-colored firepit against the wall stood on three or four rows of bright, gold bars. Leah, Theseus, and Ruth stood to their feet from two couches, both of which were deep red, long, and piled-linen. Two doors, panels of square stone, rested inside of the dirt-orange walls on each end of the back of the room, a smaller area to which my eyes found Ares. Unlike the others, Ares was already standing. He turned from the

185

sandy, gold-trimmed table in front of him, dropping our journals onto it before rushing over to me.

"You made it through," he sighs, giving me a hug. I slowly slipped out of it, still unsure of his sudden change of heart, but the fact that he cared was a step in the right direction.

"Why didn't you arrive with us?" I ask.

"And why do you have our journals?" Gale cuts in.

Ares steps back, allowing Gale entrance to the room.

"It's because of the ring on his hand."

Hannah answers Gale's question as she enters the room.

The panel in the wall shuts behind her as if it were never there, and she pours herself a glass of wine from the table with a flick of her hand.

"Please sit down children, I'm about to teach you something," Hannah tells the others. They sit back in their seats on the couch with curious faces. Hannah taps her temple, the glass of wine floating to her through the air as she mouths the word 'observant,' to me. She looks to Ares.

"Some Disciples are given rings, which allows them to portal to different places. Of course, archangels such as myself have to give you a Ring of the Angels, but I'm sure it was a gift from Aelia. Am I right, Ares?"

Ares nods, but I catch the bob in his throat as he slips the silver ring off of his finger.

"Actually, I grabbed it before I came to the solstice tonight. I thought we might need it just in case—"

"You stole from the temple?" Ruth asks, her tone laced with pure disappointment.

"It was only for precaution—"

Gale steps forward.

"And it still doesn't explain why you had our journals."

"Enough!"

I glare at Ruth before turning my glare to Gale. His mouth parts to protest but I beat him to it.

"We need to be able to trust each other," I start with frustration, "even if we have to earn it. And right now, no one in this room has fallen. Trust in that."

Leah straightens up from the couch, sending me a look, but I quickly shake my head, signaling her not to butt in. I know I told her I didn't trust Ares at the solstice, but if I was being honest, I couldn't even explain why I suddenly trusted him now. Truth be told, I think I felt guilty.

Ares had followed me to rescue Aelia, no questions asked as I had said, so I couldn't help but have an open mind about him. It was also my fault that he became the underdog amongst his friends in the first place.

"You thought I was fallen?" Ares' eyes pierce my own with such disbelief that I can't even answer.

"Look," Theseus cuts in. And we do. We all look to him, but Theseus continues with a raised eyebrow. "The prophecy says four will become one with the earth. There's no point in dividing ourselves since we're supposed to fight by Havena's side anyway."

"Then you should deal with your trust issues later," Hannah says. She steps near the firepit, giving all of us a good view of her. I can finally take in all of her features from the candlelit lighting around the room.

She had bushy, brown hair, a few streaks of grey that made her dark eyes seem even more intimidating than the way she spoke. The bridge of her nose was high, curving unconventionally, yet it was her most distinct feature alongside the mole by her lip. She had deep-olive skin, and her sharp nails reminded me of the animal claws I'd briefly seen within the hieroglyphics of the secret corridor. Compared to Aelia,

Hannah wasn't our secret mentor or protector. She was our ruler. And I watch as she takes a sip of her wine with a sigh.

"This room is the one place within the palace that allows us to talk freely," Hannah begins, "but I'll keep my words short since I've heard it's been... quite a night."

She takes another sip of her wine before speaking again.

"As you know, Aelia is an archangel and so am I. Archangels have been aware of this prophecy ever since we were anointed with our title. The war is inevitable, as is Havena helping us win it. But we were just given the task of keeping Havena alive shortly after you three received your assignment."

"And just how many people want me dead?" I ask.

The archangel looks into my eyes.

"Not people, girl—or at least not yet. I mean demons, fallen angels, Atticus himself—"

"He's alive?" Gale asks.

Hannah pauses for a moment, looking between Gale and I.

The air in my throat stiffens, awaiting her answer.

"I don't know."

"What does that even mean?" I ask.

"It means there's more to the story than you know—than we all know. I've heard rumors, but I have my own imagination running wild in regards to what happened years ago. Hopefully, those journals Aelia held on to will help you with that," Hannah explains, pointing her glass to the table. I pick up the journal with my father's name etched into it.

"My father could be alive—"

"And he could also be dead," Hannah reminds me. She doesn't wait for my reaction to keep speaking. "I've fought by your father's side before, and although I could've sworn he was a pure-hearted man, no one can predict who becomes fallen."

A weight forms in my stomach at her answer, but I push it

down and flip through the pages of his journal to avoid her gaze. I'll find out soon enough.

Hannah looks at Ares again, her eyes slithering down to his ring finger, so I turn to him with a question after following her calculating gaze.

"How did you get our journals in the portal?"

He shrugs, his eyes pleading for me to understand. "I honestly don't know. One second, I was attached to your arm, then the next second, I was in the throne room with your books in hand."

"But that's unusual. Portals are usually precise," Ruth cuts in curiously. "Did you think of a different place to go?"

"No... but now that you mention it." A spark suddenly ignites inside of Ares' eyes. "The portal must've glitched because of your blood. That has to be why, right?"

"Because of my blood?" I repeat.

"You're half-angel. It probably couldn't register the human side of you... maybe it thought there was an error inside of itself or something."

"That is... possible," Hannah adds thoughtfully. Then she waves a hand of dismissal. "But enough of the portal talk. You are here now. I expect silence while I tell you the rules—"

"Rules? Since when are there rules to war?" Theseus asks. Hannah's eyes shoot daggers in his direction. Leah tightens her lips, struggling to suppress the laugh that was making her cheeks rise, but she manages to stay silent.

"As I was saying," Hannah continues. She clears her throat and turns her gaze to all of us again.

"Although your time here is for the sake of your safety, you will be spending your days walking through the city like any other citizen. You will wear our clothes, eat our food, step in our steps... The point of this is for you to blend in. I understand Havena and the human need to learn our customs, so what better way to do that than by being inside of the city itself?"

Hannah doesn't bother waiting for our response as she continues. "We can only assume the Temple of Disciples has been infiltrated in every city. As of right now, they do not know you're here and I intend to keep it that way. There will be no leaving this room without my permission. Breakfast, lunch, and dinner will be delivered to you by one of my adversaries. They will be wearing the crest of this city, which—if you didn't know—are roses. Do not go into the city unless I know about it. If you are allowed, it is because I allowed it, but you must give anyone you encounter a false name. When you're outside of this room, you'll keep the hood of your cloaks on at all times—especially you, Havena. And lastly, do not address me by my name. I am the ruler of this city, and if my people refer to me as, 'your majesty,' so shall all of you."

There's an obvious hesitance in the air as Hannah finishes, but we all silently pretend we're still taking in her words.

Until Theseus raises a hand, that is.

"But—your majesty—wouldn't going into the city jeopardize our position?" he asks. Instead of answering, Hannah narrows her gaze at him, trailing over him from head to toe with calculating eyes.

Then Gale steps forward.

"If we spent our time hiding in this room, someone would surely find us out. Maids don't cater to empty rooms, Cupid."

"They do at your house," Ares retorts quietly. Within a second, Gale takes a step toward him and Ares leans off the table, ready to take Gale on.

"Seriously?" I step in between them, keeping them at bay

with a hand on each of their chests. "I'm not putting my life at risk because of your egos."

Gale clenches his jaw. His heart hammers under my palm, but he backs away. Ares' heartbeat is steady, and he slips my hand off his chest and into his own.

"So our objective is to blend in, but what do we do after that?" Theseus asks, bringing our focus back to Hannah.

Hannah's eyes wander between Gale and Ares before she gives an answer.

"We ready for war."

33
Havena

The sound of Leah's snoring woke me up. I sat up in my cot and looked at the other two girls locked inside of their slumber.

Aelia would scream at us for what we've done to our dresses. They were quickly thrown onto a chair in the corner of the room and we didn't bother to think otherwise of it. The gowns were happily replaced with loose trousers and long sleeves of this city, pajamas that were the softest of fabrics I've ever felt.

Ruth slept on her back, as if she would wake up ready to fight whatever made the slightest noise, but that obviously wasn't the case. Leah was sprawled across her bed, her thin blanket sprawled with her, and a monstrous sound escaping her lips.

Theseus would have a field day if he saw her.

I slipped my legs over the edge of my cot and reached for my father's journal on the wooden nightstand. It took a while for me to fall asleep after last night, and having the book next to me didn't help the questions that often crept into my head.

*Was Aelia mistaken, or did my father kill Gale's parents?
How can the man that held me so lovingly become the man in
these terrible stories? When did my mother realize he wasn't
human?*

I got up, keeping the journal in hand, to rinse my mouth in
the windowless porcelain and clay bathroom. I wish my mind
would distract me from those questions—and the dream I had
last night. It was the same one I had weeks ago, and it started
the same way. I was biking back home, my memory of meeting
Leah starts to play, and the two clouds, or beings—or whatever
I saw as a child—vanish into the forest. Then there was the
crack in the ground. The street filling with blood...

I spit out the hot water from my mouth and look at the
faucet. I had turned on the knob for cold water, but the water
that came out was sizzling from the heat.

As if on instinct, I twirled my finger. The steaming water
gushing out of the faucet fluttered for a moment. I widened
my hand, and the water slowed, and when I raised my hand it
rose to my face. My breath shook in awe as I lowered my hand,
watching the water return to its normal state. Flowing at a
normal pace.

And cold.

I turned off the faucet and clutched my father's journal to
my chest as I gazed at my reflection. Angels could bend the
elements—everyone knew that—but there was something
different about my powers. My abilities, although
uncontrolled, felt easier to summon than everyone else's. And
they were unique. I had yet to learn of another angel making
water sizzle, but I had a feeling this journal had the answers.

I headed for the common room, pushing onto the secret,
stone, panel door of my sleeping quarters to find Ares seated
on the couch with a book in hand. The firepit was lit, cackling

wildly behind him.

"Good morning," he says, his eyes slowly leaving his book. Then he registers my face.

"Good morning, Havena," he says again, clearing his throat. This time he sends me a gentle smile.

"Good morning," I return, then sit on the opposite couch.

I propped my legs up into a pretzel and laid the journal in my lap. My finger grazed over my father's name etched into the cover.

Atticus Bernheim.

I recognized it as his handwriting the moment I saw it. The way he wrote his name on the back of the polaroid was always peculiar to me, but it served as another piece of who he was. That same signature was replicated onto the cover of this journal and it proved the one hunch I've had for years.

He was right-handed like I was.

The "A" in his name had a little curl at the top of it, identical to his name on the back of the picture that I had. I was excited—and terrified—that there was more information about him in this book than just his handwriting.

"What's on your agenda for the day?" Ares suddenly asks, breaking my thoughts. I looked up to his sincere gaze.

"Same as you, I suppose."

"Then why do you look like the book is about to bite you?"

He places the book he was holding beside him and waits for my answer. I bite my lip.

"Is it bad that I think it might?"

He chuckles, low and steady, then quickly studies my face and realizes I wasn't joking. I almost let out a laugh. Maybe I had gotten Ares all wrong. From what I knew, Disciples spent years behind books rather than with other people. His social skills, or lack thereof, was probably why he was so distant.

"Knowledge is a powerful thing. Sometimes it's scary... and sometimes it's not. You'll never know until you read what's in your hands and uncover how you should feel about it for yourself," he says, gently gesturing to the journal in my lap. "You deserve the truth, Havena. Don't believe otherwise."

I thrummed my fingers against the journal as I took in his words. I did deserve the truth, it just felt like too much to discover alone. Or at least that's the excuse I was telling myself.

Deep down I knew I was scared.

So I get up from my seat.

"Where are you going?"

"Right here," I answer, plopping down right next to him. The surprise in his body made his move slightly away from me, but I put the book in my lap, which definitely caught his attention more than I did, and he scooted back.

"You trust me enough with... this?" he asks. I watch as his hand quickly, but cautiously, flips open the cover—the Ring of the Angels still on his finger.

Maybe it was just the timing, or maybe I felt my heart skip a beat, but I looked up into his yellow eyes. They studied me intensely now, with nothing but concern for my answer... Or me.

"Like you said at the solstice, I don't have a choice."

■ ■ ■ ■

We spent about two hours skimming through my father's journal, only occasionally stopping to fill in the timeline to what we already knew. We only reached a quarter of the entries before I shut the book, fighting the shakiness of my breath.

"My father... Atticus... I'm an—"

"You're an heir of Hell," Ares says for me. My lungs struggled to race the pace of my heartbeat.

Lucifer Abbadon decided to have children out of boredom, the same way he decided to toy with Lilith, the first woman on earth, out of boredom.

When Lucifer was cast out of Heaven, he roamed Earth on his own for years, for others in Heaven who thought like him were afraid of falling from God's grace. But when God first created man, Lucifer jumped at the chance to destroy them. To destroy humans. Lucifer tricked Lilith into falling in love with him, but before God could discover his spiteful act, Lucifer transformed Lilith, using his power to turn her into the first demon. When God had found out, He was furious, for Lucifer had ruined God's perfect, new, powerful creation that embodied life.

A woman.

Although many believed Lucifer's punishment was being banished to Hell, it secretly didn't end there.

It's said that Lucifer was cursed by God after Lilith's transformation, and that the very first woman created from Lucifer's blood would be the most powerful of the angels. That woman would be called The Vine, and her very existence was intended to bridge every realm of this earth together.

When she has been found, trained, and is ready to fight, three will become four, then four will become one with the earth. And soon after that happens, The Holy War will begin.

Ares' hands found their way to my shoulders, trying to console the trembling of my body, but it was too late.

My eyes had already blurred.

Atticus had researched his own father out of fear—for me.

His daughter.

I was The Vine, the threat, the woman—destined to fight Hell itself and bring the realms together. Atticus worked with Gale's parents to keep me safe—hidden—until the time was right. And they all died in the process.

"Havena?" I could barely register Ares' voice.

"Havena!"

Suddenly my breathing slowed. I blinked my focus back into the room and found Gale with his arm raised toward me, in a stance I knew too well.

He's saved me yet again, and he was standing over the threshold that held the boys' sleeping quarters. His brown hair was disheveled as if he had just woken up, but he looked rested, already dressed in casual-looking slacks for the day. His parents' journals were in his other hand and his grey eyes were filled with concern. Theseus peeked over Gale's shoulder, holding the same concerned gaze.

"Are you alright?" Gale asks. The panel opening on the opposite wall catches our attention. Ruth walks out tiredly, with a dagger in hand, and Leah trails out closely behind her.

"What's going on?" Ruth asks, alarmed and yawning.

I stood up, dropping Ares' hand from my arms, and kept my focus on Gale. I hold up the journal.

"My father didn't kill your parents," I inform.

When Aelia had given us these journals, she must've thought it would bring us together, give us the answers to the questions we had about our parents. But every time I learned something new about my family, or Gale's parents, it did the opposite.

My voice shook, but I tried to sound as firm as possible. Even though I was grateful to clear my father's name, the information I learned about myself felt worse than the accusation against him.

And no one moved a muscle to interrupt me.

"He was working with them. You see, he um... he had a twin brother... and he—"

"Rubeus fell," Ares finishes for me, standing up to rub my back. I didn't step out of his comforting touch. I felt like I'd fail to speak without it.

"Rubeus and Atticus... Abbadon."

Gasps broke out, along with the sound of Ruth's knife hitting the floor, yet Gale's face was as stiff as stone. Leah was the only one to move to the couch.

"Abbadon? What does that mean?"

"It means destruction, which makes sense since Havena's not even a Bernheim. She's Lucifer's granddaughter, and she deserves to carry his last name," Gale answers her. His voice laced every word with acid as he held up the journals in his hand.

"Your father was a Nurturer, but he had left the City of Aaron for some time after he met your mother. It wasn't until a rumor about an uprising called him back. He left you, Havena, to work alongside my parents. Their task was to close an unusual amount of rifts appearing on the Human Plane. Eventually, they found out that Rubeus was the cause of these rifts. That he had fallen. He tried to let as many demons escape Hell as often as he could. They soon realized he created a movement within the Temple of Disciples, too. He, and the Disciples who joined him, wanted a world where humans knew about us... and were beneath us. He wanted them to either serve us as punishment or perish for all of the damage they've done to the earth. For all of the damage we angels spend our lives trying to rectify. So your uncle created The Fallen. And one day our parents had found another rift as usual, but they didn't come back from that one, did they?"

Gale bitterly tosses his parents' journals onto the table, their thuds of leather cutting through the silence of the room and making me flinch. And I didn't even know what to say.

Theseus gives Gale's shoulder an empathetic squeeze.

"They didn't die in vain—"

"Yeah, but they're dead anyway." Gale slips out of Theseus' grip and walks to the secret door in the wall. He catches my step to follow him then blocks me with a barrier of wind.

"Don't."

My breath catches in my throat. Within a moment, he's gone. The panel closes behind him, blending back into the wall as if it were never there.

The air he's conjured falls to the floor.

I blink, feeling my mouth open pathetically at his departure, but I couldn't grasp the words I wanted to say. The prophecy was the only thing pulling us together—it had to be—because everything about our past pulled us apart. Everything about my past hurt him, and no matter how compelled my body felt to be near him, my existence was just a reminder of everything he lost.

My hand finds its way to the cool, metal chain resting against my chest and can't seem to let go. Any other feelings that I had for him just... didn't make sense.

"I shouldn't be here." I turn around to the group.

"My mother hid me, and what's worse is she knew about me. She knew I was half-angel, but I never knew. I spent my whole life thinking my existence was just... wrong. And now? Now, I finally know that my father, who's the reason I freaking am who I am, who made me into this—this thing—is most likely dead. And he had a brother! I have a lunatic of an uncle that wants me dead! And my last name, my stupid last name—I'm not a Bernheim. I'm an Abbadon, Leah—I'm the blood of Satan!"

The chain of my mother's necklace rips from around my neck and I toss it into the firepit. With my hand stretched toward it, I make the flames of the fire roar as it melts the reminder down.

My knees crumble beneath me and I hit the floor, straining my breath to speak through my slipping tears of frustration. Ares steps forward to stand me up, but I wave his hand away.

"And even with all of that, I still don't know who I am. I don't know what I'm doing, why I'm alive... I—I shouldn't be here!"

The flames cackle into the silent room. I can sense the hesitation from the others behind me, the hesitation to console me with affirmation, but there weren't any words that could ease my mind. I should be dead.

"You shouldn't be here," Ruth suddenly agrees. I blink my silent tears back and look to her, only to see her kneel on the floor next to me. Theseus takes a step forward, no doubt his Nurturer training kicking in, ready to defend me, but Ruth pauses him with a hand. She levels her eyes with mine.

"You shouldn't be here. You should be dead, but you aren't." Every syllable of her words are said nonchalantly. I narrow my eyes, but to my surprise, Ruth gives a small—almost comforting—smile. "People everywhere are plotting to kill you, but we've kept you safe. Your parents... they did their part in keeping you safe. Hidden. I know it sucks, but you're the key to a prophecy that promises peace. You're the key to every realm coming together. And sure, your uncle hates you for it, so what? You, Havena, will change the world. And you're going to do it with us by your side."

She stands up, gripping my arm to bring me up with her, and gestures around the room.

"We're your family," she finishes. After a thoughtful—slightly confused—moment, she adds, "You'll always have us, Havena... and your powers."

Everyone nods reassuringly at her words and a sly smile of satisfaction slithers onto Ruth's lips. She drops her arm from around me and releases a breath.

"I need a drink."

She walks over to the wine on the table. I can't help the laugh that escapes me. Only Ruth would find compassion exhausting. Leah stands up with my father's journal in hand and holds it out to me. Theseus follows her lead.

"You're The Vine—"

"And my best friend—"

"And we'll fight together—"

"Well, I'm human so I probably can't—"

"I'm having a moment here!" Theseus looks down to her. Leah rolls her eyes but looks to me with an amused smirk on her face. I take the journal from her hands and return her smile.

"Thank you... Both of you," I tell them. Ares clears his throat, and I look beside me. A shy smile is on his lips as he brings a hand up to wipe my cheek.

I don't even have to look to sense Leah and Theseus leave.

"You don't have to carry your burdens alone," Ares says. He playfully raises his eyebrows at the journal in my hands. "Plus, I'm a faster reader."

"Shut up." I swat him with the journal and he joins my laughter, which blends into the chatter happening around the circular table. Ares' warm gaze watches me gingerly for a moment before he speaks.

"When I said you didn't have a choice about who you trust, I was just being—"

"An ass?" I finish for him. He drops his gaze, but I catch his ears twitch at the curse word. And instead of reprimanding me like the first time we met, he nods anyway.

"Yes," he agrees. An amused smile creeps onto his lips as he meets my gaze again. "I was being an ass."

I bite my cheek.

"That's too bad. I think I trusted you more when you were a jerk," I say. He cocks his eyebrow in surprise and I snort.

Suddenly, he takes the journal from my hands and pulls me down onto the couch with him. I end up laughing as I land on his lap. He keeps his arm around my waist and uses his free hand to open my father's journal.

"Can this jerk keep reading with you?" he asks.

"And why would you want to do that?" I question back. He sighs as he looks at the journal, thinking of an answer. Then he looks me in the eyes and gives one.

"There are stories about you on these pages... and I want to read them all with you."

He holds his expectant gaze, waiting for a sign of approval from my eyes. And maybe I should've been more cautious. Maybe I shouldn't have let him step into a void that Gale stepped out of too quickly. But for some reason, I didn't care.

"Yes," I answer softly. A small smile curls on his lips.

"Perfect."

■ ■ ■ ■

I spent the next couple of hours next to Ares on the couch, even when Leah, Ruth, and Theseus left the room to find a place to train. It would've been smart to go with them, to see a bit more of the palace, to work on my fighting skills, but I didn't want to be smart. I just wanted a space to breathe. And as Ares and I dived deeper into my father's journal, eventually matching up his entries to what Gale had said earlier, I found myself relaxed.

Able to breathe.

Then the panel in the wall opened again. Hannah stepped out in front of Gale, and the others followed right after them. She still had the orange cloak clasped around her neck from last night, but she wore a refined, dark green dress with orange etchings embroidered within the velvet fabric. A crown of gold and diamonds rested on top of her bushy hair. And the earrings she wore, as well as the necklace and bracelet she was wearing, matched the crown on her head.

Gale stepped by her side, his face emotionless as he held a bundle of beige cloaks in his hands. Although he kept his gaze on nowhere, in particular, I knew how observant he was of me. I found myself subconsciously scooting away from Ares' side on the couch. The others crowded around the table.

"Hello, you two," Hannah greets Ares and I. "It seems you've rested well. I'm glad for it."

With a gesture of Hannah's hand, Gale starts passing out the cloaks. He walks up to Ares and I first. And although I was in front of Ares, Gale hands Ares two cloaks before heading to Ruth. Unlike me, he places a cloak in her hands.

"As I said last night, you're to blend in. If anyone on the street asks you your name, give a false one. If the smell of food catches your nose, I promise you, you'll have better food when we return. Stay with me as closely as possible."

"Just where exactly are we going?" Ruth asks.

A smirk plays onto Hannah's lips as she answers.

"You won't be coming. Instead, you—" Hannah lifts a finger to Ares, "and you will be in the Temple of Disciples."

"That's too dangerous. The Fallen want me dead," I protest, straightening up from the couch. "I thought we couldn't trust any of them."

"We can't," Gale finally says at Hannah's side. And she doesn't mind the interruption. "Ares and Ruth will act as spies, and we're to keep plotting our next move while we're here. Getting a feel of this city is just so we'll get familiar with the surroundings. We'll be prepared if something happens."

"Like what? You think they'll attack the city or something? They wouldn't be dense enough to create casualties without killing Havena first," Theseus says with a shrug—and refusing to beat around the bush.

"It'll start, whether we—or I—like it or not. In the meantime, walking around the city is a good idea. I can create escape routes or pick up a thing or two for first aid. That way, you guys can do your angel thing... Sounds like a plan to me."

Leah grabs the vase of wine on the table and sighs as she pours a drink. Then she glances around, watching the angels silently furrow their brows at her words. Ruth almost looks impressed.

"Geez, don't look surprised! I've spent the last couple of weeks reading more than I've ever read in high school..."

"High school?" Theseus asks. Leah sends me a satisfied smirk before she sips her wine, happy to know something that Theseus failed to know of.

"So you two will go—spy—and the rest of us are going... where?" I ask, changing the subject for her.

"I have a friend I want you to meet," Hannah tells me with a glint in her eye. "So, freshen up. Disciples, I trust you know where to go, but I'll give you all a half-hour to meet me in the throne room."

"Or what?" Theseus asks jokingly.

"Come late and find out," Hannah responds. Theseus bites his tongue and Hannah smirks as she steps into the secret passage.

Leah snorts after the hidden door shuts.

"You're terrible with women."

"Shut it, tiny one."

I stand from the couch as they banter again, signaling Ares to stand with me. He's already clasped his cloak around his neck as Hannah spoke, so I hand him mine. I can sense Gale's gaze on me as I move my hair to the side, exposing my neck.

"Can you clasp it?"

"Clasp what?" Ares asks behind me.

"The cloak..."

A snort escapes Gale's lips as he watches us, but it falls shortly after when his grey eyes take in Ares' hands near my throat, grazing across the skin of my neck. I roll my eyes at him, but even I couldn't deny the feeling of Ares' obliviously warm touch raising the hairs on my neck.

Gale drops his gaze.

"We have a half-hour," he announces.

Then he leaves the room.

34
Havena

The friend Hannah wanted me to meet was not what I had in mind. We met with Hannah inside of the room Aelia had sent us into. With proper lighting, I was able to take in the throne room for what it actually was.

Hannah was seated on top of a golden throne, with armrests that took the shape of a sphinx. On each side of her seat rested stone pillars with pits of fire set ablaze, and behind her rested a crest of stained-glass, forming a cross engraved into the wall. From the ceiling, rows of greenery looped from wall to wall, cascading down the sides of the room.

Hannah walked down the steps of the clay platform when we arrived, and signaled her two adversaries to give her a cloak. Instead of the orange cloak I'd seen her wear twice now, this one was a faded red. She only warned us to follow her closely, and we were off. But I wasn't prepared for what I'd see next.

The City Of Hannah was underground indeed, and the warm, firm sand that pressed against my bare feet made the limestone city even more surreal. High above us, sand pooled from the dirt sky throughout multiple parts of the city, trickling back into the Earth like timeless hour glasses. It was as if someone had scooped out a piece of the Earth, only to shove the empty space underground. Leah mirrored my gasp as we looked around, but Hannah hurried us down the palace steps.

The palace was a cave embedded into the edge of the dome, and the only thing behind it was packed earth. The city's edge.

The cave stretched into three parts. On one side, there was a hot spring. Children were playing in it, bending water and earth to their will without a care in the world. The middle cave was the entrance we had just come out of. Various angels were wearing similar cloaks to ours. Some hustled and bustled out of that entrance with several baskets of goods, their bare feet padding against the packed dirt just like us.

Hannah wanted us to blend in, and we succeeded, as long as we kept our heads down. The last cave of the palace was the Temple of Disciples. It was different from the rest of the clay structures, shining with white marble instead of orange dirt. We hurried past it, letting Ares and Ruth trickle into the midst of Disciples standing in front of the temple, then we walked into the thriving city below.

Joyful angels filled the streets, and there seemed to be a market of some sort at every turn. Colorful vendors were set up in rows, with shelves stocked with various fruits, meats, cheeses...

I could've seen more if Gale and Theseus didn't drag Leah and I's watering tongues away. Gale was following closely behind Hannah like a lap dog, and hadn't even said a word to me since we left the palace. Instead of pondering over what was running through his mind—for my sake—I decided to keep my focus on the city and its people.

After a few minutes, I started to notice the heavy amounts of children in the street. Children ran free everywhere, and the few adults I've seen amongst the young crowd didn't seem to mind their energy at all. I tugged Theseus' arm.

"There's kids everywhere but I'm barely seeing any parents. Where are the adults?" I ask. He slows down our pace a little to answer, but he ducks his blonde head up on occasion to keep Hannah's red cloak in his sight.

"The City of Hannah is named after... well... Hannah. She struggled with conceiving children, but it's said that God saw grace and favor in her. She became the archangel of this city because dirt and rock are... well... barren. And it's not set in stone or anything, but the abundance of freedom that the children grow up with is said to be this city's greatest accomplishment—aside from what they actually do."

"And what do they actually do?" I ask.

"They mostly manage the movement of tectonic plates around the world. Earthquakes, volcanic eruptions, you name it," Theseus answers. "They practically bend rocks to their will as soon as they pop out of the womb, but they can work wonders within the agriculture department, too."

"So do they do what you do?"

"What do you mean?" he asks.

"You know..." I start. "Do they become Guardians, or Nurturers, or—"

"Ah," Theseus says. His feet slow as he turns to me, nearly walking backwards as he gives me his full attention and weaves through the crowd.

"The citizens here aren't as serious as the angels of Aaron. And they're definitely not as serious as those in Adira. As you can see, the culture here is very laid back. Harmonious even."

Theseus steps beside me now, bringing our pace to a casual stroll so I can look around. And I actually see what he's saying. The City of Aaron, although happy and safe, didn't have the aura that the City of Hannah had. The angels here were filled with nothing but joy when they conversed, and as they basked in their freedom to do whatever they pleased, their eyes radiated nothing but warmth.

"Every realm has the same education system—training once we turn twelve and then going into whatever field we choose. Mostly everyone in this city gravitates toward taking care of the earth instead of fighting with it. Putting actual plants in the ground rather than demons is what most of the kids here want to do anyway. The ones who want to keep training and fighting continue their studies in the City of Aaron or Adira."

"So what of the Disciples?" I ask. Theseus chuckles.

"They're the same everywhere, little leaf. The temple here is just as crowded as any other city. Any child thirsting for knowledge usually wants to become one of their realm's teachers—"

"Hurry up, Cupid!" Leah calls back. Theseus immediately quickens the pace and I follow.

We come to a stop in the center of the city, which spreads out into a large, sandy flatland. On one side laid fenced vegetation, organized in rows with miniature streams of water separating each section. The other side of that land was strangely empty, as if the crowd purposely avoided it.

"Say hello to my friend," Hannah says, a smile on her lips.

Leah and I share a look of confusion.

"Where—"

Shrieks suddenly break out above us. Leah and I duck to the ground within a flash.

Long wings flapped over us, sloshing sand and dirt up into the air. Theseus and Gale broke out in laughter, and we blankly stared after them as they excitedly ran away from us, whistling at the creatures above. Hannah chuckled at Leah and

I as we cautiously rose to our feet.

"They're called Griffins. Half-eagle, half-lion," she explains. They squawk and roar in the sky, and their tails flow along with them. Hannah points to one of them.

"And that, right there, is my friend."

Hannah's friend yelps with delight as it flies around one of the gushing showers of sand. In an instant, it soars down from the cluster of griffins and lands onto the flatland. Other griffins in the sky start to follow its lead. Gusts of sand simultaneously fly into the air as they land onto the flat plain together, creating clouds of dirty fog, but the citizens of this city didn't mind. They hurry to greet the winged creatures with open arms and fruit.

Baskets of fruit.

Hannah gestures for us to follow her through the crowd as she walks onto the plain toward her friend. The creature found Hannah first, yet squawked at us as we approached. Hannah steps right up to it with a laugh of delight. It's silver feathers rustle under her touch, and it purrs as she pets it, turning its head to study us.

"Meet Heqet," Hannah says. I took a step closer to Heqet, only for Heqet to take a step back. Hannah cooed at the creature.

"It's alright, she's just a little nervous."

"Is she really?" Leah asks. Hannah only chuckles at the question, then steps back from petting the griffin.

"I was talking about Havena."

I sent Hannah a look before turning back to Heqet with a friendly outreached hand.

"You should bow instead—"

The griffin squawks again. I flinch with wary eyes as it steps forward, dropping its face to the ground. I step back in confusion, watching as the creature curtsies it's foot.

Then it lowers its shoulders.

"Magnificent."

Hannah's shocked whisper almost turns my head, but I reach down to pet the griffin instead. It brings its head up to purr in my hands and I chuckle with triumph.

"What's magnificent?" I ask, not breaking my gaze from the creature's eyes. They were a deep, foggy purple, and seemed to have a hint of red around the rims, mesmerizing me with their gaze of satisfaction. I invited Leah to join me, and she carefully put her hand on Heqet's fur.

"Griffins only bow to people they're fated to. They never bow to people otherwise."

Fated.

The word pulls out my last memory of Aelia.

I turn to the archangel.

"And what does being fated mean? Is it... a bad thing?"

"Nonsense, girl," Hannah answers dismissively with a laugh. "Fated means your souls were meant to cross paths with one another. It's destined. When you're fated to an animal, that bond solidifies its loyalty to you. But regardless of who or what you're fated to, the journey your souls go on together will change the course of your life."

I took in her words with a nod, and felt my eyes wander over the busy crowd of griffins and angels, searching for Gale. I found him riding a griffin alongside Theseus, their animals circling each other as they laughed with the angel children playing around the paws of their creatures.

"Can you be fated more than once?" I ask, turning my gaze back to Hannah. She studies me for a moment, then glances in the direction I was looking in. With a nod of her head, as if answering a silent question, she looks back to me.

"Your purpose in life has been prophesied for years. How it will be brought to fruition is unclear, but being fated to someone is as clear as day, child. The relationships between those who are fated are rare, however, it can become the greatest, most undeniable bond. Consider yourself lucky to even have one, but I caution you to choose the role they'll have in your life very carefully, for being fated isn't about the relationship at all—it's about the lessons within your journey together. And no matter what role you choose for that person, those lessons will always be a part of you."

And with that, she pats Heqet one last time before walking off to another griffin. My mind can't help but dance around the last sentence she said.

If Gale would always be a part of me, why were we constantly pulling ourselves apart?

"Is that why I want to be a cat lady when I'm older?" Leah asks, interrupting my thoughts. "You know? Like am I fated to cats because I love them so much or am I just weird?"

I let out a laugh as I resume petting Heqet, but my eyes find themselves sliding back to Gale.

"I think we're both weird."

■ ■ ■

The sunset peeked through the sand falling from the dome ceiling above, casting a warm, purple glow across the city. Torches on the streets began to light themselves, and angels began petting the griffins one last time before parting ways. I was sat on the ground with Heqet lying next to me, purring under my comforting hand. Out of all of the things this prophecy has done to my life, I didn't expect to be fated to a pet.

Leah had left with Hannah to roam the streets for escape

routes like she had previously suggested, and I hadn't budged from my spot since.

Then Gale approached.

"We should start heading back, it's getting late," Gale suggests.

It was the longest sentence he's said to me these past couple of hours, so I didn't respond. I just hold his gaze as I pet the griffin under my hand, and he nods at her.

"What's her name?"

"Heqet," I answer bluntly. He pulls out an apple from his pocket, and waves it to her, but Heqet grunts instead as she assesses him. I chuckle.

"She's stubborn."

"Is she?"

"Of course, reminds me of someone I know," he says, gently rolling the apple to the sleeping griffin next to us. There's a glint in his eye that makes me forget about this morning as he brings his gaze to mine again, and every other bad moment before this one. I clear my throat.

"So, where's Theseus?" I ask, standing up as I change the subject. Heqet rises with me and Gale steps closer to her.

"Wait, you have to—"

Heqet brings her foot out, and lowers her head gracefully—just like she'd done with me.

"I have to what?" he asks obliviously, stepping forward to scratch Heqet's head. She purrs under his touch.

"Bow."

His eyes study mine quizzingly, but I watch as realization settles into those grey orbs. He drops his hand and takes a step back from the creature.

"I'm fated to a bird?" he asks in surprise. Heqet lets out an insulted huff, but steps forward again anyway, lowering her head for Gale's affection once more.

Gale laughs excitedly as he pets her again.

"Yeah, well, I'm fated to two." I chuckle quietly, focusing on one of Heqet's feathers rather than Gale's gaze. I hold my breath as I wait for his words, whatever they may be.

"You say it like it's a bad thing."

"But isn't it?" I ask, turning around to face him. "Every time we get closer it's like something tries to rip us apart. What's the point of being fated if our lives just... haunt each other?"

"My life haunts you?"

"Yes, because my blood haunts yours," I respond. He bites the inside of his cheek and doesn't say anything else. My father may not have killed his parents, but the actions of his brother—my uncle—did.

I focus my gaze on Heqet's feathers again, replaying the sting of Gale's harsh words from this morning. And what sucked the most about them was that he wasn't wrong.

Abbadon is a fitting last name for me.

"Aelia says we're fated," I say quietly.

"We are," he agrees.

"And being fated isn't a choice."

"Then what's making you hesitate?" he asks. I shrug, slowly bringing my eyes back to his. He's already staring down at me as if he hasn't even looked away in the first place. And it's the fact that I looked away that tells him where this is going.

"Because deciding what we are is a tough choice to make."

Gale scoffs at my words with a small laugh.

"Maybe..." he finally says. "Maybe you don't have to make a choice just yet."

"Maybe we can just let it play out," I add.

"Maybe we can let Heqet decide for us," he jokes. Heqet

snorts at us instead and we both laugh. Gale pets her head again, then slowly brings his hand down.

"We'll have the rest of our lives to decide," he finally says. I let out a nervous laugh, then extend my hand. His eyebrows furrow at the gesture but I shrug.

"Rest of our lives, right?" I ask. He puts his hand in mine.

"Rest of our lives," he agrees. And we shake on it.

"Here's to being fated," I say, not letting go. "And hoping I'll never hurt you—"

"You won't, Havena—"

"Or destroy your life like I've already done—"

"Havena!"

I blink.

"We're not our parents, remember?"

I drop his gaze, and his hand, avoiding the sincerity in his eyes.

And the longing.

There's a moment of silence between us, with only the shuffling of sleeping griffins and our low breathing to fill the wordless void.

"Then... we should get back," is all I say, and Gale's wings ruffle out of his back within an instant. He extends his hand, and I almost take it. Almost.

Instead I turn to Heqet, who was busy glancing between the two of us with worried eyes. She studies my face a bit more, then lowers her hind legs with a nod.

"You're God sent," I whisper to her, then try to lift myself onto her back, only to slip off of her slick fur. The silvery bones at the base of her wings stuck out, but I didn't reach for them to help me up. It reminded me of when I had touched the roots of Gale's wings for the first time. He told me not to, and as delicate as they were, I assumed it was painful for him ever since.

Heqet cocked her head at me, wondering why I was taking so long, and Gale let out a laugh, retracting his wings.

"Here, let me."

"But I want to ride alone—"

Gale places his hand on my hips, sending a slimmer of electricity through my veins, and lifts me off the ground. I slide my leg across Heqet in one swift motion, seating myself onto her back. Gale drops his hands.

"I'll fly next to you—"

A huff escapes Heqet, interrupting Gale, and she nudges her head at him. When she meets his eyes, she gestures to her hind legs, which she's kept lowered.

"You won't let me fly without him?" I ask her. She huffs again as if to answer, and we both roll our eyes to Gale.

"Not unless you want me to—" but Heqet cuts Gale off once more with another nudge of her head. Persistent pet.

"I guess so," Gale sighs. He looks to me hesitantly, but I only nod, knowing I won't get back to the palace without his body against mine either way.

He slides across her back, trying to keep a decent amount of space between us. To my surprise, Heqet's legs didn't falter under the weight, but when she rose, my back slid into Gale's chest.

His arms envelop me as he leans forward, holding onto the roots of Heqet's wings.

"Is it safe to do that?" I ask, the concern distracting me from our proximity. His laugh grazes my neck.

"You tell me."

He pulls up. Heqet's wings only flap once, lifting us off of the sandy plain and into the sky.

And I scream.

The wind whips around my face, and I can only sense our altitude rising from the chill of the night's breeze.

Gale lets out a laugh, then leans next to my ear.

"Open your eyes," he whispers.

And I do.

I hadn't even realized I had closed them.

The city lights were dimmed by the underground darkness of the night, and the sand packed above us glittered like miniature stars above. It was peaceful, beautiful, and I could see the edge of this place in every direction as a blue haze washed over the sleeping city. I pet Heqet.

"You'll have to show me what she eats," I tell Gale, glancing at him behind me. "Whatever she needs, I want to give it to her."

I turn back around, ready to pet Heqet again.

But then I hear his words.

"I will."

Suddenly Heqet turns abruptly to the right, causing me to slide. Gale uses one arm to pull me into him before I fall, and we suppress the heat between us, focusing on what's caught Heqet's uneasy attention.

I recognize Ares' wings first, soaring toward us with something in hand. Once he reaches us I realize what it is, but he holds up my father's journal as he tries to regain his breath.

"A rift," he breathes urgently. "A rift is going to open again. And you know where, Havena."

35
Havena

"You shouldn't have read his journal without me."

Ares leads me into the palace, avoiding my gaze as we walk into the throne room.

Heqet had to be brought back to the flatland for the night, but Gale wanted to make sure I returned to the palace safely. He rode Heqet back to the palace steps to drop me off, and reluctantly, he also left me with Ares and warned me not to blow Ares' head off. As Ares and I passed the threshold of the throne room, I couldn't keep any promises.

Hannah and the others were gathered around a table that sat in the middle of the throne room. It wasn't there earlier this morning, but as I got closer, there seemed to be a piece of stone that had risen from within the ground. Leah was leaning over a map of some sort, but before she could send us a cheerful greeting, she took in my fuming face and didn't say a word.

The others simply watch.

"I did it because you weren't here—"

"And that's exactly my point, isn't it?" He sighs at my question, unable to argue, and offers my father's journal to me.

I snatch it from his grasp.

"Will you allow me to tell you my discovery or will you continue nagging?"

"Are you kidding me? You've read this without me and you think I'm nagging?"

"Yes," Ares simply answers. The audacity he had to use an annoyed tone towards me makes my chest heave with rage, but I catch Hannah lean against the table with a judgmental look.

I bite my tongue.

"It better be worth it," I grumble through my teeth. I shove the journal back into his chest and walk past him without another word.

"It is worth it," Hannah says once I reach the table. Ares quietly steps beside me as she continues.

"You're an Abbadon, and you're blood does more than connect your lineage to Lucifer."

"What does that even mean?" I ask, exasperated. I was tired of the damage my blood had already caused.

"It means, you have more power than we thought... Or could ever imagine really," Theseus jumps in.

"Like conjuring all of the elements without the need for training. They're all a birthright to you—unlike the rest of us," mumbles Ruth.

"There's also the possibility of locating rifts," says Ares.

"And creating hellfire," adds Leah.

"Heavenly fire," Hannah corrects. "And, I think you can control demons as well."

I look to the each of them like they're insane, but their gazes fail to falter under my own. They were serious, all of them, but Hannah's intense gaze unsettled me the most.

"Controlling demons? Wouldn't I have to be half-demon or something?"

"Not at all," Hannah answers reassuringly. "I take it everyone knows the story of Lilith?"

Everyone nods, but Leah furrows her brows.

"Lilith? That's the mother of demons, isn't it?" Leah asks.

A small smirk of pride rises on Theseus' lips but Ares answers her.

"Correct. Lilith was said to be the first woman on earth. Lucifer tricked her into loving him and transformed her blood. Together, they birthed the demons we know today."

"So I'm half-demon?" I ask. Ares goes to answer again but Hannah beats him to it.

"Absolutely not," she says. "Your blood isn't tainted by a drop of evil—otherwise you wouldn't be an angel at all. However, Lucifer's power to transform a human's blood was a hidden power your uncle Rubeus possessed. The same can presumably be said for you." Hannah gestures to my father's journal. "Ares, please show her."

Ares flips open the book, skimming over the pages to find whatever he was looking for. My mind starts traveling a mile a minute as he searches.

"But the other powers, like making hellfire or not struggling with the elements... I haven't spent enough time conjuring to know if I have those powers. How do you know for sure?"

"Because of this," Ares answers me. His eyes meet mine but he keeps his finger pointed on the page.

"Should I read it?"

"You already have," I scowl. His eyes hesitate under my gaze, but he ultimately looks down to the page anyway.

And he reads.

Today might be the last day I hold my daughter, but this last act of protection is something I must do. I followed the altar's instructions and got Havena baptized, and I can only hope that this was enough to keep her safe.

Miriam has grown distant with me ever since I showed her my wings and my city, but she continues to wear the necklace I've given her. She doesn't know that it will mask her scent from demons, but it's the least I can do for bringing her into my world.

And Havena—my darling little Heaven. I had just given her a bath last week and she conjured the water above her head. I struggled to disrupt what she'd done, but once the water had subsided, I noticed the amount of steam rising from the bath. I was so amazed it didn't hurt her.

My sweet daughter has inherited my power to create holy water, purified from the heavenly fire I know she'll conjure one day. Unfortunately, the pride in my heart is overcome with fear. I've kept that part of my powers hidden for years, to blend in with the other angels just enough so they wouldn't realize how strong I actually am, or how I've always been able to bend the elements easily to my will—and more. But now I'm afraid she may have inherited Rubeus' powers as well.

She's only a baby, but I know she will grow to be the strongest angel alive. And if Rubeus finds out she's alive, and that she can control demons like he can, I'm afraid he won't see his blood in her. He will see an obstacle, and he will kill her. And with all that I am, I can't let that happen.

The room is silent as Ares finishes, looking to me expectantly for a reaction, for words I cannot give. My hand brings itself to my chest, but the safety of my mother's necklace is gone.

And it's my fault.

"Everything was done to protect you," Hannah says gently. I nod at her words, but swallow my breath to push down the tears that wanted to escape my eyes. I drop my hand.

"So how can I locate these rifts?" I ask, masking my shaky breath with a purpose. "Are these the same rifts that my father tried to find?"

Hannah nods her head. "I would think so. Like I told you before, I've fought alongside your father. Every time we went on missions, he always seemed to know exactly what Rubeus was planning. Maybe it was because of their bond as brothers—"

"Or it goes deeper than that," I finish for her.

Hannah nods her head again.

"Regardless, we need to know our next step." Ruth says.

"Yeah, but where do we start?" Leah agrees with a mumble, scanning the map as if it'll give her an answer.

"Few Disciples in the temple of this city are fallen, but the ones who are, visibly display their markings of a vine. Word of what happened in the City of Aaron hasn't even spread here yet. I doubt genuine Disciples here know of the secret uprising," Ruth pipes in, pointing to the temple on the map.

"So why are we focusing on these rifts? Why not just kill The Fallen now? End the war before it starts?" Theseus asks.

"Because that'll be an outright declaration of war, and we never create casualties first unless we want to call for one. I understand fighters punch first and ask questions later, but The Fallen are strategic. They'll plan on opening the rifts first,"

Ares answers. He looks at me as he points to my father's journal again. "May I?"

I give him a wave of approval. My gut twists as Ares searches through the pages again. Even though he's read my father's journal for the greater good, he's read it without me.

"Here." Ares taps the page. "I won't relay this... verbatim." He slides the journal over to me before he speaks.

"Rubeus selected the profession of a Disciple, but his arrogance intensified over the years. Atticus tried every way he could to right the Abbadon name, but Rubeus took on Lucifer's views over time. Eventually, he started a revolt within the temple. It seems that history is repeating itself right now. And now that he knows Havena is alive, and possibly as powerful as Atticus had suggested, her safety isn't the only thing we have to worry about. Rubeus wants to create Hell on Earth, and he's planning to do it regardless of whether Havena is dead or alive."

I skimmed over the journal entry Ares had shown me as he spoke. Everything checked out—except for what he purposely left out. It wasn't his to tell.

My father knew of the rifts because he had dreamed them. His words recalled city streets splitting in two, and the terrible cries of demons sounding out across the earth. But what really made my breath hitch was the liquid that oozed out of the crevices.

The blood he described.

"But we don't know for sure the rifts are what they want to open. We just know they want to kill Havena, so we should kill them first," Ruth suggests. Theseus dramatically points a finger to Ruth for emphasis, nearly surprised they're both agreeing on something, but he rolls with her support nonetheless.

Hannah sighs.

"We kill The Fallen and the council of Aaron would think we've gone mad—"

"So we warn them," counters Theseus. "And the others in the City of Adira. Either way we're entering war—"

"Or, we focus on the rifts. We shouldn't make the cities panic if The Fallen wish to get an army of demons onto the Human Plane," I interject.

Ruth narrows her eyes.

"We don't know if they want to do that—"

"Yes we do," I assert. I look to Hannah, finally understanding why Ares thinks I can locate rifts. "My father dreamed of the rifts opening before Rubeus got to them. That's how he knew Rubeus' plans. Twins are said to share a telepathic bond like you suggested, so that bond with my father and Rubeus was magnified because of their blood—our blood. And I know this is true because I've seen a rift in my dreams."

They all blink at my words.

"Wait, Havena, you've seen—"

"Yes, Theseus, I've dreamt of the same rift for a second time now. I saw it the night before Gale took us to the City of Aaron and I dreamt of it again last night."

Theseus runs a hand through his hair and I look to Leah. Her eyes are wide with shock but her mouth is parted as if she wants to say something. She doesn't.

"You didn't think to tell us?" Ruth asks accusingly. "Are you that stupid—"

"She could've thought it was just a nightmare, Ruth. Being brought into our world hasn't exactly been fun, has it?" Theseus snaps. Ruth stammers for a moment, but Hannah steps in before Ruth can say something worse.

"We'll find the rifts," Hannah states firmly. "But for now, let's stay on our toes and train. You two, continue to be spies in the temple, and the rest of you, no more tours of the city. There's an armory across the hall, but please, use it discreetly. Not everyone behind these palace walls can be trusted."

"But Heqet—"

"Who's Heqet?" Ruth inquires, but Hannah ignores her.

"Heqet can take care of herself," Hannah reassures me, then she nods at all of us. "Havena's life is far more valuable than we thought. Get some rest and I'll see you tomorrow. We'll reconvene then."

Hannah leaves the table and starts toward the throne room exit before we can say anything else. Gale walks in just as she opens the doors with a flick of her hand. He sends her a puzzled look as she simply gives him a nod of acknowledgement before she leaves.

He walks over to us with a face asking for an explanation, and I spot Heqet's fur on his pants withering to the ground with every step.

"What'd I miss?" he asks.

"I'll explain later—"

"Of course you will," I mumble, cutting off Ruth. I shut my father's journal, ending her invitation to respond.

"No one reads this without me," I announce, looking everyone in the eye. I catch Leah give Ares a side-eye before looking back down to the map under her hands. Then I turn from the table. Gale steps to my side.

"What happened?"

"Ask Ruth, she'll fill you in."

"But—"

"Havena," Ares cuts in. He steps beside me as well, but I ignore them both, keeping my gaze on the panel that leads to the secret passageway. I sense Gale reluctantly leave my side.

"Havena I read without you because I had to—"

"That's a lie and you know it," I laugh sarcastically, pushing the door to the passage way open. Ares steps into the darkness after I do and the door shuts behind us. I put my hand on the wall, deciding to feel my journey to the common room, but a flash of fire lights the corridor. I turn to find Ares holding a hovering ball of fire in his palm. I drop my hand.

"Thanks," I say dryly. Then I keep walking.

Ares follows closely behind me.

"Havena, I don't understand why you're so upset."

"Read a book and find out—"

"Havena Abbadon."

"That is not my name!" I turn around and nearly catapult into his chest. Our breaths collide, flaring in unbalanced frustration, and I don't step out of it.

"I didn't keep you out of the dark or plot anything without you knowing. I literally flew to go get you so you could stay in the loop of our discussion!"

"And I'm supposed to thank you for that? Good job, Ares, you've done the bare minimum! When will both you and Gale realize this isn't about you? Or my feelings toward either of you? It's about me, Ares! It's always been about me, and my father, and my family!"

I hold up the journal.

"These are my father's words. And they're more important to me than any stupid book you've ever read!" I spit. I go to turn around but Ares grabs me back by my wrist, pulling me towards him again.

"You're right. This is about you. But you're not fighting this war by yourself—"

"Screw what the prophecy says about the four of us! You

know more about me than I know about myself because of what you've read. And you did it without me, Ares! You read without me." I swallow the crack in my voice and bite my tongue. He gently releases the fire in his palm, and it floats above us, shining a bit brighter than it did before. He brings a hand to my face, and his thumb brushes away a tear that I didn't realize had fallen.

"That night at the solstice, you asked me to help you rescue your maid alone."

"That doesn't matter—"

"And you said," Ares continues, ignoring my interruption. "You said in order to gain your trust, I had to go with you alone—no questions asked. So I followed you, no questions asked, because I knew that you would face whatever danger ahead alone if you had to. And as terrifying as your bravery is, I will never let you handle your battles alone, Havena."

His thumb keeps grazing over my cheek even though my few tears of frustration have stopped, and I watch as his yellow eyes take in all of my face.

"I am sorry, if you feel I did the opposite tonight."

"Just shut up."

I bring my lips to his before I could get my words out. His lips were soft, gliding over mine with the same hunger that I had, and his hand began to roam across my neck. Then my chest. Then lower. And even though I had my eyes closed, I sensed it.

The ball of fire he had lit before went out.

36
Havena

I kissed him. I kissed him until I couldn't breathe. And I'm not sure if I should have.

37
Gale

I couldn't sleep.

I sat up from my bed and put my mother's journal on the bedside table. I've been reading it for the past three hours, with only the subtle snores that escaped Ares' and Theseus' mouths to fill the silence of the room.

I was looking over the recollections of her hopes, fears, dreams. Me.

One of the entries I stumbled across talked about one of the last times we flew together, and it was one I surprisingly remembered. She brought me to the Human Plane, over a thick forest of some sort. My father was on the ground, working, and searching for something I was too young to understand. My mother kept me in the sky, away from the brutal fight that my father was probably having to send the demon back to the Banished Realm, yet we looked down all the same.

My parents wanted me to get a feel for the Guardian lifestyle as early as possible, but my mother thought seeing death that early in life would erase the innocence of my childhood. If only she knew that the aftermath of their deaths had the same effect.

I ran a hand through my hair with a sigh and stood up from my bed. I needed a drink.

I pushed onto the panel to enter the common room, and to my surprise, I found Havena. She was curled up on the couch in a long nightgown, with her knees to her chest and her eyes fixated on the cackling fire in front of her. She jumped at my sudden presence, but dropped the tension in her shoulders once she realized it was just me.

"Sorry," I mutter. "I didn't realize anyone else was awake."

"You and me both," she says with a shaky laugh. She moves her hair to the side of her face and I crack a smile.

"Can't sleep?" I ask. She shakes her head. I walk over to the couch opposite of her and sit down.

"I'm guessing you can't either," she says, slipping her gaze to the fire. I shake my head, then do the same.

"No... I can't."

And we sit there, as we've usually done, two parallel beings that didn't know what else to say, despite how much more we wanted to. But then she speaks.

"I just... had a weird dream, is all."

She brings her eyes to mine, and for a moment, the amber flecks seem clouded with anxiety. And fear. She blinks it away.

Despite Ruth's offer to relay the details of what happened earlier, she decided to throw knives instead, no doubt to blow off steam from their discussion entirely. To my surprise, Leah joined her, and I was left with Theseus' story telling skills to relay the information. Long story short, Havena was the most powerful angel in the room, aside from Hannah, yet they had talked about her like she was merely a weapon.

"You've dreamt of another rift?" I ask concerned.

Havena's eyes widen from my words, but she gives a quick nod to my question.

"This one was different. I mean the blood still bubbled over like usual—"

"Whoa, wait, you're dreaming of blood?" I ask. She shyly nods her answer again. Air swirls around my fingers, and I pull the couch opposite of me closer.

"Stop! I doubt Hannah will be happy with you redecorating the room," Havena whisper-shouts from her seat, but a laugh escapes her throat anyway.

"Don't care," I mutter. I lower my hand once the edge of her couch hits my knee.

"How graphic are these dreams?" I ask. She simply bites her lip as I lean back, waiting for her answer.

Now I realize why my mother was concerned. Guardians are trained to stomach gruesome situations, and even though my father urged me to get an early start with it, I couldn't imagine the kind of suffering that entered Havena's mind when she was at her most vulnerable. When she just wanted to sleep.

She drops my gaze with a sigh and brings a hand to her hair, twirling the ends as if it'll help give her the words she doesn't want to say. But she knows she has to.

And I'll sit here until she does.

"How graphic, Havena?" I ask again gently.

She meets my gaze.

"It always starts the same," she finally says, then fixates her gaze onto the fire. "It's almost like a memory. And I'm five years old again, staring at the clouds like I used to do with Leah. But it takes me back to the one day I saw those blurs in the sky. I passed them off as clouds for years, but now? Now I don't know."

A laugh of disbelief escapes her throat as she looks at me. I nod my head, signaling for her to continue, and allow the small smile on my lips to settle. That was when she first recognized The Sight, and she didn't even know it.

Then the humor falls from her eyes.

"The dream changes. Or transforms? I don't know... It's like I'm actually there, waiting for the rift to open. It gets quiet—too quiet—and it feels real. I can actually feel the hairs on my arm raise. Then the street splits, glowing with a red that reflects onto the houses around me... And then there's blood."

She drops her gaze back to the fire, and I can see her throat bob before she speaks again.

"My body wakes me up before the blood starts to spill, but I already know what happens next. I've always felt it coming."

"Felt what coming?" I ask. She finds my eyes again.

"The demons... their screams," she says.

My breath seems to freeze.

There are protective wards in Hell that usually allow enough space for one demon to slip through a rift. By the time a demon has passed over, the protective ward repairs itself. While one Guardian seals the rift on the Human Plane for precaution, another Guardian hunts the demon that escaped. More than one demon coming through a rift meant that the protective wards were malfunctioning, and if they were completely destroyed, then all of Hell would break loose. All of it. The only thing I can do is run a hand through my hair, and Havena just watches me. But it's just a dream. It has to be.

"I didn't mean to scare you. I thought they were just nightmares... This is why I didn't tell anyone—"

"I'm just... processing your words," I reassure. "I've been trained to fight whatever comes out of rifts, but what you saw... it's just.. not something I'd want to dream about... The dreams scare you, don't they?"

She bites her lip again before she answers with a simple nod. And I can't blame her.

I've never seen a rift actually open, I just knew the process of them opening. And that Rubeus wanted to open as many as he possibly could in broad daylight.

"It's terrifying," she admits. "It doesn't happen every night, but I—I also think that it's just a memory. My father wrote about it in his journal, so maybe... I've just... inherited the memory from him? And in a sense it's... different. I can't say it's better than the one I had tonight but... it's different."

"How different?" I ask. She just shrugs.

"Because the dream tonight showed a rift in a different place. It didn't happen back home."

I take in her answer, realizing what she was trying to say.

"This one wasn't a memory." I state. She nods her head in confirmation. "You can actually sense where the location is then? Where the rift will open?"

"Yes... I think so," she confirms softly, then her eyes widen with realization. In an instant, wind erupts from her fingers and she slides her couch back.

"Ares was right," she huffs, standing up from the couch.

"Ares? What do you mean Ares?" I ask, but she ignores me and I watch her open the panel to our room.

"Ares, Theseus, get up!" she calls into the room. I hear Theseus' grumble of protest, but Havena makes her way into the girls' room, probably waking them up gentler than the other two.

"Theseus, it's important!" I hear Ares yawn, and he steps out into the common room. He pauses at the sight of me on the couch and studies the room a bit longer.

"Have you two been up for long?" Ares asks, but I can sense

the actual accusation beneath his words.

"You tell me."

He glances to the fire, then to Havena, who was now walking Leah and Ruth out of their room.

Leah immediately sits on the couch, visibly tired from being woken up from her sleep, and Theseus stumbles out of our room with an obnoxious yawn. Her eyes pierce him like daggers.

"Goodmorning, Leah!"

"You're so loud, Theseus. Jesus!"

"You're so loud, Theseus. Jesus!" Theseus mocks. He moves to sit next to her on the couch anyway. Ares glances between them with annoyance, and to my surprise, Havena picks up on it.

"Don't say His name in vain," she says, looking to Ares. He sends her a small smile of appreciation and she returns it, and watching it happen forms a pit in my stomach. I catch Leah's eye roll and we both share a look. Neither of us say anything about what we've witnessed.

"You were right," Havena tells Ares. "I think I know where the next rift is."

"Then get on with it," Ruth says grumpily. "The faster you tell us, the faster I can sleep again like that idiot over there."

Ruth gestures to Theseus, who's eyes were now closed as he leans back into the couch.

"Open your eyes, Cupid," Leah nudges him.

"I'm not asleep. I'm simply... resting."

"I'll give you something to make you rest for good—"

I clear my throat, cutting off Ruth's threat and stand up from the couch, crossing my arms. Even Theseus opens his eyes.

"Sleep can wait," I say firmly. I nod my head to Havena.

"You were saying, Have…"

Havena stammers a bit. "Right. I—uh, I had another dream, and the rift was inside of a building somewhere."

She looks to Ruth. "There was mosaic tiling on the floor, in a circle in the middle of the room. And there's a design on it, a carving of some sort. Roses?"

"The seal of Hannah?"

Ruth instantly looks to Ares.

"The rift is inside of the temple," she says in surprise. Ares' eyes widen as if he's just realized it, too. Then they flash with anger.

"The Fallen wouldn't destroy the holiest place of this city—"

"But they will," Havena tells him, gently placing a hand to his arm. Her touch seems to calm him down. "And we have to be ready when they come."

"So we sneak into the temple and then what? Wait for it to happen?" Theseus asks.

"Yes."

"Obviously, you bird."

Leah and Havena answer his question together. He throws his hand up in surrender, but looks to me to be the voice of reason.

"We'll sneak into the temple," I decide, giving Havena a nod for her plan. Theseus sighs back into the couch and closes his eyes again. Ares speaks up.

"Then we need a plan," Ares says. "The seal of the temple is in an area where the Disciples of this city go to socialize. Sometimes they pray, eat, read… It's hard to miss since it's right there when you first enter, and it was busy when Ruth and I spied the last time. We can pass off as Disciples because that's what we are, but what will the rest of you do?"

He looks to everyone for an answer, and they all stay silent, pondering his question in their heads. Except for me.

"We'll divide ourselves, split up into pairs. We'll draw less attention that way," I suggest.

"We could do that, but girl Disciples usually socialize with other girls. Plus there's three of us and three is usually a crowd, Gale. How will we hide Havena?" Ruth asks. She catches Leah's raised eyebrow. "Disciple guys tend to be..."

"Sexist?" Leah asks. Ruth snorts, glimpsing at Theseus, who still has his eyes closed. His ears, however, had perked up.

Listening.

"Our culture is not as intense as the Human Plane, but the trait of arrogance reeks off of boys all the same, doesn't it?"

"Ouch—"

"In that case," I say, cutting off Theseus' remark. "We'll blend into every corner of the room as much as we can. Ares and Ruth, you know the temple like the back of your hands now." They nod in confirmation and I continue. "You two will be the ones to lead us in. We'll wear the cloaks Hannah gave us to go into the city. Ruth, you'll wear the hood of your cloak and so will Havena. It'll hide you both well enough and you won't look out of place. Still remember to keep your head down—just in case. Once we're inside, Theseus and I will keep toward the back of the room, monitoring The Fallen. Ares and Ruth, you'll be placed in the front of the room, doing the same. Leah and Havena, you will sit closest to the seal. Keep in conversation with each other—even if you have to pretend. Just as long as no one will think about talking to you. And lastly, if we see anything out of the ordinary, just stay on guard and don't engage—unless it looks like The Fallen will harm someone."

"But what if one of The Fallen approaches Havena?" Ares

asks. "Or what if the rift opens and knocks her out? What if—"

"I'll be fine, A," Havena says as she gives his arm a reassuring squeeze. *Since when has she known his nickname?*

She turns from him and sends me a nod. "If I see the seal, I'll know when it'll open—"

"But how can you be so sure?" Ruth asks.

"Because it's her blood." Theseus' input surprises us all, snapping our attention to his no longer exhausted face. His eyes stared intently at all of us and none of us at the same time, a distinct look he wears when deciphering the energy of a room. I quickly realize he's focused his ability on just one person, but he's already locked his eyes to hers.

"It's your power, Havena, not ours. Lead the way."

38
Havena

"Absolutely not!"

Hannah stands from her throne, her hand flying toward the throne room doors, to which she throws open.

"Out," she orders to the adversaries by her side. They rush down the clay steps as swiftly as Hannah crosses her arms, glaring down at the six of us with pursed lips. She doesn't utter another word until the doors slam shut.

We stood in front of her, prepared for her disapproval with our bellies fed, our cloaks on, and our weapons hidden beneath the fabric. With Disciples on my left, along with a Guardian, a Nurturer, and even a human on my right, Hannah had no reason to worry about my safety. Yet still, she did.

"I will not put Havena in the middle of crossfire. The Fallen could have orders to kill her on sight."

"Will all due respect, your majesty, we weren't asking," I tell her. Ares takes hold of my hand. If my knowledge of how he viewed higher powers has taught me anything, he was reminding me to speak more respectfully.

So I tried.

"I dreamed of a rift last night and it's inside of the temple—I know it is. If I can just see the rift, even if it's for five minutes, I'll know for sure when it'll open."

"And how will you know for sure, hm? You didn't even know what you were capable of last night. But now that you've slept on it, you suddenly do? It's just a guess, child. A wild goose chase—"

"I can feel it," I snap back. Ares squeezes my hand. I sigh. "I don't have all of the answers when it comes to my family, but I know what I feel. And my father did, too."

The others simply watch, witnessing the two of us stubbornly challenge each other through our silent gazes. Finally, Hannah lowers her eyes from mine with a defeated sigh and leans back in her throne.

"The pride of my city is found within its children, but like most things in life they grow over time, form their own thoughts... opinions..." She murmurs dramatically, mostly to herself, and waves a hand of dismissal.

Then she looks to Ares.

"If there is a sliver of commotion and her life is at risk, use that ring on your finger," Hannah advises. Ares glances down to the silver band.

"Of course," he says, but Hannah has already turned her gaze to me now.

"As for you," she says, her voice firm and steady as she gives her order, "stay on guard."

I give Hannah a final nod, to which she returns.

Then we leave.

■ ■ ■ ■

The temple I had imagined from Ares' description didn't calm my nerves as we walked into the actual building. As soon as we walked across the threshold, my eyes took in all of the Disciples throughout the peaceful room. The majority of them were spending their time talking to one another in hushed voices, while others sat alone, eating their lunches or studying their books in arms reach to pass the time.

The walls were lined with hieroglyphics, and I tried my best to follow the stories etched into the stone as fast as I could. Animals, people, angels, food. Altars, stars, crosses, the moon. The sun.

The Son.

I quickly realized these were recollections of scripture, Christian, Islamic, and Jewish ideologies combined, painted into two-dimensional Egyptian masterpieces. This room was quiet, sacred, historic—and we managed to blend in all the same.

Just as Gale had planned, Ruth and Ares branched off to the front of the room. I kept my head down, allowing Leah to lead me to one of the stone pews that circled around the temple's seal. The seal on the floor was carved into the center of the room, with roses etched into it just like I had dreamed. The only thing that threw me off was how the seal was outlined by a thin ceramic fountain, something I had not seen in my sleep.

Then it dawned on me.

Once the rift opens, the fountain would turn to blood.

"So... do you know when the rift will... you know..."

Although she was asking me in a hushed whisper, Leah's hands briefly mimicked the boom of an explosion. And even though no one else sat in our pew, I suppress the snort that wanted to escape my throat.

"It won't explode, or at least I hope it won't," I explain with a smile. She returns it. "Just give me a few more minutes to sense it, I guess."

I didn't want to explain that I was trying to sense when the blood would come—it would be too scary and hard to explain—but as Leah nodded with her furrowed brows of confusion, I held my breath.

"Should I keep talking to you or let you concentrate?" she asks after a moment. I drop my eyes to the seal again. For some reason, they couldn't help being drawn to the fountain.

"Not sure. We're supposed to be blending in, but I don't think that'll be possible for me anyway," I say jokingly, mostly to myself. Leah nods, then shifts in her seat to look behind her, in the direction of Theseus and Gale. I don't follow. We couldn't risk the hood of my cloak falling. Or having one of The Fallen recognize me.

"Well, those two are enjoying themselves," she sighs. I nod at her words, and unfortunately blink. The water in the fountain had just flickered for a split second.

Or so I thought.

It was steady now, just like it was before, flowing gently within the silence of the room.

"Maybe I was wrong," I huff, looking to Leah. "Maybe my dreams are just that—dreams—and I know where rifts will open but I won't know—or don't know—when they'll open."

"Or maybe you should've read your journal," Leah says matter-of-factly, "and not Ares."

Her eyes sweep over to Ares' direction, and the annoyance slivering over her gaze doesn't go unnoticed.

"What's wrong?" I ask. I tried to keep my tone as neutral as possible, but I couldn't mask the defensive raise of my eyebrow.

I kiss the guy once and suddenly I'm possessive?

Leah, thankfully, doesn't notice, but I watch her lip curl as she nudges her head in his direction.

"Your father knew the extent of your powers so you should trust what your father wrote. It's like what Theseus said, it's your blood—your powers. Gale may think he's our leader, but this is your show. And Ares shouldn't have invaded your privacy. I know the dude reads a lot but..."

Leah turns to me now, shrugging off her explanation to change the subject. "Whatever, I saw you giving him a mouthful after you left anyway..."

I feel the heat rise in my cheeks even though I drop her gaze. "Right..."

"Right?" Leah repeats puzzled. Then she takes in my face when I look up at her again. "Oh, you're doing the thing, Have!"

"What thing?"

"Your nose—the nose thing! It crinkles when you lie. Have, you can't lie to me, I know you!" she says it all hurriedly. I shush her, and with an eye roll she lowers her volume. "What happened last night?"

"I yelled at him."

"Then what else?"

I shoot her a look, but her determined eyes press on.

So I tell her.

"I kissed him."

"You kissed him?"

"I kissed him," I repeat.

"No—you don't get what I'm saying—You kissed *him*?" she asks in disbelief. I nod my head and she sighs.

"No wonder you were so nice to him this morning," she says.

"Hey, I didn't expect it either... well... that's a lie, too... I initiated it."

"And he kissed you back?"

"Yes, that's usually what happens when two people care for each other in that way—"

Her snort interrupts me and she turns her thoughtful gaze to the seal of the floor.

"And to think you didn't trust him," Leah finally says softly, pondering the next question in her head.

"What made you change your mind about him?" she asks.

I can only shrug.

"He feels safe," I explain. "I don't have the stupid question in the back of my brain that wonders if I'll hurt him. My family has hurt too many people already, and with Ares I... I know that my family's past decisions don't affect him. He can come out of this stupid prophecy without feeling the weight of what my family has done to the world. It's not personal to him... it's just another stupid quest in his eyes."

Leah studies my face for a moment, searching for more meaning behind what I've said. Unfortunately she finds it.

"So you chose him because he's the safer option?"

I blink.

"What other options do I have?"

A crack echoes into the room. The hushed room goes completely still, and every pair of eyes turns toward the seal on the floor. My gaze immediately takes in the split tile in the center of the floor. A low rumbling settles underneath the ground and I stand from my seat. Leah stands as well, along with the other Disciples around the room.

The rumbling stops, and even though everyone has brought their gaze to each other, whispering about what had just happened, I keep my focus on the fountain, at the calm water that was beginning to bubble.

"Have, Ares is calling us over," Leah tugs on my arm.

I don't move.

"Have, Ares needs to get you out of here! Now!"

The seal crumbles in on itself, the tiling falling deeper and deeper into the earth. Leah tugs me back hard enough and we fall into the pew. Wind gushes out of where the seal once rested, swirling forcefully into the room and whipping the screaming faces of everyone in its path. Disciples start to rush out of the temple, but my eyes glance to the ones who stay behind, who've started ripping their clothes to expose their tattoos of a vine.

The Fallen.

Within a moment, Gale and Theseus drop down in front of us. Their cloaks no longer hide their armored bodies, and their wings were drawn to their fullest length. Theseus goes to bend down, to shelter myself and Leah from the scene with his wings, but I step out of it.

"Protect her," I order, gesturing to Leah. Theseus doesn't object, only cocoons her with his sharp feathers. Fire flashes from the tips of his fingers, and he sets up a perimeter of fire behind us, blocking The Fallen by the entrance from reaching us. I step next to Gale, with his sword already drawn and raised, ready to fight. I slide my own sword out of the sheath on his hip.

He turns to me with a glint in his eye.

"I knew you'd rather fight," he says over the wind. I smirk at him, then get into my own stance. Ares couldn't portal me out of here even if he wanted to.

He was occupied with Ruth on the other side of the room, fighting The Fallen. Ruth fights with a long dagger in each hand, slicing through The Fallen as if they were merely blades of grass. She was untouchable, dodging every ounce of their blood that slipped into the air, moving at the same pace of her knives.

Volant.

Ares, however, was conjuring the earth, blocking and hitting his enemies with the weight of rubble when he wasn't using his bare fists. Watching him fight sent a fire to my stomach.

A rumble erupts from the broken seal again, catching my attention. The seal was now a pit in the ground, yet the fountain around it remained intact, untouched, until an ear scratching screech sounded from the depths of the pit, and the water became blood.

"So how do we stop this?" I yell to Gale. He turns to me.

"We fight whatever comes out of it." As if on cue, multiple screeches erupt out of the hole, and I watch as Gale's face flushes at the blood-curdling sound.

"How many come out of it?" I ask nervously. He gulps.

"Usually one."

A black mist rose out of the pit, and my hands nearly trembled as the cloud split itself into sections. Three black silhouettes emerged from the mist, and their skeletal bodies were covered with the thinnest of leathery skin. There was no meat on their bones, and the size of their ribs seemed to match the size of their hands that scourged around the room, as if they were looking for something. Someone.

All three of them screeched again, and their pale, white faces were dominated by the gaping hole of their mouth, leading to a black void of nothingness. Their ash-colored eyes held nothing but pure evil and disdain as they gazed around the room. Then, one of them fixed their gaze onto Ruth.

Her body was turned from them, too concentrated on pulling her dagger out from the back of one of The Fallen.

"Ruth!" I shouted as loud as I could.

Gale had left my side, flying as fast as he could to reach Ruth as she turned, but it was too late. One of the creatures was already reaching for her, preparing to take her in its grasp.

"No!" A voice boomed into the temple.

A flash of light crashed into the creature, and its scream throttled the blood in my veins.

The other two creatures rushed into a corner of the ceiling, away from the blinding light as they watched their companion deteriorate into ashes. All that was left was the glowing armor strapped to Hannah's body, and her face looking at the other creatures with revenge in her heart. Her wings were like Aelia's, the feathers bright, like illuminating flecks of the sun.

Hannah looked down to Gale, who had reached Ruth in time and cocooned her with his wings before the creature could take her. Take them both. Then Hannah turned to me.

"Use your power!"

The creatures screeched again, as if they were trying to silence her. And when one dove for Hannah, the other dove for me.

I dropped my sword.

Theseus shouted behind me.

"Havena!"

But I knew what to do.

The creature was fast, merely a few feet away as my hand guided the bubbling blood from the fountain, engulfing the demon in front of me. I brought up my other hand, letting the fire erupt from my fingertips and kept my eyes open, watching my powers collide into the creature. It's scream scoured out like nails on a chalkboard, and it's ash eyes flared in pain, almost pleading for me to stop as it held my gaze.

I kept going, fighting the strain in my body until the creature was nothing more than dust on the ground, just like

Hannah had done before. Finally, my arms dropped to my side. I didn't even notice I was screaming until I watched the demon's last remaining piece of ash wither to the ground. I fought through my faltering eyelids with a haggard breath, watching the others. Hannah retracted her wings as she landed onto the ground, spreading the ashes of the creature that she'd defeated.

Theseus rose from the floor, helping Leah to her feet. With a wave of his hand, the fire behind us was gone, and so were The Fallen behind it. They'd gotten away.

Ares began stepping between the rubble to reach my side, but the weight of my eyelids didn't stop searching the room until they landed on Gale.

Ruth was behind him, hugging herself with fear in her eyes as Gale stepped away from her. His clouded, brown wings flowed behind him, and the last thing I saw was an image I've seen so many times before.

His hand stretched out towards me.

39
Ares

"It's been too long."

I stepped away from Havena's bedside and turned toward the others. Leah, Hannah, and Ruth stood against the wall, watching and waiting for Havena's eyes to open just as I was. Except I hadn't moved from beside her since I carried her limp body out of the temple.

And I beat Gale to it.

We had equally overestimated and underestimated Havena's powers. I had never seen an angel conjure two elements at the same time in my life—let alone conjure blood—and the words in her father's journal didn't compare to what I had witnessed.

"Earth, air, water, fire. All four elements that every angel trains to control, yet a half-human girl is capable of conjuring blood?" I ask in disbelief.

"And the only person who understood her powers in the first place is dead," Ruth spits, clearly referencing Havena's father.

"And let us be glad that she isn't," Hannah snaps. "She's tapped into a part of herself that she didn't know existed and it's much more overwhelming than The Sight. We're lucky that she's still breathing."

Leah lets out a shaky breath. "So she'll be fine?"

Fine. She'll be fine. A scoff escapes my throat.

"*Fine* isn't good enough."

"*Fine* is better than dead," a voice interrupts.

The bedroom door was ajar and we look toward Aelia. She stood in the doorframe, gingerly gazing upon everyone in the room before resting her eyes onto Havena.

"God's grace, it's good to see you, Aelia," Hannah greets. A smile of familiarity spread upon her lips. Aelia returns it.

"God's grace, Hannah. I came as soon as I heard. Some of the fleeing Disciples used a portal to reach the Temple of Aaron. They told us the news when they arrived."

Aelia cautiously stepped to Havena's side, immediately bringing her hand to Havena's face, checking her cheeks and forehead. "How long has she been like this?"

"About four hours," I answer quickly. It's been four hours too long since the attack on the temple of Hannah, and Havena hasn't bat an eyelash since. "She took down one of the demons that came out of the rift—"

"One of them?" Aelia interrupts in shock. "How many of the demons escaped?"

"Three of them," I answer. She looks to Hannah for confirmation and Hannah simply nods.

"Is that unusual?" Leah asks.

"Highly," Aelia replies. She takes a careful seat on Havena's bed. "The Banished Realm is contained by holy enchantments, spoken through the tongues of appointed archangels on Christ's day of resurrection. This protection is supposed to keep demons from leaving Hell's depths—"

"But how? The City of Aaron hasn't had an appointed

archangel for... well, since forever," I interrupt. "Archangel Aaron was the first priest of the Israelites, and like you, Hannah, the city he looked over was named after him. Archangels are supposed to be immortal, but Aaron's death was always an inconsistency. The City of Aaron has been governed by the Holy Council ever since he passed."

Aelia simply smiled.

"Well, of course *you* know our history," Aelia tells me, almost in admiration. "Even so, you've just discovered not too long ago that I am an archangel, have you not? I am the Archangel of Aaron, and I've been spending my time as the secret head of the Holy Council for several centuries. We may be immortal, but no creature on this earth is invincible. I was appointed as Archangel ever since Aaron's death."

Leah goes to ask another question, but Aelia waves a hand of dismissal. "That's a story for another day, dear."

"Well, one story we need to hear is how more than one demon travelled through that rift," Ruth mumbles.

"Precisely," Hannah answers. "Some demons are determined to fight through those barriers we've created. Even if passing through inflicts the sensation of hellfire upon their skin, they don't care. Their desire to wreak havoc on humans is stronger than any pain they will ever feel."

"So what happened then? Three demons decided to fight the barriers together and got through?" Leah asks.

For once, I didn't have an explanation for the questions everyone was asking. All my training as a Disciple blinded me from the work Guardians and Nurturers did. From the work Gale and Theseus, and many others, were accustomed to.

They've been trained to fight whatever comes out of these things—these rifts—and all I knew was the word of God and how to teach it. No matter how many perspectives I could have on our sacred text, I didn't have the experience to fight through the recollections I've read on paper.

But Gale did.

"Rubeus is behind this, and make no mistake, he's trying to alter the wards to his will somehow," Hannah says. Aelia grunts in agreement.

"He's not an archangel, but he is the prince of Hell..." Aelia adds. "My guess? He pushed as many demons as he could onto the barrier until one of the areas weakened. It's just like he tried to do years ago. In his eyes, this is a small victory for his plan, and in due time, he'll strike again. Make no mistake of it."

"So those things that attacked me will come back?" Ruth asks, turning to Hannah.

"What even were they?" adds Leah. I bit my tongue so Hannah could answer.

"We were attacked by Als." Hannah cleared her throat, but the crack in her voice didn't go unnoticed as she began to explain. "They're demons that feed on fertile women. Before they take your life in here," she places a hand to her heart, "they absorb the life down here."

Hannah places a hand to her stomach now, and although Ruth had a stone-like expression on her face, she subconsciously brought a hand to her stomach as well.

"Rubeus sent them here to taunt you," Aelia points out.

Hannah simply scowls.

"And he'll pay for it."

"Then why did it reach for me first?" Ruth asks.

"Because you're a Disciple," Aelia answers. She gently nods to Ruth's stomach. "You can't start a family after the age of thirty. You have to decide to conceive earlier than most, and taking away your choice to have a child—"

"Is just evil!" Leah gasps.

"Demons always are," Hannah sneers.

Ruth drops her hand from her stomach, and it somehow finds a way to the knives strapped to her thigh. She gulps.

"I'll go—uh—help the others," she says quietly, and no one stops her from leaving the room. Aelia looks to Hannah.

"She wants revenge."

"We all do," I respond. Aelia raises a brow, but before she can ask her question, Leah cuts in first.

"So we'll be prepared for when they come back, right? There's not going to be any more rifts, are there?"

"Yes... and no," Hannah answers. "Rifts are unpredictable, but I ordered the few Guardians we have here to patrol every street and every nook of this city. Disciples have been posted alongside them, blessing the area and the waters of this land for extra protection. I've already advised the angels here to paint lambs' blood above their doors so no demon can enter. Hopefully, we'll be able to sense whatever disturbance Hell wants to bestow upon us if they come again."

"And I've done the same in Aaron. Some of our Guardians will arrive here shortly to give you the numbers you need. I've already sent word to Adira. I can only imagine they're taking the same precautions, if not more—"

"But how will we know who to trust?" I ask, interrupting Aelia. They all look to me for elaboration. "How do we know which Disciples to trust?"

"Because the ones who are fighting with us haven't defiled their title. Those are true Disciples. But the ones that have betrayed us are most likely on their way to Lucifer's palace, preparing for war as we speak," Aelia answers. Her calm gaze mirrors her voice as she studies my stature. "You know the ones we don't trust, young one, and I'm sure you know them quite well by now."

"The Fallen," I answer. I look to Havena again. The only thing that calmed me down as we waited for her to wake was the steadiness of her breathing. A reminder that she was alive.

"No matter the plan we set into motion, Havena is our first priority. Her well-being will always be our first priority."

I look to Hannah, her lips parted with hesitation from my words, but I didn't care.

"Swear to me."

Hannah's eyes widened. A promise between two angels is sacred. If an angel can't fulfill what they've promised, they'll lose their powers. Turn human, with only their wings to remind them of what they once were. And some angels would rather choose death. Hannah stammered.

"I-I guarantee you that I will keep Havena safe—"

"Swear to me," I interject sternly. "That whatever we plan from here on out, Havena's well-being will be our first priority."

Hannah looked to Aelia before looking back to me. I couldn't decipher the look they shared, but Hannah looked defeated as she brought her eyes to mine again.

"You have my word, Ares. I pledge on my life," Hannah vows.

"As do I," I return. I lingered before leaving, letting my gaze fall upon Havena one more time.

She'll wake up. She has to. Because Havena can't die yet.

Not now.

40
Ruth

I didn't leave that room to help Gale and Theseus clean the temple. Screw that. I almost died from the hands of petty, maternal demons.

My knife hit the clay bullseye etched into the armory wall. The first night we slept here, I needed a place to blow off steam for an hour or two, and this armory sat right across the hall from the throne room. It was probably stupid to go snooping around—and to use this room before Hannah gave us permission—but I wasn't going to be caged inside of my sleeping quarters with a pair of brittle humans.

Besides, our cover was blown now anyway.

I slipped another knife from my thigh and watched it glide off my fingers as I threw it at the target. It clanged to the floor, and I let my scream of frustration roar.

I threw another, but that fell flat too.

"Don'tScreamAgain!"

Leah's voice sounded out behind me.

I turn, only to find her with both hands covering her ears in caution. She lowers them once she realizes I won't scream again.

"Why can't I scream? Because your stupid human ears are too fragile for my voice?" I ask bitterly.

"No," she simply says with a shake of her head. "You shouldn't scream because you need to put what you feel into words, not... a scream."

I rolled my eyes as I turned my attention back to the bullseye and bit my lip. The human was right, but I wouldn't tell her that. My hand slid to my knives, only to feel the absence of their presence inside the leather band in my thigh.

Leah snickers.

"It's not funny!" I grumble, then walk up to the target to collect my daggers. Leah follows my lead.

"It's not funny," she says matter-of-factly, meeting me at the target. "I couldn't imagine a demon taking away my choice to—"

"Have a baby?" I ask bitterly. "Start a family? Force me to find someone that would want to marry a barren woman?"

She parts her lips, but doesn't say anything as I pluck a single knife out of the target.

"You're right. You can't imagine a demon throwing the strain of your occupation back in your face. You're just a human for crying out loud—"

"I'm trying to empathize with you!" she says frustratedly. Her cheeks began to redden and I turned away, setting my sights onto another dagger on the ground.

Unfortunately, Leah trails my steps.

"I get that I'm human, and I get that you've trained your whole life to fit into some perfect-angel-mold because you're some perfect-angel-being, but if you haven't noticed, none of that matters right now! You almost died! I don't even know why I care about you when all you've done—this entire time—is be rude to me! If you want to focus on yourself, fine, I'll just leave you to it—"

"I like women!"

My breath caught in my throat as I watched Leah's face flush at my words.

"And I-I've known," I stammer. "I've known even when I was with Gale. And I love him, I really do, but it'll never go deeper than what it is... And I—I didn't even realize I wanted kids in that way until that demon nearly took that choice away from me. I've read Hannah's story, but I never thought her struggle to conceive children would ever be my reality. But now? Now I'm... I'm confused because I don't know of a woman that's going to get me pregnant. Do you? And you—Leah, you annoy me because... you just do! So back off... please."

I inhale, finally able to catch my breath, but I only watch as she simply blinks.

"Are you—I mean, so you're—I mean—"

She shook her head with a sigh before speaking again.

"So can I wear rainbow T-shirts here or will angels yell at me for it?"

I pause, taking in her face to see if she was serious.

Then she grins.

"You suck," I chuckle, nudging her arm. She takes a step back with a chuckle of her own but doesn't turn to leave. "And no, it's just—we're not like the Human Plane. The homophobic verse in the bible was introduced in 1946—by man—and doesn't exist before then. The actual translation condemns pedophilia."

"So you're in the clear?"

"Sort of," I wince. "Sexuality isn't a big thing here, nor is race if you haven't noticed, but it's one of those situations where no one really acknowledges it, and it just becomes..."

"Erased," Leah finishes with a thoughtful expression. "Where I'm from, people like to say they don't see color. But living inside of a colorless world is so boring to me. No colors are the same, and I'd like to see every color there is one day, rather than erase what they represent."

I felt my eyes widen with surprise.

"Exactly."

Leah smirks, then takes another step back.

"I'll just... leave you to this." Leah nods towards the bullseye, "and 'back off'... for now."

I watch her walk away, and she almost reaches the door before I call out to her again.

"I only said that to push you away."

Her feet slow at my words, and she turns to me with furrowed brows before I continue.

"I just... don't bother telling anyone... please?"

She gives me a small smile.

"I wasn't planning on it."

Then she's gone.

I saunter back to a good throwing distance from the bullseye, and subconsciously twirl the knife about my fingers before I throw it. A smile creeps onto my lips as the knife glides off my fingers, hitting the bullseye right in the center, and I can't slip the heat from my face as I reach for another knife. I bite my cheek.

I should've realized it sooner.

Leah and I were fated.

41
Theseus

"You know, if you tried a little harder there'd be a bigger flame." Gale lowers his hand from the rubble and points it towards me, but I counter the wind he sends at me.

We were busy cleaning the temple—or whatever was left of it—along with other citizens throughout the city that volunteered. I would say that word had spread quickly, but so had the sound of screeching demons, screaming Disciples and crumbling rock.

Most of the debris has been restored, thanks to the conjuring hands of this city's angels. The angels of Hannah handled conjuring the earth with ease. They always made it look as simple as breathing, so I definitely noticed the side eyes that occasionally found Gale and I as we helped them clean up. Especially since Gale was pathetically conjuring fire to meld the clay seal of the temple back together.

"You've always been better at this," Gale points out. He steps back, gesturing his head at the seal. "Fire is your thing anyway."

"But you need the practice. I may like fire the most but I

can conjure every element. You, on the other hand, sir Gale, are simply pathetic with flames."

Gale crosses his arms, defeated, so I mirror his movement.

"Ah," I breathe in, "a stance of failure."

"Hey!" Gale lowers his arms, and so do I. "I don't care about fire—or this seal right now. We're wasting our time here. We should be—"

"Watching over an unconscious Havena and waiting for her to wake?" I ask.

"Exactly!" he answers with a grin.

He takes a step to leave but I grab his arm.

"I wasn't serious."

"Well, I am," he says, but he stretches his hand toward the temple's seal again. His eyebrows furrow in concentration as he keeps talking.

"I should've caught her when she fell."

"You should do a lot of things, but you already don't because of her. Or should I say, how you view her?" I retort.

He manages to create a small flame.

"That is not true!"

"The octave in your voice says otherwise," I point out. He turns to me and drops his hand. The flame he's created is gone.

"What have I not done because of her?"

"We—Or should I say you?—have nearly spent two months with her and she's barely practiced conjuring the elements."

"Because she took a liking to air first."

"Or, because you're biding your time with her ignorance. You also didn't show her, or Leah, the city. Did you know how weird it was to teach Leah our city through drawings?"

"It was a dangerous idea. They snuck out anyway—"

"And even with all of the excuses running through your brain, you still haven't kissed her."

"I—Well, that has nothing to do with the prophecy, Cupid."

"You're telling me that you being fated to her, and then falling for her, has nothing to do with the prophecy?" I ask. Gale drops his hand and turns to me again with visible surprise in his eyes.

"How do you know that?"

"Because I'm a Nurturer!" I exclaim. "In case you've forgotten, I'm the most empathetic being in any room. I can literally distinguish the energies of anyone in sight, and it doesn't help when you two shock each other when you touch sometimes. It's weird. I can practically smell the lust in the air—"

"Have you told anyone?" Gale lowers his tone, bringing his voice to a serious whisper, and I shake my head.

"Of course not," I answer, matching his volume. "Your feelings for each other have amplified your bond. I don't understand why you shock each other though—"

"Well... that's exactly why I haven't kissed her," Gale reasons.

I narrow my eyes for a second, then it clicks.

"You both may think disregarding your bond will make our assignment easier, but if anything your bond will make us stronger once you two figure it out. The four of us—you, Havena, myself, even Ares—become one with the earth, remember? You'll regret not acting sooner," I advise. Gale takes in my words slowly, then I watch as he drops his gaze to the seal with a raised hand.

"If our enemies found out we were fated—or even romantically involved—we'd be liabilities to each other. What if someone goes after her so they can get to me?"

I can only chuckle at the suggestion. "I'm pretty sure if

someone tried to kill Havena, she'd kill them first."

He looks to me wide-eyed.

"Not helping?"

"No!"

"I just mean," I sigh, "that every demon, or weird cult member—or whoever is on Rubeus' side—is trying to kill all of us anyway. I'd like to see my best friend find some kind of happiness in his life. Instead, you're clouding your head and letting it slip through his fingers."

"Well, your best friend has other things to worry about," Gale mutters. "She's with Ares now, and we have a seal to meld."

I've heard that tone too many times in my life, especially when certain conversations were over. It didn't mean Gale had given up hope, just that he'd accepted the situation for what it was—even if it's created a grudge he'll never let go of.

It reminded me of the day he took up his father's sword for the first time. It was only Gale and I, training in his armory like we'd always do. Ares and Ruth were trying to be Disciples at the time, so they didn't need to fight as much as we did.

Gale stopped halfway through our sparring one day, and I thought he'd just complain like he had done in the weeks prior. It was always the same complaint: that he wasn't connected to his weapon—or any weapon—and couldn't fight like he wanted to. He picked a different blade every week, trying to find the one he could call his own. I figured he held a grudge because I kept landing him on his ass, but as we polished off our weapons to end our training time, he lingered in front of his parents' swords.

Then he chose his father's.

"Everything was meaningless until the Lord gave it meaning," I remind him. Gale's eyes flicker to me for a moment, but stay latched onto the steady flames that finally begin to form in the disheveled seal.

"And every action from your body is a reflection of your heart," Gale finishes with a smirk. The earth within the seal starts to shift, and I watch as the clay pieces begin to melt into each other, until the once broken seal was nothing more than smooth, recovered pavement.

"Hey, look at that, you've balanced your thoughts. It's kinda like controlling fire, isn't it? An act of balancing the flames."

"So you've wasted your time teaching me that instead of how to conjure fire?" he asks.

"No. I taught you both—obviously. Your parents' wisdom can literally be used for every situation, did you forget?" I reply.

"Of course not. But what if I just set your hair on fire since, you know, I'm good at it now?"

"That'd be a very bad reflection of your heart," I caution.

"Is that so?—"

"Anyways," I interject. I rest my arm on his shoulder and start leading him toward the temple exit.

"Anyways," Gale mocks, taking charge of the conversation again. "Let's leave my love life alone. We should be trying to figure out where the rifts will open again."

"Fine, any idea where to start?" I ask. We step out of the temple and into the dusty evening. The streets were just starting to clear out, and as far as my eyes could see, lamb's blood was painted above the thresholds of homes in the city. Some have even painted the entirety of their door with the blood.

Regardless, Hannah made a good call.

"My parents mapped a few of the rifts in their journals. They closed them, but... we can start there," Gale replies.

"So you think Rubeus will strike in the same places he did years ago?" I ask. Gale shrugs.

"I had that same thought!"

We turn our attention to find Ares a few feet away. He was leaning against the marble column of the temple, looking at the city with a pomegranate in hand.

"Hannah and Aelia said the cities are taking as many precautions as they can. The only place Rubeus can attack without opposition is the Human Plane now," Ares explains.

"Aelia is here?" I ask, and Ares nods his head. "Has Adira arrived as well?"

Ares shakes his head.

"Adira is still in her city. Aelia is with Havena and the others. They're watching over her right now, but she should be fine."

"Then why aren't you there?" Gale asks.

Ares shakes his head again, and for the first time since the Summer Solstice, I see sincerity in his eyes.

"I couldn't stay there any longer. We were just watching her breathe, not watching her wake up," he says. He solemnly looks out to the city with a sigh before speaking again. "I just keep thinking about how once she wakes up, we'll have to use her powers again."

"Once she wakes up, we'll make sure she's okay and go from there," Gale counters nonchalantly. Despite his calm demeanor, I could hear the Guardian in him giving an order.

"She's going to jump into the action anyway, you know how reckless she gets—"

"We won't know until she wakes up. For now, we'll figure out the prophecy stuff while she rests," Gale asserts. Ares studies him for a moment, then nods defeatedly.

"I'm not disagreeing... I'm just... fine..." Ares mutters,

mostly to himself. He perches off the column.

"I'm going to check on her again. Care to join me?" he asks. Gale clenches his jaw, holding back the words I know he wanted to say, so I jump in instead.

"We'll catch up with you later, A," I suggest amiably.

Ares gives a somber nod of his head before he leaves us.

"That question was a test," Gale says when Ares is out of sight. "A test to see if I still care about her."

"Well, you do, so why is it a big deal?" I ask. It's not like Gale has been hiding his feelings for Havena. Or if he was trying to, then someone needed to tell him that he sucked at it.

I began to trust Ares again the night we arrived in Hannah. From the very beginning, I noticed Havena didn't trust Ares like we did. During our time in the market, I focused on Havena's energy. Her unease was overwhelming, but I closed my eyes and found the source of it in the room. At first I figured she just didn't know Ares on the same level Gale and I did. But it wasn't until his departure from our assignment that made me distrustful of him. She relaxed into our world a little easier when he wasn't around, and the way Ares spoke of Havena and Leah—of humans—had me on edge. Not to mention his random reappearance, which made it easier to believe he was fallen at the Summer Solstice.

Fortunately, Havena's hunch about Ares had been wrong. As I watched them grow closer—their hugs longer and their eye contact less calculating than before—I had to remind myself that Ares was never that charismatic to begin with, even when we were kids. Yet as we began to lower our walls for Ares again, Gale continued to build his up. And though I wouldn't mention it, a part of me blamed jealousy.

"Because," Gale starts, "I don't trust him. He just tried to see whether my distrust in him stems from my feelings for her or... or something else. But that's not the case, and he knows that now."

"So you didn't answer... because...?" I ask, still not following.

"Because if I joined him to visit Havena, then he would think I'm just jealous. But my silence just confirmed that I'm not jealous! I'm onto him and his game... whatever it is."

I slowly nod my head, trying to link his reasoning with the wordplay the two had shared.

Gale chuckles at my expression.

"There's a reason you're a Nurturer and not a Guardian."

"Yeah, because I didn't pick that profession," I say matter-of-factly, to which Gale snorts.

"No, Cupid," he replies. "Nice as you are, you're quite dim within the strategy department. No wonder Leah likes you."

He doesn't wait for me to walk to the palace entrance, and I'm left replaying his words in my head before I trail behind him.

"Wait, Leah likes me?"

42
Havena

Drip. Drip. Drip.

I opened my eyes to a cold, gloomy, stone room. Candles were set up throughout the perimeter, illuminating just enough for me to take everything in. Rows of wooden pews mirrored themselves across the floor, leading up to an altar at the end of the room.

I knew this place.

Then I held up my hands. They glided through the air like mist, blurring with every movement I made as if the matter of my body didn't exist. I was no longer human, angel, or being. No longer here, but present.

Was I air itself? Maybe a ghost... But did I die?

The groan of a door sounds behind me, along with a cackle of thunder, and I look toward the stained windows to find rain pattering across the glass. Then I turned to find hushed voices entering the chapel. Then my father.

I blink, and suddenly, I'm looking underneath his face. I only had the polaroid of us to go on—but just as I had thought—I shared his eye color. I brought up my hand, only to gasp at the fingers staring back at me. My hand was so tiny compared to his face, and my fingers were no more than little stubs. Atticus looked down to me, smiling with nothing but love in his eyes. Then he looked back to the second person, the person across from me, and the love his eyes once held was replaced with worry. I turned my head, and what sounded like a babble to them, was another gasp from me.

"Once you do this... she will no longer remember you."

Mr. Pelowski, the man I thought was nothing more than the owner of Mrs. Patty's Marketplace, spoke those words to my father. Then he looked down at me with hesitation in his eyes. He was a bit younger than how I knew him, but I'd recognize those wrinkled eyes and freckled skin anywhere. I felt the feeling of cool liquid touch the back of my bobbing head.

I looked back to my dad.

I had his eye color. I knew it. The words he wanted to say couldn't find their way past his lips, and when I tried to say them for him—to say I love you—the babble of a baby was the only thing that sounded into the room. His eyes crinkled at my voice, then he turned to Mr. Pelowski.

"It must be done."

His hands that held me were replaced by the hands of Mr. Pelowski. I tried to speak some more, to tell him not to do it, but the babbling tongue of a baby was silenced by the water Mr. Pelowski lowered me into. It filled my mouth, my nostrils as I tried to scream, and the mere seconds I spent under there felt like forever away from my father. Mr. Pelowski brought me above the water, and my eyes immediately latched onto my father as I cried the cry of a baby. His body looked faded, as if he were stuck between two planes and erasing before my very eyes. My hands reached for him, but he only looked to Mr. Pelowski.

270

"Once more."

Then I was underwater again.

The water danced over my eyes, but the blurry figure that was once my father had vanished entirely.

I broke the surface tension of the water again, the absence of baby teeth allowing me to feel the liquid sputtering over my gums and out of my mouth as my eyes darted around the cathedral. They found nothing more than the cold stone of the room, the withering candles in every corner, and Mr. Pelowski. I wasn't crying anymore, and I watched as Mr. Pelowski moved his gaze from me, to nothing.

"It is done," Mr. Pelowski said to no one. "She will be safe."

43
Gale

I nearly jumped.

Havena gasped for air as if she's never held a breath of air in her lungs her entire life. Her amber eyes blazed across the room, flashing from face to face as if she were unable to register where she was or who was here with her.

"I can't breathe," she sputters. "I can't breathe."

A whirlpool of wind started to churn in the air around her, and I immediately brought my hand up, ceasing it, but Ares made it to her bedside before me. He stared into her eyes, with nothing but concern in his, and held onto her delicate shoulders.

"I'm here, Havena," he reassures. Her eyes latched onto his, widened with fright, but they focused on the intensity of his gaze.

"I'm here," Ares repeats. "Right here."

She brought her hands up to his arms, holding onto him as her breathing began to slow, as if he was her anchor. And in that moment, as the whirlpool of wind diminished from around her, he was. With a clenched jaw, I lower my useless hand.

"I saw him," she says. Ares furrows his brows.

"Who'd you see?" he asks gently.

"My father," she answers with a breath. She turns to the rest of us, her eyes widening with realization as she begins to recognize us. "Aelia, I saw my father."

"Are you sure dear?" Aelia asks gently, now stepping to Havena's side. Aelia had stood by my side as Havena woke, holding her breath as she witnessed the debacle, but now she sat down on the bed, and took Havena's hand into her own.

"You should rest—"

"I am rested," Havena protests. "I need to go, I need to—"

She gestures her body to move off the bed, but Ares grabs her arm and pushes her back down. Havena huffs as Aelia locks her into place, too. Then Havena looks to the rest of us for back up.

None of us try to step in.

"You've been out for too many hours, Havena," Ares tries to reassure. He moves a piece of her hair out of her face, and she doesn't fight his touch.

"All the more reason to get up," she retorts.

"I'm sure you saw your father, and it must've been a wonderful dream," Aelia starts softly. Havena gives her a look, but Aelia continues. "Trust me when I tell you that we'll listen to you when you're properly rested. Make no mistake—you're strong—but your powers took a lot of energy out of you. And you can't fight anyone when you're a withering vine, dear. We'll worry about Rubeus in the meantime."

Havena slid her gaze over to Ares.

"It wasn't a dream," she asserts. Aelia turns to him, waiting for his response and watching his mouth part pathetically. I even think I see Aelia's mouth tighten into a thin smile as Ares struggles with the pressure of his answer.

"We're just... worried," he finally says, to which Havena rolls her eyes and reluctantly settles back into the bed.

"I'm alive. There's nothing to worry about except the war."

"Precisely," Aelia chimes in. "And I'll worry about that while you stay here."

"And Ares?" Havena asks with a raised eyebrow. She settles her wishful gaze onto his as she continues. "Can Ares stay?"

I could barf.

Aelia shakes her head in response. "There shouldn't be a rift anytime soon, especially since the seal has been restored, but we'll be putting up protection wards here for extra precaution. It always helps to have a Disciple there to guide our prayer, so for now, the Guardian and Nurturer will be by your side."

Aelia pats Havena's hand, ending their conversation, then rises from Havena's bedside. Ares leans over and gives Havena a kiss on the forehead, and I watch her close her eyes at the touch. She doesn't protest his departure any further as he rises from her.

I keep quiet as Ares follows Aelia out of the room, and stay quiet as Havena brings her gaze to Theseus and I. As soon as the bedroom door clicks shut, Havena jumps from the bed.

Within a blink of an eye, her feet trip over themselves. My feet move forward as she nearly falls, but Theseus catches her for me.

"Easy, Vine, you've just awakened," the Nurturer chuckles, but the comment is cut short. He immediately stands Havena upright, and her eyes widen as he abruptly steps away, bringing his hand to where she's just touched.

"Are you alright?" she asks. The concern in her voice corresponds with the alertness of my body. Theseus removes his hand from his arm just enough for his eyes only. He blinks profusely at the sight, and before I can ask to see what he's seeing, he lowers his hand completely. A small welt on his shoulder has formed, as if he's been burned, and he looks to Havena.

"You've just conjured fire... on my skin..."

"But I—I wasn't even trying to," Havena sputters, sitting back down on the bed.

"Air, fire, yet you still haven't conjured earth or water... "

I ponder out loud and Havena shakes her head.

"My father said we conjure our powers easily. I just can't... control them all yet..."

Her eyes slide off mine and study the clay wall behind me.

"What are you rushing into, Havena?" Theseus questions. Our eyes snap to his face as he gestures to his arm. "I'm hoping it's worth me being burned."

"I'm sorry."

"You'll live."

Havena and I speak at the same time.

Theseus looks from me, to Havena, then back to me with nothing but a look of surprise in his eyes. I should share that same look—I've never seen an angel burn another angel from a simple touch—but I didn't care about Havena's powers.

I cared about her.

"The bond of the fated," Theseus simply mutters to the floor, but Havena meets my eyes.

"Are you alright?" she asks me.

Theseus sighs dramatically at the question. He goes back to studying the mark on his skin while we ignore him. I fight the curl on my lip at her question.

"I think I should be asking you that," I respond.

A small smile forms on her lips as well.

"I think I'm tired of questions. I only want answers."

"Yeah, me too," I mutter, replaying Ares' kiss on her forehead.

A knock sounds on the door, followed by a maid holding a tray of food. The maid places it onto Havena's bed and smirks, as if the rumble of Havena's stomach served as gratitude toward the food. Even so, Havena says her thanks, to which the maid gives a curt nod and leaves the room.

Havena only picks up the bowl of sliced fruit from the tray, and I watch as she nudges the rest of the food away from her, including the full entree that could only be served to royalty.

"You need to eat." The words escape my lips, breaking her thoughtful gaze on the bowl in hand.

"I'm not staying long," she simply responds, then pops a grape into her mouth. My eyebrows furrow in confusion at the words. Even Theseus stops poking the burn on his arm to look at her, but she only nods toward the food. "I'm getting out of here."

"Just where exactly are you planning to go?" I ask.

"A church I think, I saw it while I slept—"

"You don't think it was just your mind playing tricks on you?" Theseus interrupts. I cross my arms, waiting on her answer as she chews her food. Finally, she puts the bowl down.

"It was a memory, not a dream," she tells him. Then her eyes falter. "At least I don't think so..."

"And you know where the church is?" Theseus asks confused, but her mouth's occupied by her chewing again. I almost tell her to think this through, just in case we run into a problem like the night Ruth found her in the City of Aaron, but I stop myself. She's just confided in me about the dreams she's been having, and I'd rather help her decipher them instead of letting her go about it alone. I didn't want her running off on her own again.

"I'll tell you when we sneak out," she says to him.

"When do we start?"

"When we what?"

Havena's eyes widen with surprise as they settle onto me, ignoring Theseus' question entirely.

"You're coming?" she asks.

"It'd be smarter to bring me over anyone else," I respond.

A small smile slides onto her face as she takes in my words, and I knew her brain was recalling the time she snuck out of my house with Leah.

"It'll only be for a little while," she reasons, then she turns to Theseus. "You don't have to come if you don't want to."

Theseus turns to me, his face silently telling me to talk her out of the idea.

I don't.

"So, what are you planning?" I ask her, to which Theseus dramatically slumps into the wall. "Do you know the building we're looking for?"

Havena pulls a silver ring band from underneath a fold in her bedsheet, and I immediately recognize it.

"Ares will kill me if I let you hang onto that," I sigh, but a slimmer of excitement ran through my veins at the thought of making him mad.

"Of course he will, but he'll kill me first for letting you two leave in the first place," Theseus says to me.

Suddenly, he pauses and turns to Havena.

"I thought your blood altered the portal's destination. Remember when Ares arrived here on his own?" he asks.

"Yeah, but he just thought it was the half-human side of me glitching or something," she reasons. I perk up.

"You're still half-human right now, Have—"

"And I'll still try to portal with or without you, Gale," she reminds me. But if that were true, she still wouldn't be here. Besides, I literally gave my word a second ago, and we both knew I wouldn't let her leave without me. She slips out of the bed sheets, sauntering up to me with determination in her eyes as she slides the ring on her finger.

"This dream really means something to you?" I ask cautiously. She only nods. "No rifts? No demons? Yet you still feel called to it—"

"Because it wasn't a dream," she asserts. Then she brings her voice almost to a whisper. "It was a memory of my father."

We hold each other's gaze for a moment, our mirrored understanding intensifying with every split second. Staying behind wasn't even an option anymore, not when the spontaneity of this plan would lead us to something so personal.

"Think of where you want to go, then say, *'Ahket,'*" I mutter softly. Her eyes widen with appreciation at the information.

Then she grabs my hand.

"Safe travels to you two!" Theseus declares with sarcastic cheeriness, but it's simply background noise as I stare into Havena's eyes.

"I'm nervous, Gale. Why am I nervous? I don't know why I'm nervous," Havena rambles. She laces her fingers through mine and tightens her grip on my hand. I can't even fight the smile I've been hiding behind my lips anymore.

She's been collecting bits and pieces of herself in a shoebox for most of her life, and although the memory she's just had of her father wasn't tangible, it was sacred. And for the second time in her life, Havena's uncovered another piece of his existence.

And I get to protect it.

"I'll just wait here until Ares discovers you're gone... and then I'll lie to two archangels about where you've gone... and then I'll die because of it," Theseus mutters to himself.

Before Havena can question her recklessness again, I say the word for her.

"*Ahket.*"

■■■

The sound of our feet becomes muffled by the sound of thunder. Our arms are linked as we look around through the rain, our bodies getting damper by the second as we stand in the middle of an alleyway. I blink, taking in the brick walls that were barely illuminated by the streetlight.

Havena suddenly pulls on my arm, and we step out of the alleyway onto a busy sidewalk. The sound of honking cars and chattering people quickly register in my ear, but Havena's already tugging me across the street.

"Where are we going?" I shout over the noise, but Havena doesn't answer until we reach the other side of the street. She brings me onto the steps of an old, neo-gothic building. Two symmetrical pikes of stone guarded the large, wooden door, centered at the building's entrance. I can't even comprehend why they'd keep something so old in the middle of all these modern, glass structures surrounding it.

"St. Patrick's Cathedral," Havena tells me. I drop my gaze to hers and she gestures her head toward the door. "This is where I was... in the dream."

I reach for the door handle and push, but it doesn't budge.

"It's locked?" Havena asks in surprise. I only laugh, bringing my hand down to the lock on the door. I conjure just enough air to mess with the mechanics.

"Well someone isn't a church girl. You can't recall the hour your church opens?" I tease.

"Funny," she only retorts. "My mother didn't bring me to church, it was probably too dangerous.... Besides, I only know this one because it's famous."

I pause. "So... you believe in God, right?"

She almost laughs, but the click of the lock catches her attention. She pushes open the door.

"After you," I say sarcastically, but she's already one step ahead. I follow behind her anyway.

Archways uplifted by stone pillars line the marble room. Wooden pews lead our eyes to the altar at the very front of the room, adorned with pianos, podiums, a few lit candles, and golden assortments of holy relics.

There's no one else here, so I flick my hand toward a few of the hanging candle chandeliers. They illuminate the room just enough for us to see. I almost walk down the shiny, marble aisle by myself, but Havena's hesitation catches my attention. Instead of heading toward the altar, she walks toward a brochure stuck underneath the leg of a pew. I step closer to see what she's picked up. A wedding brochure. She starts walking down the aisle as she reads the cover of the brochure. And I step by her side.

"So..." I start.

"So..." she says, not paying attention to me.

"What does it say?" I ask. She stops staring at the names of the couple on the front and begins reading the inside.

"Welcome to our wedding. We are happy to have you here with us today. This blessed union has been—"

Her breath falters ever so slightly before she closes the pamphlet, lowering her hand.

"What did it say?" I ask.

"Nothing."

"Havena?"

She slows her steps, but keeps her gaze toward the altar.

Without looking at the brochure, she quotes it.

"This blessed union has been brought together by destiny."

A moment of silence passes as we walk.

"It doesn't say fated," I point out.

"Sounds close enough," Havena says.

"I know we said we wouldn't decide—"

"Because we shouldn't," she interjects.

"But I'm not afraid of being with you," I counter.

"No, Gale—I'm not afraid either. We're just... dangerous together." She tosses the brochure from her hand, and it glides into the air before settling onto the floor. The frustration in her eyes was daring me not to listen.

"If someone held a knife to my throat and said they'd let me live in exchange for your life, even though my death would save millions, would you do it?" she asks.

"Without hesitation," I answer without missing a beat. She simply chuckles, the tone of it laced with disappointment before she drops my gaze.

"That's why we shouldn't," she says to the floor.

"Why? Because I want you to live?" I ask.

"No, because you'd simply die without a cause," she snaps.

Her eyes latch to mine in exasperated defeat.

"You'd be the cause, Havena," I argue. "Would you not do the same for me?"

"It's not the same thing, Gale, and you know that... Too many people have died in my name. I don't want to be your cause." She almost turns from me, but stops herself short. "If Ruth hadn't found out I was The Vine, she probably would've thrown her knife at me like I was just target practice. But then you showed up. You always show up! And now that The Fallen know my face, they're going to try to kill me and you're going to show up and try to stop them. And you shouldn't have to do that because I'm The Vine. I'm supposed to be the biggest threat in the room."

A smirk rises to my lips.

"You want to test that theory?"

"I'm serious—"

She steps out of the way of my fist, cutting her words short, and stares at me wide-eyed. I keep myself in my fighting stance.

"I won't fight you inside of a church!" she brings her voice to a hissed whisper. I can only laugh because there's no one else here.

"Words for the weak," I taunt with a shrug, then throw another punch. She dodges it again, and instead of fighting her urge to hit me, she lunges at me.

Her punches soar toward me swiftly, forceful, strong, and if my reflexes had faltered for a second, one of the six punches she sent my way would've knocked me out cold. I've trained her well.

Her eyes flicker to my mouth, taking in the amused smile forming on my lips as I block every blow she sends my way.

Then those amber eyes burn with fury.

Suddenly, she brings her knee up, trying to connect it into my side. But I grab it, pulling her into me. Her eyes flash in surprise, but she quickly recovers with determination as she wraps her leg around my waist. As swiftly as she can muster, she tries to plunge her elbow into my chest to push us both down to the floor—but I'm too fast. I drop my hand from her leg and grab her wrist. Then the other. As I restrict her hands behind her back, she huffs in frustration.

"That's cheating."

"Is it?" I ask seriously, then push her into my chest. I can feel her heartbeat rap against mine as our breaths collide. Her eyes, as mad as they were, flicker to my lips, softening by the second as they dart between my mouth and my eyes.

"The bullseye's on my back," she practically whispers, her voice ashamed. Her eyes are pleading for me to understand the risk of us being together, even though we both know I already do. I just didn't care. And with her lips hovering so close to mine, I could only mirror her volume.

"Then let the arrow rip through both our hearts."

She closes her eyes with a sigh and pulls back.

I release her hands.

"I can't choose whatever this is... Not now... or probably ever." She turns from me. I run a hand through my hair, letting my silence speak for me instead. I could only bite my tongue as I watch her turn away—like I've done so many times before. But as her feet moved her body further away from me, I no longer wanted to.

"You chose Ares."

Her feet freeze at his name, but she doesn't turn around.

"Loving him is safer for the both of us," she says.

"You chose Ares, Havena," I repeat to her back. "Just like you're choosing that lie!"

She turns around.

"And you chose Ruth during the solstice, Gale!"

So that kiss is what this is about.

Despite the daggers in her eyes, I take a step forward.

She takes one back.

"I know what you saw, but it meant nothing. I didn't kiss Ruth—she kissed me," I reason. She only scoffs at the sincerity in my voice and drops her gaze to the floor.

"Havena—"

"Rest of our lives, remember?" She brings her gaze from the

floor and settles it onto me. The distance we had between us couldn't hide the exhaustion in her eyes, and I could only look at her in silence.

"We have the rest of our lives to figure it out," she says, keeping her voice strong as she blinks her strength back. Then she points to the altar at the end of the aisle. "There's just too much we have to do first."

She turns from me with a breath and keeps walking down the aisle. I trail behind her, letting the pattering rain on the windows take up the noise in the room, muffling the sound of our feet on the marble floor. *If the weight of this war didn't exist, would we choose each other then?*

She reaches the altar before me, and when I step by her side, she keeps her gaze on the golden podium, letting her fingers trail over the brittle pages of the bible in front of her.

"This can't be the only worthwhile thing here," she mutters. I swallow my breath, ignoring the slight shake in her voice. I knew she was trying to occupy her mind with something else other than our conversation, and I wanted to mentally punch myself for it. Then she closes the book and steps around the podium to look around. I almost follow her lead, until my eyes catch a glamoured shimmer etched into the bible's cover.

"*In principio erat Verbum et Verbum erat apud Deum et Deus erat Verbum*," I mutter the glamoured words.

"Huh?" Havena asks, distracted.

Her hand was curiously guiding her to different places on the altar, touching the various fabrics, rosaries, candles and crosses that were scattered about. I clear my throat, then gaze back down to the words only meant for angel eyes.

"It's latin," I declare a little louder. "*In principio erat Verbum et Verbum erat apud Deum et Deus erat Verbum*."

Havena pauses her curious hand, which was currently holding a candle, before she turns to me.

"What does it mean?" she asks.

"You don't know it?" I return. Her look of confusion only intensifies. Then it dawns on me. Latin is a dead language to humans. I almost laugh.

"In the beginning was the Word, and the Word was with God, and the Word was God," I translate. She puts down the candle and starts to walk back to my side.

"How would you interpret it?" she asks, reaching me. I shrug.

"I've been told this scripture was just referring to the bible, since it's about the Word and all," I answer.

"It sounds like it's talking about communication itself," she murmurs, letting her finger trace the words. Then she shrugs. "If writing existed in the very beginning, we'd have journal pages of Eve's frustration toward Adam."

"So, The Vine has discernment and a sense of humor."

Havena and I turned our eyes behind us, our minds registering the figure in the middle of the aisle, to the frail voice we've just heard. I go to put a hand on my sword, but Havena places a hand on my arm to stop me.

A withering chuckle escapes the figure's mouth as he starts taking small steps closer to us. The man was short, and the cloak around his body made him appear stocky. His feet scraped across the floor slowly, as if moving took a great enough effort from his bones. As he came closer, allowing enough light in the room to illuminate his face, I understood why.

"I haven't seen you in a long time, child," the old man says.

The old, ivory cloak around his shoulders had more color than this man's freckled skin, and the tips of his white hair matched the grayish, blue of his eyes. He looked to Havena with familiarity, and his eyes crinkled in happiness as he took the both of us in. He extended his hand.

"My name is—"

"Mr. Pelowski," Havena sighs in relief. She throws herself into a hug with the man. A hearty laugh escapes the old man as his frail arms engulf her. The hug is brief, but loving, and as Havena leans out of him, his wrinkled hand takes hold of hers.

He fully cups their hands with his free one, only for his body to go rigid. His eyes glaze over into the back of his head.

"You've come for your father."

44
Havena

I held my breath. Mr. Pelowski's eyes seemed to flush into flipping pages as he blinked them back into their normal grayish-blue state. He releases my hands.

"What are you?"

Mr. Pelowski barks with laughter at my sudden question.

Then he turns to Gale.

"And you've come because... well it's not my place to say," Mr. Pelowski mutters with a knowing look in his eyes.

"Mr. Pelowski... how did you... what did you just do?" I ask again. The old man turns back to me, a gentle smile remaining on his wrinkled lips.

"I was your father's mentor," Mr. Pelowski answers gingerly. "Atticus chose the path of a Nurturer. And when he came to this plane, he didn't want to lose his skills. He wanted to continue his work down here."

He shuffles past me and begins walking up the altar steps. Without a second thought, I follow. And so does Gale. We politely take one step at a time, slowing our pace to keep behind the fragile, old man in front of us. Once he reaches the top of the stairs, Mr. Pelowski begins shuffling to the ornate, bronze bathtub on the altar.

"You've come here because you've uncovered a memory," he announces. "A memory of your father that you shouldn't have seen, but alas... the prophecy..."

"How do you know about that?" I ask. It was a stupid question, and as Mr. Pelowski turned back to me, he knew that I knew it was a stupid question, too.

"Why, I was there Havena!" he exclaims.

But then he studies my face for a moment.

"Ah, you mean how have I accessed your mind?" he asks. I nod my head. Mr. Pelowski gingerly touches the bathtub, as if he's reliving the memory.

"The day of your baptism was a cover up," his frail voice starts. "You're very gifted Havena, and because of that you are a threat. Your father knew that since you were young... very young."

He turns toward us again, and I feel Gale place a reassuring hand at the small of my back as Mr. Pelowski continues.

"Your father thought his brother, Rubeus, would somehow find you and kill you once he discovered what you could do. At first I thought your father was just paranoid. You see, half-angels don't exhibit any signs of inheriting our powers. There may be a certain tug on the wind, or a flutter of water they can create, but nothing out of the ordinary for a half-blood. Nothing as powerful as a pure-blooded angel—or at least that's what Disciples in every realm have taught us pure-blooded angels since we were younglings.

"One night—just like this if I remember correctly—your father rushed in here with you bundled in his arms. Only about three months old I think. He said you had conjured holy water and I didn't question it. You were the first half-blood

I've ever seen, but I could sense that you were just as capable as a full-blooded youngling. I've never seen your father so adamant about something—even more adamant than when he decided what necklace he wanted to gift your mother."

Mr. Pelowski cracked a smile at me, and I tried to return it just like I've done so many times before when I worked for him, but I could feel my breath freezing in my lungs as he spoke. As if he could read me like a book, his face softened.

"I erased your memories of him that night, including the memories of you ever using your powers. As much as I regret making you forget a part of who you are, you must understand that we did it to protect you. Atticus wished he could visit you all the time, but he knew it would risk triggering your Sight. You would've seen past all of the other glamour around you. I didn't hesitate when he asked me to check in on you from time to time. He asked the same of your parents as well."

The old man gestures to Gale. "And we did. I monitored you until the day you left, I even made sure your mind couldn't detect the glamoured beings that showed up in the grocery store while you worked for me. God willing, they didn't know who you were, and you didn't know what they were. But I knew what had happened when I showed up to the market that one morning. You and Leah left the room so organized and I just knew. And when it was reported that your mother had suffered a heart attack... that you and Leah had run away..."

Mr. Pelowski's eyes dropped from mine. The sadness trembled in his hand, which he leaned onto the bronze bathtub to steady. He turns his gaze to both of us now.

"I am sorry for your losses on this journey. Both of you have my condolences," he says gravely. Then he gestures to the pews.

"I assume you'll have questions," he says. He turns from us, expecting us to follow him again—and we do. I turn to Gale, and he looks to me without hesitation, his eyes signaling me to ask my questions first.

I shake my head, but he only stops me in my tracks.

"I've mourned enough—"

"So have I," I interject his whisper. He goes to cut me off but I bring a hand to his face. A part of me felt as though touching him was a mistake, but it's a gesture that had to be done. He looks into my eyes so gingerly, as if my touch has re-centered him.

"Go," I tell him softly. He takes a deep breath as I drop my hand, then turns away from me. I trail behind just a little bit before he reaches Mr. Pelowski.

"You spied on Havena with my parents, so you knew them well?" Gale asks. Mr. Pelowski nods as we start to sit on the pew next to him.

"I'd rather say I knew your parents well enough. When they came to this plane to work, they took shelter here, in this cathedral. It was almost as if they knew what was going to unfold before it happened. After Havena had been born, your parents visited here maybe three or four times. And it was always just to pray... Rose and Nathaniel always just wanted to pray...

"Shortly after they spoke with Atticus, all three of them were assigned to stop the rifts Rubeus had made. Atticus had already left his family behind to secure their safety, so naturally, Rose, Nathaniel and Atticus became their own little family. They all knew each other when they were children, but it was as though the assignment had brought them all together again for this one cause. And they fought for it until the very end."

Mr. Pelowski studies Gale as he finishes, monitoring Gale's hesitance to even breath throughout the recollection. I grab

Gale's hand and give it a squeeze.

"What happened when my mother became pregnant?" Gale asks. I catch the small waver in Gale's voice, but whether Mr. Pelowski picked up on it, I didn't know.

A small smile forms on Mr. Pelowski's face.

"I can't tell you much. Most of those memories you have for yourself, but I can say we all were overjoyed. From what I remember, Rose held her belly every day after she told us the news. Of course, the three of them moved back to the City of Aaron for her sake—and to spend time with you before your brother was born. This place wasn't designed for the comfort of a pregnant woman, you know? But I can tell you this. Your father Nathaniel, as stern as he was, would linger over his weapons with your name on his lips. He was thinking of which weapon you would choose for your own." Mr. Pelowski's gaze drops to the sword at Gale's hip with a nod. "I believe fate has made you choose the one he wanted you to have."

Gale leans his head back, blinking back the tears in his eyes. He pushes out a deep exhale to recover, then lowers his gaze back to Mr. Pelowski, who only had patience in his eyes as he looked upon Gale.

"I only have one more question," Gale says earnestly. "How did they die?"

Mr. Pelowski nods understandingly, but straightens up in his seat nonetheless.

"I can't say," he starts. "I don't want to say I wish I knew, but I also don't want to say they're not dead. I joined the search party of angels to look for them, and the only thing we found were their weapons and supplies... unidentifiable bodies burning on the ground... We could only assume the worst."

I give Gale's hand another squeeze, and he looks down at it with a shaky laugh. Mr. Pelowski looks down at our hands with a knowing look, then looks to me.

"You have a question on your mind too, Havena," he points out. Gale looks up to me now.

"Go," Gale whispers, using my previous words against me.

Despite his sad eyes, he squeezes my hand this time, and doesn't release the pressure before I speak.

"Why are your powers so... different?" I ask Mr. Pelowski. He blinks, as if he were expecting another question, but nods nonetheless. I couldn't bring myself to ask about my father.

"They're different from what you're used to, but that's only because you're young," he says with a small smile. Before I can speak again he continues.

"Nurturers have a certain power. One that can... alter the mind. Think of it as taking the glamour we use to conceal ourselves from humans, and then utilizing it to the next level. I don't know the specifics, just that it's a God given gift for some who become Nurturers. Over time, and if the Nurturer finds a skilled mentor, they can access that power, and then go on to access the mind."

"So reading minds, erasing memories—"

"Altering memories. Implanting feeling, hallucination, opinion," Mr. Pelowski adds. My eyebrow raises at the information and he chuckles as he takes in our faces. I could only assume Gale was making the same face of astonishment I was.

"The power is only given to those who God deems worthy, but you may find that the ones who do have this gift will utilize it in their own unique way," Mr. Pelowski reassures. "If there is one thing this power has taught me, it's that God's gifts cannot be deciphered by whom it was not made for."

He gingerly looks toward the huge cross bolted into the far wall, his eyes glistening with admiration as he looks upon it.

We follow his gaze, taking a few moments to listen to the sound of pattering rain echo into the room as we take in the information we've been given. Then Gale breaks the silence.

"We should head back," he whispers to me softly. His thumb brushes across my knuckle as I respond with a nod. Then we stand from the pew.

"I'm glad I saw you again," I tell Mr. Pelowski, and he turns his gaze to us.

"And it was nice meeting you, sir," Gale adds.

"I hope to see you both again," Mr. Pelowski says.

We all share a warm smile as Gale and I turn from him, going near the stony wall to open a portal back to the City of Hannah. The sound of a creaking pew catches my ear just as Gale says, the word, 'Ahket'.

"Remember this children," Mr. Pelowski calls, now standing from the pew. The wind of the portal starts lapping behind us as the old man yells.

"Prophecy and special knowledge will become useless, but love will last forever. Even now, my knowledge is partial and incomplete, but the gift of prophecy reveals only part of the whole picture. When the time of perfection comes, and these partial things become useless, love will remain. Love and God's kingdom will always remain!"

Gale wraps his arm around mine, bringing me into the portal before I can respond. As the portal closes, I swear I hear Mr. Pelowski shout one more time.

"Love will remain!"

45
Havena

My boots stepped into something mushy, and my face was immediately met with something wet.

Droplets of something wet.

"Havena, the portal glitched!"

I turned to Gale, who was still linked to my arm and looked down at me through the rain.

"You're the one wearing the ring!"

"Well, you're the half-human!" Gale reasons.

I almost snap back until I hear his voice.

"Havena!"

My head whips around.

"Ares!"

Within a flash I'm in his arms. I didn't even realize how much I wanted to be in them. Ares squeezes me into his body.

And I don't fight it.

"Where the Hell did you go?" he mutters into my hair.

I shift my head to his face.

"You just cursed, Ares."

"And I'll do it again if you leave again," Ares sighs. "I

might've scared Theseus a bit though. I don't think he's heard that many swear words come out of me in his life."

My laugh escapes my lips. I take in his soft smile, his warm golden eyes, his caring heartbeat...

"Where are the others?" We turn our heads to Gale, who I forgot was standing a short distance away.

"We set up camp back that way," Ares says, gesturing his head behind us. I remain under his arm. "When we found out you left, Hannah gave me another ring—very reluctantly might I add. I can't tell whether she dislikes me or the fact that you left. Possibly both. But apparently one archangel's ring can alter another. I had to wait for you to portal again so I could send you here instead."

"And where is here exactly?" I ask.

"Your birthplace," Ares says.

"My birthplace?... As in—"

"Yes," Ares whispers. "You're home."

I shift my body out from under his arm.

"Why are we here?"

"I know why," Gale interjects. His feet squelch in the mud as he steps beside us, a smirk of bitterness on his face.

"Ares and I agreed that revisiting the rifts our parents had closed might lead us to the rifts that were going to open. Didn't we, Ares?"

Without another word, Gale turns, heading in the direction of the campsite. My eyes slither to Ares in confusion.

"Fill you in as we walk?"

"Please do," I grumble in response. Ares extends his hand and I rest my hand into it. Our feet trudge over the mud in sync.

"Your father and Gale's parents marked the locations of rifts they had closed. Gale and I discussed it earlier, and he agreed with me, that we might be able to find clues about Rubeus' whereabouts if we visited them. You know? To see if there's a pattern just in case history repeats itself. We would've told you—I would've told you—but you were asleep. And when you woke up, you were so focused on that dream you had. I know you wanted to jump into the action of it all, but Aelia wanted you to rest. And I was worried. With your powers being new to you... this whole journey being new to you... it's overwhelming. When I went back to check on you, I didn't think you'd just sneak out..."

"And I didn't think you'd portal me back to my childhood," I finish with a chuckle, squeezing his hand.

The elevated streetlights in the distance told me exactly what I needed to know, as well as the row of parallel trees opposite of that huge slab of concrete. The freeway.

"So a rift opened inside of this place?" I mutter, mostly to myself. Ares grunts in agreement anyway.

"We'll investigate it in a little while, best before sunrise so we can get an early start to the day. That way we can portal to the other rifts that are marked nearby."

"Sounds like a plan," I say. Ares pulls me into his side once more and plants a kiss into my hair. We walk to the campsite in silence, our body heat keeping us comfortable through the drizzling rain. Soon enough, I spot wavy, blonde hair.

Theseus had built a small cave around the fire, a dome of dirt of some sort, protecting the flames from the drizzling rain, and was busy roasting what looked like sausages over the flames. He sends me a wave, his hair damp and clinging to his forehead, then Gale nudges him, grabbing the sticks in Theseus hands which were now smoking from the fire.

"I'm going to go sleep," I say, turning to Ares.

He furrows his brows.

"You sure?" he asks, and I nod my head. His lips quickly find their way to my forehead again, then he steps aside. I watch as he heads toward the fire.

Ares sits on Theseus' side, avoiding the tension between Gale and himself, and Theseus obliviously starts to fill Ares in on their conversation. Gale turns his head in my direction, his grey eyes watching me while Ares is distracted. My feet hesitate for a moment, but with a small shake of my head, I turn away.

I chose Ares.

A light catches my eye, so I walk toward one of the two tents nearby, only to hear a laugh escape the well-lit tent—which tells me I'm walking to the right one.

What I assumed to be the boys' tent was a few feet away, and not under a protective tree branch that kept the rain from pattering onto it.

"Have!"

Leah squeals as she hugs my leg. It's only been a second after I crawled through the worn, fabric flaps of the tent. Ruth throws a pillow at Leah, who pulls away from me while in a fit of giggles. It was unusual to see Ruth smile, but I couldn't stop the joy on her face from mirroring onto my own. She looked less threatening for once.

"I told you she wasn't dead," Ruth says, sticking out her tongue to Leah.

"Well geez, I could have been—"

"That's what I said!" Leah cuts me off. "Just because Ares has that stupid ring doesn't mean he can keep Havena safe. That's what Gale is for."

"I'm not completely helpless!" I counter.

"Of course you're not. Men always forget roses have thorns, then they cry when they prick their fingers," Ruth snorts.

I end up scooting onto the floor between the girls and their blankets, getting myself comfortable and slipping off my boots.

"Whoa, Have, you're drenched," Leah points out.

"Well, that's how rain works, I guess," I laugh, poking her side.

Ruth sits up at the spectacle.

"You've conjured the air before right?" she asks me.

"Yeah."

"And water?" she questions. I wince.

"Sort of?"

"Good enough. Just go like this." Ruth brings her hand up, and within a second the water from my clothes begins to disperse. I feel air trembling over my body. The droplets from my slacks rise into the air, shrinking and shrinking until they disappear. And within a few seconds, my slacks dried.

"Now your turn," Ruth encourages.

Leah sits up to see my try.

"Okay."

I sit up in a pretzel, hands on my knees, and focus. I try keeping my gaze on the tent zipper, meditating on my power.

Nothing.

"It's alright. Just try not to think about it as much. Let it flow," Ruth guides. My furrowed brows meet her eyes in return and she sighs. "Think of it as... vaporizing the water. Go on."

So I let the elements do their thing. I close my eyes, and after a moment, the sensation of trembling wind spreads over my body. After a few seconds, my top gets dry.

"Holy shit," Leah mutters. Ruth and I can only laugh.

"You should've trained me instead of Gale," I point out. "Why didn't you?"

"Because she's difficult," Leah jokes. Ruth cocks her head at Leah, but her eyes hold a playfulness I've never seen before.

"Because I'm a Disciple," Ruth corrects. I lean back as Ruth crosses her arms. "Guardians are the fighters of our realms. Beyond their blunt feathers and stupid swords, they can teach you everything you need to know about combat. Gale just... decided to teach you slowly."

"Then what about Theseus?" asks Leah. "Besides teaching me a few ways around a knife, he was actually pretty book-smart."

"A dagger, little lamb..." Ruth corrects with a nod, but it's not condescending at all. "And Theseus is well... a Nurturer. When we were kids, he seemed to be good at everything. Fighting, public speaking, understanding others beyond the surface... As easy-going as he pretends to be, I think he chose the hardest profession because... it's a hybrid of everything we are..."

"The knowledge of a Disciple..." I found my voice filling the silence, my gaze fixated on the roof of the tent. "The strength of a Guardian... The empathy of a single being..."

"All leading to a profession that many angels avoid," Ruth adds, "yet I can't picture him as anything else..."

There's silence for a moment, a pause in the world before Leah lays back down. Ruth blinks before turning to put out the fire in the lantern. Then, we settle into the tent filled with darkness.

After a few minutes, Leah's light snores sound into the tent. Ruth's back faced me, yet I still heard the curse she muttered as soon as Leah's snores erupted.

Normally I would've chuckled, but a feeling in my bones told me to cherish this moment. I kept my gaze on the ceiling instead, just at the peak of the tent where it pointed toward the sky, to the stars hidden behind the fabric. Something didn't feel right.

"Whatever happens next, don't come after me."

Ruth turns on her side to face me with worried eyes.

"What are you talking about?" she whispers. I shake my head.

"I don't know," I lie. "But, if something were to happen to me, don't lose yourself trying to find me. Spend your time preparing for the war."

"You don't think you're going to die, do you?"

Ruth props herself up on her elbows, but her tone of concern makes me shake my head in reassurance.

"No," I lie. "Nothing like that..."

"Gosh Havena, always the dramatic! Why are you speaking such... things?" Ruth huffs with a small sigh of relief. She lowers herself back down again.

There was one part of the prophecy that I couldn't find an answer to, and as I lay here tonight, I can't help but think that my first dream of a rift brought the answer to me a long time ago—I just refused to see it.

My blood will bridge every realm of this earth, and that action will most likely call for my death.

I blinked away the tears in the darkness. If I had to die to save the world, then so be it. Despite what everyone else has said to console me, the burden of this prophecy did fall on me. Not Gale. Not Ares. Not Leah, Theseus, or Ruth.

Me.

I lie to Ruth one more time tonight, though the slow rise of her lungs told me she was already beginning to drift into slumber.

"I don't know."

46
Ares

"I won't show you my hometown if we're flying over it!"
Havena exclaims with a laugh.

We awoke an hour before sunrise. I wanted to get a jump start on the day, spending as little time as I could stalling to find the rifts. There were so many rifts marked inside of Atticus' journal, but the one right next to Havena's childhood home made the most sense to visit. If Rubeus wanted to make a statement, to come back to where it all started, he'd do it here with a dramatic entrance. I just didn't realize the forest was going to be this dense as we moved through it.

And though I wouldn't admit it, I personally didn't mind.

Being alone with Havena, and away from the group, made everything easier. It was one of the reasons why I split the group up the way I did. Gale seemed even more jealous once I broke us up into pairs, but no one else seemed to mind. Leah and Theseus couldn't survive without arguing for five minutes, yet they never seemed to tire of each other's company. Ruth didn't really care about who she explored the forest with, so long as the person tagging along was fast and could keep up with her; which left her with the Guardian of the group.

Of course, that left me with Havena. Havena became easier to talk to and easier to joke with when we were alone, especially when our relationship didn't have the eyes and ears of everyone else eavesdropping in.

"But if I flew without my glamour, then I'd get to show off the beautiful being by my side," I joke. Havena nudges my arm, but she chuckles with me before moving aside a tree branch.

"And that's exactly why you won't. If you flew without your glamour then everyone on this plane would see you. We can't risk it," she counters. I cock my head.

"Since when do you know about glamour?" I ask.

"Since I was five," she answers smugly. "I remember seeing these two clouds that weren't actually clouds, but—um—now that I know of angels, I can definitely say they were angels."

"You sure it wasn't just your imagination as a toddler?" I tease.

She turns to me with a smirk.

"I'm still half-angel, of course it wasn't my imagination," she reasons. I nod in understanding and we continue through the thicket. The sky was becoming a hazy orange, indicating the sun's quick arrival. We were almost there.

"Do you think angels should stay hidden?" I ask to her back after a few minutes. She slows her steps to actually think of an answer, then steps by my side. There was no longer a leader or follower as we walked. Just companion.

"I think," she starts, "that you stay hidden for a good reason."

"And what reason is that?" I ask. She shrugs.

"The realms already have so much peace and... there's a distinct order in every city... It should remain protected," she answers earnestly. "The Human Plane wouldn't know how to handle that way of life, or how to incorporate it into their own lifestyle. They'd call it communism... or witchcraft."

"Communism?" I ask.

"It's a joke... about an economic structure?... I'll tell you later." She smiles at me. "But I guess what I'm trying to say is that... humans are given freewill like you guys, but with that freewill we do a lot of good, and sometimes a lot of bad. From what I've seen in the realms, angels do a lot of good, and make it their mission to do a lot of good, even though humans will never realize it. God designed it that way for a reason, and it's been working for centuries."

"Yeah," I scoff, "until now." Havena stops her steps. She then places a hand on my arm to stop me.

"Hey, we're going to win this war," she reassures softly as she places her hand on my cheek. "And when we do—"

"I'm flying you over your hometown in broad daylight."

"Only if we're glamoured!" she protests, but a laugh escapes her mouth anyway. I put my lips on hers, feeling the joy in her heart speak through her lips.

"What's this for?" she murmurs onto my mouth.

I pull away, mirroring her smile.

"For you."

I wink, then turn around to continue our journey. A part of me wishes I had stayed in that moment a little longer, to feel the delicate touch of someone who saw decency in me for just a second more, but when a gust of wind wraps around me, pulling me deeper into the forest and out of Havena's arms, I know that moment is short lived.

"Ares!"

Havena's cry echoes through the thick, oak trees as she tries to keep up with my soaring body. My eyes could barely keep up with the cracking of twigs and branches against my skin. Then my back hits something hard.

Black spots blotch my vision, and I took in the dead, grassy clearing that Havena was just rushing into. I hear his malevolent cackle as his feet shuffle by my head.

He conjured the wind to stand me upright. It circles around me, bounding my body in front of him as he stands behind me, elevated on the old, stony ledge of the well.

The rift we were looking for.

My vision blurs but his words ring in my ear.

"Hello, daughter."

47
Havena

"You are not my father."

"Oh? Well, I'm certainly not your uncle... But then again, how would you know?"

I almost blink at the man standing before me. I had his features, and as he stood on the well's ledge, releasing Ares' head from his grasp, I hated him for it. But what I hated the most was his question—because I didn't have an answer to it.

The only thing layered in this man's eyes was disappointment as he gazed upon me. And as we studied each other for the first time, a moment I've dreamed would overwhelm me with happiness, I found myself not caring about who he was. He was the enemy.

"Your very name was inspired by Heaven," the man says calmly. His voice was slick as honey, but a knot formed in my stomach all the same as I heard his words. "An attempt to rectify our last name in the eyes of the angels. Yet you, my seed, are the prophesied key to stopping my plans. Your childhood best friend is named Leah. Your mother, Miriam, bless her heart, died a short while ago. I apologize for the mess my demons made with her body. But you see, daughter, I know everything about your life, and you don't know a single thing about me."

"You have no right to talk about my mother!"

The man cocks his head at my tone, unphased by my words so I press on. Rage begins to boil in my blood.

This couldn't be the man who tried to protect me in his journal. The man who loved me when I took my first breath.

Then I remember his powers.

"You sent me that dream, didn't you? Why make me remember my baptism? Why make me remember you?"

I watch as his amber eyes falter for a moment, as if he's trying to recall the memory—or suppress it.

Atticus quickly composes himself with a sinister smile, erasing any hesitation he's just shown me. I can't tell if he's lying or if he's hurt.

"Why not?" he simply asks.

Then his fingers grip Ares' head again.

"No!" I shout and unsheathe my sword. Atticus cackles at my stance, sending a gust of wind at me like I was nothing more than a sheet of paper. Wind whips away from my skin, and the air I've conjured immediately counters his. One thing was for certain: He's my father.

"Yes!" Atticus shouts with excitement. "I expected nothing less from my daughter. You. Are. Powerful, Havena!"

His wings erupt from his back and I bite my tongue, withholding the gasp that wanted to erupt from my throat.

They're like nothing I've seen before. His feathers were stripped of their splendor, limply hanging from their stems like they've been burned to brittle. The bones of his wings were strong and black, like branches of iron holding onto dead autumn leaves. The most distinctive feature? They flared up, which only meant one thing. He was fallen, and his wings bent in the direction he fell. Upward.

The man I held so dearly in my heart because of a photograph—my father—couldn't be saved.

"I sent you those dreams, and if you were as smart as I thought you were, you would've known why."

I almost blink, but then I remember he's a Nurturer.

Well... was one.

"If that's true then why didn't you alter my mind instead? Was this your plan all along? To use my baptism as a facade so I could join you later? Did you really think I would drop everything to be by your side? After all of the vile things I've heard? The things you've done?"

"A word of advice if you will." Atticus nearly yawns, ignoring my questions. "It's easier to frame someone else for your deeds when they're blinded by love. I learnt that the hard way, when I tried to save my brother."

My hand almost falters from the weight of my blade.

"What?—"

"Your uncle fell before I did," Atticus bellows. "And every time he made a stupid mistake, I was to blame! Angels of every realm refused to associate with me. Half the time they thought I wasn't pulling my weight. They thought I let Rubeus do whatever he pleased on purpose. But I wasted most of your childhood years trying to find him, hoping he could be saved. He was my brother, but he couldn't be. Not in the eyes of the angels. And in the end, when that damn Guardian tried to kill my brother, I killed him. So I guess the angels were right about our kind. Our blood. For when I killed her husband, my brother nearly ripped out her throat."

My chest tightened as Atticus began to thrum his fingers against Ares' unconscious skin.

"To my surprise, Rubeus died from that Guardian woman's hand. It wasn't your mother—no, no—this woman was far more beautiful. Ten times more beautiful because of the angel blood in her veins. And of course, more powerful. Strong and resilient—"

"Don't talk like you knew either of them!" I shout. "You killed both of them!"

"Did I?" he asks. "Oh child, there is so much you do not know. So much that I could teach you."

"I know you're fallen and that's all I need to know." I take a step closer, my sword becoming sturdier in my grip, urging me to kill Atticus. To save Ares.

"Fallen? Who has fallen, girl?" He simply chuckles at my words. "Fallen is nothing but a word for children that scrape their knees. We are the Shadows of Heaven, child. And we have finally brought ourselves to the light! My brother was right when he thought humans belonged beneath our feet. It's a pity I joined him so late, but it's not too late for you."

Atticus stretches out his hand.

"Join me, Havena, and prove me wrong. Embrace your name. Erase all of what you once were. A sad, lonely, neglected, human girl. A Bernheim. You will be praised by my side, and you will be my daughter. An Abbadon!"

"And what if I don't?" I take another step forward. "What if I kill you, right here, right now, and you leave Ares alone?"

"Ares?" He asks. He looks down to the head in his grasp, then deviously looks back to my gaze. "Why, do you care for him?"

"I will kill you."

"Why do you care for someone who's betrayed you?" he asks.

My feet scrape the grass like lead at his words.

"No more lies!" I yell.

"You couldn't separate the truth from the lies being told to you, Havena—even if your life depended on it. Your ignorant mind burdens you!"

His voice booms into the air. The intensity seems to hush the forest as his echo travels through it. Birds caw at the disturbance, exiting the safety of the trees to escape the danger so near. I keep my sword raised and swallow my breath.

"Come with me, Havena." His face suddenly floods with sincerity, but I knew better than to trust it. Before I can open my mouth he proves me right and speaks again. "Come with me, and I won't kill Ares."

"If that's true then release him."

"You're in no position to negotiate, girl!" He hisses. "Do not test my patience."

I take another step forward, my sword still raised.

"Take another step closer without begging and I'll kill your little friends, too."

My blood runs cold.

"You don't know where they are," I say through my teeth.

"Want to test that?" he asks, yet he doesn't wait for my answer to explain. "Before you decided to explore this forest, it was Ares' idea to split up, wasn't it? To go into entirely different directions... But the ratio was weird, didn't you think? Of course you didn't. With the way your friends stick together I'm sure it became four versus two quite quickly. But of course you stood by lover-boy here while he led you right to me. Your friends are on their way to the second rift I've opened, and no demons have escaped through that rift... yet."

His slithering smile of satisfaction inspires my feet to move, but then he jerks Ares' head. That boy's unconscious face begins to bore itself into my memory. Ares played me, and yet I still wanted to save him. I had to.

"Down on your knees. Or they all die," Atticus commands.

"Don't kill them," I plead.

"Then don't test me."

Atticus' eyes narrow, signaling me to get on the ground. I sheathe my sword, keeping my gaze on Atticus as I lower my knees. A smile of triumph slips onto his face as I kneel.

Defeated.

"That's more like it."

48
Ares

My eyes felt like bricks as they opened. Havena was kneeling on the ground, and Rubeus had his hands around my head.

"No!" Havena cries out. Rubeus tightens his grip. My hands instinctively tried to claw at his hands, but I couldn't move. I was still bound by his restricting wind. I could feel how delighted he was to watch his niece squirm under this situation.

"Don't kill him! I'll go with you just don't kill him," she breathes out. Her wet eyes gazed upon my face with nothing but fear. Fear of losing me, fear of losing another person at her expense. It's like she's told me before, she didn't want anyone else dying for her.

"I'll go with you," she says. I shake my head as feverishly as I could. Rubeus loosens his grip.

"Promise me."

"No!" I shout, but Rubeus tightens his grip to cut me off again, and I can feel his nails dig into my skin.

"Don't... Have..." I struggled weakly through my breath,

hoping she'd understand.

It was a trap, it had to be a trap. And even though the hesitance in her eyes revealed her ignorance to me, I knew she didn't care. Not if this promise could save my life.

"I promise. I'll go with you... I promise," she says. I drop my eyes in defeat and stop struggling. Rubeus' laugh sounds through the air, like acid in my veins.

"Excellent," he slurs. Then he releases me. I fall to my knees, and in an instant, thick, iron chains weigh me down, wrapping around my wrists and feet. I didn't have to look behind me to know that chain descended into the well. Rubeus moves his hands around my head, ready to snap my neck.

"What are you doing?" Havena asks hurriedly.

"It's okay," I tell her. She brings her fearful, confused eyes to me, and the void I would leave in her heart was already starting to sink into my own. Still, I knew better. I knew to follow the plan I couldn't apologize for.

Not yet.

"It's okay," I reassure, "it's not your fault."

"I promised," Havena pleads to Rubeus quickly, "I promised that I'd come with you. You can't hurt him. You can't kill him."

"This isn't your fault, Have—"

"So lover-boy didn't tell you the next part, did he?" Rubeus asks coyly.

"P—Please, father. I don't care, just let him go." Havena stammers.

She's said it all with a haggard breath, and my heart winced with every word.

She would care when my actions have been revealed. She would care when Rubeus reveals who he truly is. And as Rubeus tightens his grip on my face one last time, I realize I wouldn't be the one to tell her.

When I made that promise to Hannah, I knew she wouldn't be the one to turn human. I knew that I would be.

It was all a part of the plan.

Befriend Havena, make her trust me, make her train with me... I even let her fall in love with me. And that part was the easiest—to include her inside of a world we both knew she didn't belong in.

Everything fell into place so smoothly, and I couldn't have done it without the Ring of the Angels. Archangels, as a whole, embody all of what angels are. They have access to the strength of a Guardian, the knowledge of a Disciple, the emotional capacity of Nurturers, and even powers that go beyond the elements. With a Ring of the Angels, average angels like myself can do more than what we've been told. We weren't just capable of creating portals with their rings—we could change the entire world with it.

When Rubeus revealed to me that I could tap into any of their secret powers, he showed me the most dangerous of them all. A gift only given to a handful of Nurturers throughout the earth.

I could manipulate the mind.

Toying with Havena's mind was easy, for her fears resembled the fears of any other human girl. A broken heart. She longed for security ever since her mother died, and I gave it to her.

Or so she believed.

It was almost humorous, watching her mind become infatuated with me while her body had no idea why. From the moment she kissed me, I knew she fell into my hands.

All I had to do was bring her to Rubeus, and as he promised, I would become the first Archangel of the Banished

Realm.

I had sacrificed Havena's wellbeing because it had to be done. I had to evolve. And the damage of this world didn't compare to the pain she'd feel from a broken heart.

What is broken in this world needs to be fixed, what is incorrect must be corrected, and other Disciples like me couldn't wait for Revelations to correct it. We couldn't sit around while our world overpopulated with non-believers, with mere humans who insisted on knowing everything about the world whilst destroying it. Pollution, oil spills, genocide, war. Sin. Sin. Sin.

The biggest misconception of Disciples is that we obtain an inflated ego from the knowledge we absorb overtime, and that misconception has always angered me.

Our thirst for knowledge intimidated others. And the other angels—our kind—singled us out every time we spoke against the humans. They couldn't see that angels were the chosen leaders of every land. Including the Human Plane, the land of mankind. The Fallen had formed because of this. We didn't wish to create this movement because of our egos. We were doing this to paint the world in an entirely new image.

A righteous one, without the human race.

And it was the only reason I came back to Gale's manor.

I kept my gaze on Havena, trying to reassure with my eyes that I would be fine—and to my surprise—that I loved her. But I watched her mirror my gaze with regret in her eyes. I couldn't bear to see her blame herself for my fate, so I shut mine. Soon enough, she'll regret not killing me herself.

Rubeus stopped thrumming his fingers against my face.

And my neck snapped.

49
Havena

"No!" Ares' limp body nearly fell to the ground, but Atticus' hand held Ares' head, keeping him upright. My breath knocked itself out of my body as I stared at what was left of his existence.

The bones of Ares' neck had splintered out of his skin. His eyes were closed yet his mouth slanted open, as if he were witnessing the blood trickle down his neck and onto his own dead body. I fought the whimper that wanted to escape my mouth and shakily unsheathed my sword as I rose to my feet.

My father had taken enough people from me, including the life of a boy I was growing to love. And for that, he would pay.

"Oh, the fire in your eyes! You're my daughter indeed," Atticus announces joyfully. "What fun it will be to spark that flame with your dear, old father!"

"You are not my father!"

"Ah, ah, ah," Atticus taunts.

The sound of wings turns my ear, and the next second, Gale drops down by my side. Ruth follows suit, along with Leah and Theseus. Atticus takes us in, calculating our weapons and strength, but that glaze of amusement on his face sends a ripple under my skin. I wanted him dead.

"Looks like the gang's all here." Atticus pouts his lips satirically. Then his hand, holding Ares' head, flies backward. My blood runs cold as Ares' body falls backward into the well. "Shame. I'll just have to kill the rest of you."

"And yet you're destined to die by her blade," Gale retorts, but he slightly steps in front of me, giving me time to recover from Ares' removal as he covers me.

My breath trembles as it enters my lungs.

"Is that so?" Atticus asks. Then he lifts his left hand.

Grunts of agony sound around me simultaneously, and I watch as Leah drops first, screaming in pain. Then Ruth. Then Theseus. Then Gale. They wither to the ground, barely propping themselves onto their elbows for support, squirming in excruciating pain.

Suddenly, a whirlpool of wind restricts my body. My arms fall to my sides and my legs stick to each other as if they've never been apart. As much as I try to move, my mouth is clamped shut.

I can barely lift a finger.

Atticus cocks his head, and I try to mask the terror in my eyes as my body moves closer and closer to where he's standing, but he sees right through me. I'm his daughter after all.

His eyes slit with amusement when I reach his side, then he turns me toward the others, letting me witness their pain as the wind pushes my bound body to the ground in a kneeling position. Their groans ring in my ears, but I still can't move.

"Who should I kill first?" he asks me with a wave of his right hand. A gust of air leaves my mouth and I can breathe again. Speak again. The others seem to regain a bit of strength, their cries turning into coughs of recovery, but they're still weak. Pinned under Atticus' power. And my mouth doesn't waste a second.

"You won't kill any of them. I've promised to come with you."

Atticus looks at me with boredom in his eyes, then turns back to the others.

"Hmm, what about the Nurturer?" he asks excitedly, ignoring me. Before I can protest, Theseus curses from the pain. His body starts to turn red as he begins to wriggle and gasp in exertion.

My heart clenches.

"Enough!" I growl. Atticus waves a finger, and I watch as Theseus' pain falters back to the same tolerable level as the others. Atticus laughs, then looks down to me.

"I was a Nurturer, too, you know. To think your daddy issues haven't led you to a man like me," he sneers at me flatly.

"They don't deserve this. I've agreed to go with you!"

He only studies my face for a moment more, then a smile slips onto my father's lips.

"It's only a bit of blood fun," he says connivingly. I narrow my eyes in response, my chest heaving with rage, yet he perceives my silence as confusion with a raise of his brow. "Shame, I heard you took down the demons in Hannah with heavenly fire. I thought you'd be as strong as me, if not stronger."

Then he turns his gaze to the others, oblivious to my breath catching in my throat at his words. 'Blood fun,' he had said.

Blood conjuring.

My eyes quickly settle onto Gale, wincing at the struggling limbs in his body because I now understood the pain he was in—and the power causing it.

The flexing veins in his body were throbbing across his muscles, itching to break and burst under his skin.

"Yes... that's the one," Atticus murmurs thoughtfully. I

turn my head to find him staring down at me with a sinister smile.

"You care for the Guardian," Atticus says with confidence. I hold my breath, watching as he motions his finger toward Gale.

Gale's thundering cry pierces my ears. A sound I never want to hear for the rest of my days, but I focus my gaze on his body anyway. Just like I had planned.

C'mon, I say to myself, *C'mon, c'mon.*

I push into my mind, willing for this to work.

For the intent.

I close my eyes.

Gale gives out another scream, curdling the nerves in my body.

I flinch at the sound, as if his cries will never fade from my ears, but then I hear it.

"Impossible."

Atticus' whisper of disbelief opens my eyes.

Gale's heaving chest was starting to calm itself, and his skin, which was once clinging to his once throbbing veins, began to smooth itself out, diminishing his pain. He lifts his eyes to mine as he brings up his knee, then the other one, and as he rises from the ground, panting with sweat trickling off his skin from the attack, pride glazes over his eyes as he looks to me.

I now knew I was stronger than Atticus, but I could do more than counter his strength. By blood, we share the same powers, just like he had assumed in his journal, but my powers will always overpower his. Because whenever he chooses to churn someone's blood into an excruciating tide of fire, I'll always use my powers for peace. For good.

Gale lifts his hand, gesturing to the silver band on his finger.

Aelia's ring.

"The ring of an Archangel. It's full of wonders, isn't it? But you wouldn't have known since archangels have disgraced your kind since the day your father fell."

Gale glimpses to me again, proud of the lie he's made to protect me, then he drops his gaze.

I longed for him to look at me a moment longer, but I knew if he did, then we'd both be caught. He didn't want to risk giving me up—or the extent of my power. Then Gale twirls his sword, and starts to walk closer.

I could feel Atticus' hesitation, and I didn't need his words—or lack thereof—to prove it. His hand trembled. And as Leah, Ruth, and Theseus panted to their feet in recovery, Atticus threw up his hand. A streak of fire—hellfire—erupted in front of them, blocking them from following Gale across the grassy plain.

In this moment, Gale was invincible, the blood in his veins now steady, impenetrable because of the power I possessed. But Atticus didn't know that power, and relief washed over me as realization trickled into my brain—because Atticus never will.

I am The Vine of this prophecy: I grew up in New Jersey, in a rickety house across from a forest that I wouldn't die in—I refused to. My enemies destroyed the one place I called home as an attempt to destroy me. Destroy my bloodline. But my blood has already bridged every realm of this earth—because I am human. And no matter the title or realm of birth, I also had angel blood in my veins. And the most important part, four has already become one with the earth.

Gale's element of choice was air, Theseus' element of choice was fire, the dust that made up Leah's human body was earth, and the element that allowed me to conjure blood, to manipulate the liquids of a living body as if it were my birthright, was water.

Gale's assignment was complete, and I was ready for The Holy War to come. And unbeknownst to many, the one thing that amplified my power wasn't because I was an heir of Hell. It was because God placed people in my life that I had to fight for.

It took me so long to realize the purpose of this journey, but by some weird trial of fate, I finally understood. There was only one feeling that every being with a heartbeat was destined for.

Love.

As I gazed upon Gale, hearing the sound of his blade twirl in the air once more as he prepared himself to fight for me, one thing was for certain. I'd fight for love until my last breath, even if my father didn't.

Then Atticus placed his thin hands around my head, gripping it like I watched him do to Ares only moments before. Gale's body goes still.

"Release her," Gale demands. Atticus' chuckle tremors through his body, including his fingers.

"She's promised to go with me, Guardian. I didn't specify whether dead or alive," Atticus spits. My blood runs cold as the confidence that was just in Gale's face flushes out of it.

"Release her. Now!" Gale barks. I hold my breath.

"Tsk, tsk, tsk. Down boy. Drop your sword and I will," Atticus suggests slyly. It was a trap, it had to be, because even though Atticus knew he could no longer conjure Gale's blood, he didn't speak like he was out of options. Goosebumps prickled across my arms, warning me of something more sinister up Atticus' sleeve. I just didn't know what it was, or if I had the power to seize it.

"No!" I almost squirm from my outburst, but Atticus' grip

on my head tightens, making my body go still with panicked adrenaline. One false move on my part could kill me. Gale's eyes widen with hesitation as they glaze over me with worry. His blade falters for a moment.

"Have—"

"No!" I tried to keep my voice firm. I blinked away the stinging of my eyes to study his, but I knew what Gale wanted to do. Every cautious centimeter of a step he took closer to me told me what he wanted to do. "Don't choose me, Gale, don't you dare make me your weak spot."

He shook his head in denial, but I couldn't let him try to save me. A single tear fell down my cheek as my voice cracked.

"This is how it plays out, okay? Don't make this choice. We don't have to make a choice right now, okay? Let me go."

"It's not just your decision, remember?" he says, as if there's no other option. If I could only shake my head to tell him I didn't remember, I would—even though he'd know it was a lie. Besides, I can tell from his eyes, he's already made up his mind. Gale made up his mind from the moment he first saw me. He'll always choose me, even if it meant choosing me over himself. I rush out my words.

"Don't you dare."

"We have the rest of our lives."

"No—Gale!"

He drops his sword. Atticus' hand flies off my face toward Gale, serving as the only opening I would get, and I push myself into my father.

Then we fall back, into the rift.

Atticus' cackle rings in my ears as we fall, but I still hear my name echo off the walls from the top of the well. Gale's face reaches the rift's opening just in time for me to burn the memory of his face into my brain.

He was terrified, then he was gone, because I had brought my hand up and conjured heavenly fire along the walls of the well. The stone began to crumble in on itself above me, crashing down to race Atticus and I back into the realm of Hell. And as I sealed the rift from the inside, I only had one thought.

My family.

Leah. Theseus. Ruth. Gale. All of them safe, all of them loved, all of them alive.

I heard the screeches first, then the walls around me started to blur, washing over my vision in ragged hues of red as we sank deeper into the earth.

Then I closed my eyes. I only wanted to envision Gale's eyes staring back at me, like they've done so many times before, even during the moments I was too afraid to look back into them. But still, I knew he stared.

The last thing I felt was the heat against my skin. So I took a deep breath, and braced myself for the hellfire below.

EPILOGUE: GALE

Dirt. Rubble. Impediments of soil that blocked any chance I had of entering the rift and following Havena.

And even still, my knees settled into the ground as my hands began to pluck and plow at the earth that had crumbled at the touch of Havena's power. Completely sealed from the inside and no longer a well. No longer a rift.

"Gale." Theseus' voice barely sounded in my ears. My hands continued searching through the rocks, ignoring the scuffs of their surface that scratched my skin. Then I heard it. Even over the unsheathing of Theseus' sword, I heard it. The shrieks.

And within a blink of an eye, I saw red.

The shriek sounded out again, this time ringing in my ears as if it were right in front of my face.

I blinked feverishly and my vision cleared, revealing the face of a foul demon inches from my own. It's yellow eyes writhed in agony and hate, a look of confliction that only fueled the anger surging through my veins. The demon's mouth opened just enough to bubble over, the saliva seeping down its scaly skin until it slid over the metal of my blade in its chest. I twisted my sword, watching the creature's last breath subside weakly into the air. And with a tilt of my sword, the corpse slipped onto the ground.

My chest heaved with rage, so I blinked again in realization, trying to calm the unregistered anger in my body. Then I lifted my gaze from the corpse and turned around.

Three other bodies were on the ground. Sprawled apart and sliced to pieces, bits of their scaly skin clung to whatever it could hold onto, but the black liquids of their blood oozed from their bodies, seeping into the earth. Their eyes, lifeless yellows and frozen with terror, were unexpectant of their lives coming to an end so abruptly. So suddenly. That's how fast I came for them.

They didn't deserve the roots that began to pull their existence into the ground, slowly replacing their bodies with flowers and grass, as if they didn't exist in the first place. Their bodies of death supplying the earth with the nutrients it needed to create life.

I settled my gaze on Theseus, who's hand was out towards me and the deceased, and who was, no doubt, reciting the hymn we use to hide the demons we kill. I didn't have to squint to see him—the clearing was open enough. Leah was next to him, her face distorted in fear even though she had a bow and arrow in hand. She pointed the weapon to the ground, as if she didn't get a chance to use it.

The flap of wings drew my gaze to Ruth above. She held my gaze, her hands over her mouth in horror. And I knew why.

Ruth has acted tough ever since we were kids, like she was born to be a fighter, but deep down we both knew she couldn't stomach the sight of a slaughter. Not like this. So when she flew into the air, showing Theseus the way as he hurried after me with Leah in his arms, I knew she didn't expect to witness what I had done. None of them did. But I didn't even know they were there.

I just saw red.

Ruth lowered her hands, but I caught the nervous inhale of preparation she shook off before she dived. And as she flew toward the ground, soaring to meet me in the middle of dead bodies, I flew up.

I flew home.

■■■■

It only took a few minutes to reach the manor, and whether it was because of the adrenaline in my bones, or the panic in my heart, I didn't care. My legs had a mind of their own as soon as my feet hit the ground, and I didn't bother to retract my wings as I rushed through the frosted manor doors without hesitation.

"Gale!" Ruth calls out, but I didn't care.

I flew up from the foyer floor to the landing on top of the staircase, leaving the sounds of Ruth's staggering footsteps behind me as I headed down the hallway and entered my room.

"Every action of your body is a reflection of your heart!" Ruth calls out from behind me.

My hands grip my desk in the middle of the room, holding its edges to steady my vengeful breaths. I didn't need the reminder, but Ruth's inclination to stay by the door as she tried to console me was a smart call because one thing was certain: I wanted Havena back. In this moment, my heart urged me to hurt anyone who would try to stop me from getting her in my arms again.

"Don't you dare use my parents' words against me. Not right now!"

"Then don't do something reckless," Ruth warns with caution.

I run a hand through my hair with a sarcastic laugh at her words. *Reckless. She thinks chasing after Havena is reckless.*

I sigh, lowering my head to calm my breathing as Ruth takes a steady step closer to me.

"Theseus and Leah have gone to the city of Hannah to get our things. Let's at least wait for them so we can come up with a plan, so we can just... think!"

Inhale. Exhale. Inhale. Exhale.

Ruth ceases my silence.

"You could've died fighting those demons on your own," she says quietly. A bitter scoff of amusement slips out of my mouth.

"But I didn't," I say, turning around to latch my gaze onto hers. "Because that's my job, Ruth. I'm a Guardian. I kill those creatures to protect everything God built. And I was given this assignment to protect her, Ruth—to protect The Vine."

She goes to interrupt me but I shake my head. The words lingering in my mouth turn my throat dry.

"I failed her today."

Ruth's eyes falter at my defeat. I watch her mouth part pathetically for a rebuttal, but it's cut short by the sudden sound of footsteps in the hallway that catch our attention.

Leah rushes into the room with a sigh of relief when her eyes land on me. Her hand clutches the strap of the duffle bag that hung from her shoulder, her knuckles white from the weight, but she slides it off her shoulder effortlessly as she walks over to hand it to me. With a huff she speaks, "I grabbed what I could."

I receive the duffle bag, and just as I give her a curt thanks, Theseus stalks into the room.

"The house is secure," he announces.

"And no one followed us from the Human Plane?" Ruth asks. A snort of derision escapes my throat, interrupting Theseus' words of confirmation, and I lean off the table.

"Doesn't matter, I'm not staying here," I affirm. "I have to go get her."

"We don't even know where to start!" Ruth counters firmly. Leah bites her cheek and steps back toward Theseus, who only watches Ruth and I converse with calculating, worried, eyes. "You're diving head first into a danger that you don't even know how to find, but it will surely find you first, Gale—"

"I don't care, I'm going after her! I can't just leave her—"

"She left Gale—"

"She did not leave!"

My shout threads into every inch of the room, and the only thing muffling the echo of my voice is the thickness of the stone walls. I turn, exasperated, to find the trio examining me with worried eyes. Their mouths waver with hesitation, but even I knew nothing in this moment could calm me down.

"She didn't just leave," I tell them, urging myself to speak with a calmer tone. Theseus steps forward with a reassuring hand, but I step out of his reach with pleading eyes. If only he understood that leaving wasn't her choice. And that she pushed herself down that well so Atticus wouldn't kill me.

"She didn't just leave," I repeat quietly. The bag slips through my fingers, spilling its contents onto the floor. The room stays silent as we watch the first aid, the food, the books and a bit more exit the bag. My eyes immediately recognize Havena's shoebox—the one that she kept throughout the years to give herself an identity. The one that she used to preserve the childhood her parents didn't give her.

I kneel down, picking up the polaroid that's escaped the withering cardboard. She had only told me about this picture once. Her father was holding her in his arms, and she couldn't have been more than a week old.

"She didn't just leave," I say once more, flipping over the polaroid to find her name resting underneath his. As much as I wanted to rip this picture to shreds, I knew I couldn't. Not because Havena would give me an earful for it, but because it was the only evidence she had of Atticus, of the loving father she had built in her head. And even though he had betrayed her imagination, she would still find forgiveness in her heart for him somehow. I knew she would. Because regardless of what he's done, he was the only piece of lineage she had left.

"He made her promise to go," I remind them, holding up the picture. Then I started shuffling everything into the bag again. "We should've warned her about angels making promises. She didn't have a choice in the matter, not after she had given Atticus her word to follow him."

And despite Havena's ignorance, I only had myself to blame, because the last memory I have of her eyes told me all I needed to know. Her only choice in that moment was to save me, the rest of her life be damned.

I rise from the ground, slipping the bag onto my shoulder.

"I'm going to get her back."

Leah takes a step forward at my words. "We're coming with you—"

"He's not asking us to follow him," Theseus interrupts

softly. Leah's eyes darted from me to Theseus, searching for the realization she didn't want to acknowledge. But Ruth understood, and she shook her head with wide eyes.

"What're you going to do? Ask Atticus for an invite to dinner? You're only way in is to become fallen!" Ruth exclaims firmly. I almost turn away, allowing my silence to serve as my answer, but she too, steps forward to touch my arm, to anchor me from the recklessness of my plan—or lack thereof. And I let her. "You can't denounce your faith for her—"

"I won't," I lie. I turn my attention toward the books on my desk again, and my eyes immediately begin searching for my bible. The others don't stop me as my fingers begin rummaging over the golden pages.

"There has to be an entry point somewhere. We just have to interpret something right? Use our discernment?" I suggest hurriedly.

Theseus steps up to the desk.

"That's not how it works—"

"So I just let her go?" I challenge.

His mouth fails to waver at my indignant tone.

"We'll go where you lead, but we get her back together," he says firmly. I study the seriousness of his proposal as Leah cautiously walks up to his side.

"We just... need a clear head if we're going to get her back," she says softly. I study her gentle gaze, too, watching her hopeful eyes ask me to calm down. "She's my best friend—"

"And I'm fated to her," I reason as calmly as I can. She shares a look with Ruth, but nods understandingly nonetheless. My fingers start skimming the bible again, trying to find any reference to the gates of Hell.

"There just... there has to be something we could use, somewhere—anywhere. Can we please just think of something?" I ask with a frustrated sigh, mostly to myself.

"I can't believe I'm saying this," Ruth mumbles. My fingers pause their fiddling and we all bring our attention to Ruth. She runs a hand through her hair with an anxious sigh, then walks over to the map on my wall.

"Judaean Desert," she points. "You know the story. Jesus was taunted for forty days and forty nights. He was practically tempted with food every hour by Lucifer himself. We know how regal the archangels are—"

"So Lucifer would be just as regal, if not more. He would use his etiquette. He would've dined with Jesus within his own dwelling," I mutter, walking over to the map and settling my gaze onto Israel. I grab a pin and stick it into the wall.

Into the Judaean Desert.

"Hell has to be there—"

"But it's just a hunch," Ruth reminds me.

"Then it's a risk we have to take," Theseus adds. We turn from the wall to face him. He sends me a curt nod, and with his arms crossed and his eyes stern, I knew he would join me.

"We'll figure it out," I say.

"We should be planning this out more, I won't denounce my faith for her! And we're literally about to dive into hellfire. Head first!" Ruth says with urgency. I shook my head.

"Doesn't matter," I respond.

"We can figure out a loophole—we always do," Theseus assures to Ruth. Then he turns to me. "But this is your call."

The last bit was more of a reminder than a warning.

"I know."

"You don't seem afraid of what happens next," Leah says, looking to both of us anxiously.

"I'm terrified," I respond in a heartbeat. I look down to my hand, hoping to feel the tug that led me to Havena before I even laid my eyes on her.

There's nothing there.

"There's no need for a plan," I say after a moment. "We need her. It's a part of our assignment to protect her... and we're going to go get her."

Without another word, I turn toward the balcony. My wings ripple from my back as soon as the summer breeze greets my footsteps on the cobbled stone. Turning around to persuade the others wasn't an option—I would do this alone if I had to—but as my ears twitched at the sound of wings erupting behind me, I knew that saving Havena was no longer up for debate for them either. We were a family, and the only end goal of our plan was to restore our family.

Even if I had lied.

We didn't just need Havena because of the prophecy—we needed her because I needed her. The prophecy said Havena's blood would bridge every realm of this earth, but if that called for her death, then I'd risk being fallen. I'd risk losing everything I am to protect everything she is. And I'd do it again a thousand times over, if I could just do it first.

With one flap of my wings I soared into the air, into a quest that even the strongest prayers might fail to protect me from. Because I was heading toward Hell. I was heading toward the Judaean Desert.

I was heading toward Havena.

ACKNOWLEDGMENTS

To my closest friends, whose love and support for this story inspired me to publish it in the first place: Arelis Rodriguez, Giovanna Maia, Marjorie Murillo, Melissa Saravia, Mirna Canon, Rosanna Corona, and Thiffany Fernandes. I cherish our friendship more than you know.

To my amazing grandmother, Cynthia. Your love for literature has been passed down to me and it is the greatest gift I have ever received.
Thank you.

To my mother, Dionne, I thank you for your encouragement and kind words that carried me through 3AM writing sessions. You're the strongest woman I know, and I will carry your strength with me through every season of my life.

And lastly, I'm eternally grateful for God's grace. This story would not be here without my faith.

CHECK OUT A SNEAK PEEK OF BOOK TWO IN

TRIALS OF FATE:

HIS DESCENDANT

PROLOGUE:
HAVENA

My room felt colder tonight.

I sat against the headboard of my bed, my eyes alert as I stared at my bedroom door. Every few minutes—or every few seconds—my hand would rest upon the butterknife I had picked up from dinner, hidden within a fold of my black, silk sheets.

Silence has accompanied my surveillance for about an hour now, an hour which apparently showed no signs of danger within these four, marble walls.

"I'm an idiot," I mumble. After a breath of defeat, I plunk the butterknife into the vase of roses beside my bed. Strangely enough, they were a gift from my father. Ares must have told him I loved roses, and when Atticus first showed me this room, pointing out the vase and expecting me to show him gratitude for his small act of decency, I could only shut the door with a controlled breath. He will never see me break. I couldn't even crack a smile as I looked upon those vibrant, red petals now, and I don't think I ever will again.

Besides reminding me of Ares' betrayal, they were also the only living thing in this realm besides me and my father. But like the rest of the creatures here, they haven't exactly died yet.

Demons, from what I discovered quickly, don't have heartbeats. As soon as they transform into a servant of Hell, they lose more than just their life.

They lose their soul.

Most demons are like talking animals, acting on their primal instinct to murder, deceive, devour. They breed with each other to repopulate the Banished Realm, scouring within their caves along the realm's edge.

But the ones who had the choice of transforming were mortal once. Human. And you can tell by their eyes.

When humans die, and their Day of Judgment isn't kind, they're sent to Hell. They stare into one of the three pits outside, horrified by the suffering they'll endure for an eternity until Lucifer gives them another option. With hope, the damned accept Satan's offer, thinking they'll be free from the pain they've already paid for with their life.

But they're not really free, are they?

Their freewill is gone. Their bodies are no longer warm. Their blood, once as red as these rose petals, turn to ink. And worst of all, their minds are changed. Their orange eyes signify the alteration, serving Lucifer's bloodline until the end of time.

But if there's one thing I've learned since I've been here, immortality does not mean invincible. When transformed demons find death again, they'll be sent to the circle of pain they tried to run away from in the first place.

And the very screams outside of my bedroom window

prove that.

I keep the candle lit as I get under my blanket, shaking off my knowledge of this place before I sleep.

It's a place of trickery, fear, manipulation.

Death.

So I close my eyes to tune it out.

■ ■ ■ ■

"There, your hand follows the stroke of the brush—yeah, just like that."

I smile at his direction, watching him guide my hand with the paint brush anyway.

Outlined on the canvas before us was a beach from my childhood. It was a tragic recollection of course—the artwork resembling the talents of a toddler. But even so, my back was against his chest as his arm moved with mine, working upon the canvas like we were making a masterpiece anyway.

He snakes his arm around my waist now, but just as he does my hand slides the blue paint into the sand.

I pull my hand back, my body rigid from the mistake, but then he leans his head on my shoulder, bringing his other arm around me.

"It's beautiful," he simply says.

"Don't lie to me," I mutter, but my body relaxes into his embrace. I feel his chuckle across my neck.

"Fine," he starts. "It's the worst painting I've ever seen."

"Hey—"

"And it's beautiful." He plants a small kiss on my shoulder and slowly starts to sway as I laugh, bringing my hand back to the painting to finish the sky.

"You're such a delicate creature, Gale," I point out. There's silence as I keep painting.

"I'm delicate?" he asks after a moment. He stops swaying and shifts his head, no doubt looking at me instead of the painting.

"Mmhm," I answer, avoiding his gaze. I can sense his smirk.

"Then you are just as delicate in my eyes," he says softly.

I laugh.

"Are you sure?" I counter playfully.

Then I turn my face toward his.

My eyes blink into darkness. Within a second my body sits upright, my eyes adjusting to the dark with the assistance of a small flame flickering in my palm. The candle on my dresser has extinguished itself, the wax smaller, with frozen drops of it trickled along the side. Time had passed, that's all.

My eyes sweep over to the door. I raise my hand, conjuring air around the bronze handle and give it a tug. It's still locked.

I turn to the butterknife now, still in its place and settled into the vase on my bedside table.

Just as it was before I closed my eyes.

With a sigh, I dim the flames in my hand, watching the darkness swallow the light.

My hand finds its way through my hair and I take a breath.

I'm just paranoid. *Paranoid, scared and.... and...*

I settle back into bed, pulling the sheets up to my chin to distract myself from my thoughts, but I couldn't fight this feeling of loneliness. And that dream I've just had felt too real.

Too many parts of my heart were screaming for it to be real, as if I could just burst through my bedroom window and turn that dream into a reality. I close my eyes, taking a breath to remind myself that wasn't Gale. Just my head.

And rather than dwell on the mistake my tired mind had made, I chose to sleep, for the color of Gale's eyes were a feature I'd never forget. And one thing was for certain.

His eyes weren't blue.

KaliVictoria makes her debut as an author with the first installment of the Trials of Fate series. She is a city native and lives within the tri-state area of the United States. Visit her on Twitter and Instagram (@itskalivictoria). Learn more about the Trials of Fate series at instagram.com/trialsoffateseries.